TOO CLOSE TO HEAVEN

"Tessita," he said.

Tess closed her eyes. "Señor, I beg you, do not address me so."

"Why not?" He stepped closer, until their bodies were nearly touching—until she had to look up into his fiery eyes and saw his mouth hovering so close that she had only to stand on her toes to kiss it. "Does it make you want me, too?"

"It doesn't matter if I want you, Señor Morales," she said, far more steadily than she believed possible. "I am not free."

Now he looked at her mouth, and lower. "My hands remember the feel of you, Tessita. The softness, the eagerness."

"Please," she whispered. "Have you no honor?"

At last he backed away. "*Sí,*" he said and she heard in the word a fine disgust. "More than I wish, señora, or else you would now be mine."

Books by Barbara Samuel

A Winter Ballad
A Bed of Spices
Lucien's Fall
Dancing Moon

Published by HarperPaperbacks

Dancing Moon

⋊ʒBARBARA SAMUELᕁ⋉

HarperPaperbacks
A Division of HarperCollinsPublishers

HarperPaperbacks
A Division of HarperCollins*Publishers*
10 East 53rd Street, New York, N.Y. 10022-5299

This is a work of fiction. The characters, incidents, and
dialogues are products of the author's imagination and are not to
be construed as real. Any resemblance to actual events or
persons, living or dead, is entirely coincidental.

ISBN 0-06-108363-1

HarperCollins®, ▰®, HarperPaperbacks™, and
HarperMonogram® are trademarks of HarperCollins*Publishers* Inc.

Cover illustration by Diane Sivavec

First printing: September 1996

Printed in the United States of America

Visit HarperPaperbacks on the World Wide Web at
http://www.harpercollins.com/paperbacks

❖ 10 9 8 7 6 5 4 3 2 1

For Ramm Samuel and
Roger Freed, who were surely brilliant
outlaws together in another life.

ACKNOWLEDGMENTS

Heartfelt thanks go to the employees and dedicated volunteers at El Pueblo Museum in Pueblo, Colorado; at Bent's Fort in La Junta, Colorado; and at the Martinez Hacienda in Taos, New Mexico. These people spent hours answering my endless questions, looking up obscure details, and providing a magic I could not have found in research books alone. Two people in particular were a great help: my mother, Rosalie Hair, who patiently found the books I needed over and over again, and Callie Goble, who knows everything about everything, and was especially helpful this time. My historical mistakes are, of course, my own.

PROLOGUE

Arkansas
Spring, 1844

In her high bed, with its counterpane of white chenille, Tess Fallon burned. She thrashed and tossed, fighting the kindly slave who tended her wounds with a poultice made of some foreign herb.

No, not foreign, Tess remembered. The plants were native here, only foreign to her. The slave, a woman named Marie, wrapped long lengths of cotton soaked in the mixture over Tess's back and arm and breast. The fabric cooled her hot wounds.

But one wound would not heal. The newly seeded babe in her belly was lost. Blessedly lost. Tess wished to bear no child to a man—even a native Irishman from her own village—who could horsewhip other human beings. Including his own wife when she dared to interfere.

A candle burned at the bedside and the poultice was gone. Tess lifted her head at Marie's urging. "Come on, chile, you got to drink this now. You got to drink."

Water spilled on her lips. Tess thought to let it fall, but her mouth opened of its own accord to catch the liquid. Cool and sweet, drawn straight from the brook. It soothed her fever-parched throat. With a gasp, she breathed in, and drank again, deeply.

"That's right," Marie murmured. "Drink, chile."

Tess dropped back to the pillow and looked at Marie. The slave was impossibly round, as people never were in Ireland, with large breasts and a full face and ageless black skin, smooth as a stone in spite of her fifty odd years. "How is Sonia?" Tess asked.

"She's alive, thanks to you."

Tess nodded. Relieved to hear the news that Sonia had survived, she fell into a slumber unmarred by Seamus McKenzie, or bullwhips, or hunger, or pain.

When next she awoke, she began to plan.

1

Arkansas River Valley
Fall, 1844

Tess gratefully jumped down from the wagon of the Spanish traders. "Are you coming, Sonia?" she asked.

The pregnant slave nodded slowly. Her skin looked dull. "In a minute," she said. "Let me just stretch out my back."

"There is no hurry," said one of the wives of the traders, a woman with hair as black as coal. Her eyes were kind as she took Sonia's arm. "Walk a little." Over her shoulder, she said something in Spanish to her husband, a lean man with a thin mustache.

He turned his lips down in agreement. "No hurry."

Wearily, Tess headed over the grass toward the river. Her body ached, not only from the long, long journey from Independence, Missouri, down the Santa Fe trail to this flat, plain land. She ducked into a thick stand of cottonwood trees that would offer privacy. Tess tended to the needs of her body, then unable to resist the lure of cold, fresh water, she moved toward the bank of the river. She splashed her face, feeling grit sluice away.

A sharp, long cry pierced the stillness. Tess froze, listening. There were all manner of beasts in this new place, not like in Ireland, where cows and dogs and cats gave the only music. Here she had seen bears and wolves and a small dog they called a coyote that was most frightening of all.

It came again, a whooping, terrifying sound, as high and eerie as a banshee's wail. That was no animal. Her mouth went dry.

Indians.

A shard of terror stabbed her, making her heart stop for a breathless second. She heard the horses, and an abbreviated scream, and more whoops, all undercut by the soft, soothing chuckle of the river behind her.

She thought of Sonia, and scrambled to her feet. *Oh, no. Not this.* They had come through too much, come too far. Grabbing her skirts, she ran through the cover of the trees, staying low. Near a small scrubby bush, she knelt to look out.

A swarm of black-haired savages, beautiful and terrifying at once, with their long limbs and paint, had already done their work. The trader's wife lay on the ground, her head bloody, the black hair gone. Before Tess's horrified eyes, the wagon master was stabbed viciously, and the Indian who did it gave forth a blood curdling cry.

Tess looked for Sonia, and saw her hiding behind a wagon wheel, in the shadows. For the moment, she seemed safe.

An older Indian, with hair as long as Tess's own and shining in the sun like the wings of some great bird, gave an order. The others circled toward him.

Sonia crouched where she was, and Tess could see her rigid grip on the wagon wheel. Just then, one of the warriors rounded the wagon one more time. The instant he spied Sonia, she rolled backward, out of his reach, and broke for the trees where Tess hid.

The Indian lifted his bow and fired cleanly. Tess screamed when the arrow pierced Sonia's skirt. Sonia stumbled another three steps, then fell to her knees. The warrior swung down gracefully from his pony. Sun glinted on his knife.

As long as she lived, Tess knew she would never forget the look of him, painted with bright color like the ancient warriors of her own land, who'd fought nearly naked like this, covered only in paint. She would never forget the cold way he moved toward Sonia, his knife upraised, his face as calm as if he were going to butcher a pig.

His was the face of a soldier, accustomed to war and killing. But Tess had learned to fight herself. She thought of her body painted blue like her ancestors, and grabbed a thick branch from the ground.

She bolted from her hiding place, making a high, wild sound of her own, wielding the huge stick in front of her. Before she reached him, the Indian had squatted by Sonia, grabbing her head roughly in one hand as he lifted his knife with the other.

Tess swung her club, and it caught him on the shoulder, knocking his knife away. He scrambled for the weapon and sprang to his feet. Tess ran straight at him, swinging the club. He lunged at her, slicing the thick wool of her traveling costume as if it were bread. She lunged back, thrusting the branch out before her, and hit him in the chest. He grunted, then ducked her next swing, and gave a swipe with his knife that nearly slashed her face.

A blind, red rage was upon her. She could hear only the race of her blood, the grunt of the warrior, and the harsh grate of her breath.

To the death, she would fight him. She had come too far, had fought too hard, to give up now.

Joaquin Morales was the first man to get to the edge of the mesa. It was nearly dusk of an October day. Bitter wind, the scourge of the high plains, swept the desolate scene below. He halted and held up his hand silently to

signal the two men with him. All three paused at the edge
of the bluff.

Joaquin stared grimly. An overturned wagon had
spilled bags of trade goods and camp supplies into the yellow grass nearby a stand of cottonwoods. The last rays of
sunlight came over the Rockies to the west, shadowing
ground churned by the feet of many horses. Bodies were
strewn over a wide area. Even at a distance of a hundred
yards, Joaquin could see two had been scalped. Arrows
protruded from the bodies of the others.

"Reckon it's the Arapaho," Raul said. It wasn't a question. He lifted his head and scanned the horizon, squint-
ing against the light.

"Damned Armijo." The curse came from the third man,
Roger St. John, late of the British army.

Joaquin nodded. Armijo, governor of Nuevo Mexico,
had been warned some weeks before to release kid-
napped Indian captives. He had not even bothered with
a reply.

Now the Indians had taken their revenge.

Turning his horse, Joaquin rode down a smooth slope
in the bluff. The others followed. Up close, the scene was
even more grim. Five men and two women had been
slaughtered, their belongings scattered like tumbleweeds
over the prairie. Joaquin saw a pair of lace-edged pantaloons caught on a yucca, flapping in the hard wind like a
flag. He kept alert for the sound of returning Arapaho, but
heard only the silence of death.

"Pack the horses with the clothes," he said. "We'll sell
them to the Kiowa at Hunter's Break on our way back."

"What about the food?"

Joaquin narrowed his eyes, gauging the weight of the
foodstuffs, all packed in hundred-pound bags. "Leave all
but the coffee. We'll sell it at Bent's Fort. The rest will
slow us down."

Raul dismounted, nodding, and began to collect the
scattered goods.

"It's bloody heartless," St. John protested.

"Heartless?" Raul snorted. "What good is any of it to these folks?"

"But—"

Joaquin looked at the dying light over the mountains. "Leave it if it turns your stomach, amigo."

St. John shrugged and dismounted. He picked up a blue dress and shook it out, then tossed it over his shoulder.

Raul shot Joaquin an amused glance, and Joaquin met it with a half-grin. St. John was learning quickly. What seemed heartless in civilization was often simply a matter of survival here.

The three men were comancheros, tradesmen of the plains, carrying everything from fabric to food to various tribes on a circuitous route that covered hundreds of miles. They'd left Taos a month before on a permit that would expire in a few short days. Raul, an escaped slave from Mississippi, had been riding with Joaquin for more than five years, and took pleasure in needling a former British officer with more spirit of adventure than good sense. They all needled one another—it was the way of men. But today there was no time. They had to make camp by dark.

As the others gathered usable goods, Joaquin rode in a circle around the site of the ambush, uneasiness crawling on the back of his neck. He did not fear the Arapaho, for their mission was vengeance and had been accomplished, but he had a sense he'd missed something.

He listened intently for any slight sound, moving slowly toward a grove of cottonwoods that shaded a long stretch of the Rio Napestle. The Anglos had christened it the Arkansas, for reasons Joaquin had never bothered to decipher. They had a lust for naming things their way, these Americanos. They blushed to call the blessed mountains by their true name, too. They were invisible at this distance, but Joaquin thought of the way they rose in perfect voluptuous points, and smiled. *La Tetas de Madre*—The Breasts of the Mother. What else?

To his left, a trio of magpies suddenly screeched and flapped their wings. Joaquin halted. He peered closely at the trees and scrub oak. It might only be a war with a squirrel, but he'd learned to investigate such cries.

The smallest gasp reached his ears. At the same moment, he spied a scrap of blue fabric through the branches. Hand on his rifle, he dismounted cautiously and strode forward, calling out, "Who's there?" in English, then in Spanish.

No answer. The magpies screeched again. Joaquin shoved aside the brush, seeing now the broken twigs and scuffed dirt he should have noticed on his first pass.

At the foot of a cottonwood, huddled in blankets, were two women, one white, one black. The white one stared at him in speechless terror, her eyes wide in her scratched, dirty face. The black woman, obviously the lady's slave, was cradled against the other's breast, a gash over her head, as if a knife—

Joaquin cursed. He knelt, instinctively reaching out to touch the slave's face, to see if she were feverish from the wound. The white woman shrunk back, keeping her arms around her slave. She made a quick, savage noise of warning.

"I won't hurt you," Joaquin said. "I want to see if she's alive."

"No!" She clutched her slave closer. "Stay away."

He realized how he must look to her with his serape and long black hair and moccasins. She stared at him as if he were Satan himself.

"I won't hurt you," he repeated. To illustrate his good intentions, he put his rifle down and even lifted his serape to take the knife from his belt, which he put beside the gun on the ground.

He held open his hands, palms up. Still she stared. He'd never seen such eyes—strange-colored, almost too big for her small face. Wild hair, the color of piñon nuts, tumbled in loose curls over her shoulders. Her jaw was hard, fierce. And she was protective about her slave. Perhaps she feared they would steal her.

"She's alive," she said, and Joaquin caught the singing lilt of her words—not an American English, but not quite like Roger's British, either. "She's hurt."

"Show me," he said. "Maybe I can help her."

The woman stared at him a moment, then abruptly turned and murmured something in the slave's ear. Gently, she shifted and tossed back the blanket that cloaked them.

Joaquin sucked his teeth as the blood below was revealed. It stained both dresses in blotches. The Anglo apparently knew something of healing, for the wound on the dark woman's thigh was packed with mud and herbs. "An arrow?" he asked.

She nodded, pulling the blanket around them again.

Rocking back on his heels, Joaquin looked at her without speaking. The pair puzzled him. The white woman looked like a lady—the dress was well made and of a style he knew rich women wore.

But he had not known many ladies to care so much about their slaves. "You must come with us," he said.

She made a wordless motion of protest, as if she wished to blend into the bark of the tree.

"Night will soon fall, and the wind will freeze you to death." He lifted his chin toward the black woman. "She'll die."

The white woman stared at him. Again he noticed her eyes. Not quite gray. Not green. Somewhere between the two colors, like the shallowest edge of a hot-spring pool.

She clasped her arms around her slave more tightly.

In sudden decision, Joaquin stood and strode out of the hidden place. "St. John!" he shouted.

Roger came over. "What is it?"

"Women." Joaquin pulled aside the branches to show him. "She's afraid of me. Coax her out and let's get someplace we can make camp before full dark."

"Will do."

Joaquin glanced over his shoulder. The woman still stared at him with distrust. It was a look he'd seen many times. Letting the branches go behind St. John, he went to join Raul in the business of collecting usable trade goods.

Tess watched the dark man depart, her hands trembling. She had never seen anyone like him, seemingly civilized in his speech, with the same lilt to his words as the Spanish traders who'd been killed. But not civilized, in his wild clothes, with the impossibly long, black hair, bound by red cloth at the nape of his neck. Not civilized, for he wore a blanket and leggings.

Now a white man in the same strange clothes knelt next to her. At least he did not have the fierce dark features of an Indian, but blue eyes, red hair and a reassuringly crooked smile. Even his British voice was undaunting. Whatever evil the Brits brought upon Irish heads—and heaven knew it was a load—Tess had never seen them scalp anyone.

"Your friend is quite ill," he said and held out a hand to put on Sonia's cheek. "How long has it been since the attack?"

"A few hours." Tess closed her eyes at the remembered horror. "They came so fast," she said.

The Brit nodded.

"So fast," she repeated. "It was terrible."

"Why didn't they kill you?"

"Some other men fired guns at them." She had been breathless with exhaustion by then, but the old Indian had called, and with swift grace, the warrior dropped his knife and rode off. "I hid from them. Sonia played dead." Tess was still furious at herself for allowing *these* men to find her.

"It'll be a true enough death if you don't come with us. You'll both die out here alone," he said. "We'll help you get where you're going."

"I'm afraid of that other man."

The Brit shook his head. "He won't hurt you." He stood up. "Come on."

Against Tess's neck, Sonia stirred, and a broken moan

sounded low in her throat. Bleakly, Tess realized there was really no choice. "We're going to Taos to meet my husband," she said finally. "Can you take us there?"

"Taos is where we're going. Who is your husband?"

Tess felt the pressure of lying all through her as she stared at the kindly face, but she would not deviate from her plan now. "Seamus McKenzie," she said without blinking.

The Brit shrugged. "Never heard of him, but that don't mean much." He stood and whistled, a bright, loud sound, like some exotic bird. "I'm going to get Raul to carry your woman, there. Guess you can ride with me."

Tess said nothing. She held Sonia close, taking comfort in her warmth. Below the blanket, she moved her hand on Sonia's arm.

A third man appeared, and Tess started, gripping Sonia closer. He was tall and black and had made no sound whatsoever as he came through the brush. Tess looked at his feet as if he might have floated. They were enormous, as were his hands. His sparse beard was grizzled with white, and in his narrowed eyes, Tess saw his hatred.

Once, he too had been a slave. She would have gambled all the money in her hems on the assumption.

"This is Raul Libre, ladies," the Brit said, as if they were all at a tea party in a drawing room. "They're coming with us, Raul. If you'll carry Rose Red, I'll take Snow White."

For a long moment, Raul stared at them with a flat expression. It would be amusing, him thinking her a great lady, Tess thought, but it was important that she maintain the ruse or she and Sonia would be in grave danger. If he were an escaped slave, he'd know as soon as he heard her speak that she was no plantation belle. She'd have to think of a lie to convince him if it came to that.

Jaw hard, he squatted and tossed off the blanket covering Sonia. Immediately, his face thawed. "Let's do this nice and easy," he said in a rough, low voice. She heard the long vowels and soft consonants of the South. "Move up and I'll see if I can lift her."

Tess eased forward. The man's big hands seemed surprisingly gentle as they slipped beneath Sonia's legs and back. With a grunt—Sonia herself was no slight maid, but a strappingly tall woman with long muscles and a babe in her belly—he gathered her limp body and stood. Tess jumped to her feet to give him the blanket, but she'd been sitting so long in the same position, her legs nearly buckled. She hobbled toward Raul and tossed the blanket over Sonia. Raul gave her the same odd look as the first man had given, then abruptly turned and took his burden out of the hidden place.

The Brit steadied Tess with a hand to her arm. "Are you hurt?"

"No." She rubbed her knees and took an experimental step. The tingling eased. Picking up her once-fine blue cloak, she threw it around her shoulders and followed after Raul, anxious not to lose sight of Sonia.

2

They made camp in a high arroyo Joaquin favored for its convoluted twists and turns. This time of year, there was no danger from the sudden waters that had carved the shallow canyon in the desert, and the ten-foot walls gave protection from the hard wind.

The three men had an unspoken routine. Joaquin built a fire of mesquite and a handful of cottonwood branches while Roger took out the food that would be their supper. Raul tended the horses.

His eyes on the woman, Joaquin fed a bit more wood to the fire and put the coffee pot on a nearby rock to warm. The slave had stirred during the ride, and the Anglo woman now coaxed water to her lips, murmuring quietly. Joaquin narrowed his eyes once more, trying to understand their odd relationship. When the slave drank and settled back on the blanket Raul had laid in the soft sand for her, the white woman took off her cloak and put it over the slave.

He stood and went to his saddlebags and took out a serape, striped in yellow and white. Knowing the woman was afraid of him, he didn't go too close, but held it out to her for a moment before tossing it to her lap. "It will be very cold before long," he said. "Put it on."

Warily, she put it around her, looking once at Joaquin to see how to drape it. "*Gracias,*" she said.

"You know my language?" he asked, surprised.

"A little from the traders, that's all. I'm trying to learn what I can."

The garment gave her a different look, covering the fine but soiled dress. With an impatient gesture, she freed her hair from below it, and the corkscrew curls tumbled around her shoulders and down her back. It was very long and very wild, and it made him smile. So much life in that hair.

"What?" she asked, wiping at her face with the back of her wrist. "I've not washed in days. I must look a ragamuffin."

"Ragamuffin?" Joaquin echoed. He squatted and took the coffee from its place and poured some into a tin cup. The scent was rich, the steam heartening. He handed it to her. "What is a ragamuffin?"

She accepted the cup and closed her eyes to smell it, as if it had been a long time. Joaquin found the gesture moving, and looked away to give her privacy. When he looked back, she was watching him.

"A ragamuffin is a grimy little child," she said.

"Ah." He smiled. "You will see many of them in Taos."

She sobered, looking toward the fire over his shoulder. The pale yellow light bled her eyes of any color, and he saw there was a worry in them. He waited.

After a time, filled with the lonely sound of the wind moaning over the prairie, she looked at him. "What else will I find in Taos?"

He lifted a shoulder. "It's only a village, like any village."

"Are there Indians?"

Ah. She was afraid. "Many," he said with a nod. He poked a stick in the fire. "But they will not hurt you. We live in peace with the Comanche and the Utes and the Navajo, and there is a pueblo of Taos Indians there, too." The peace was being disrupted by Armijo, but Joaquin saw no need to add to her fear.

"And you, sir? Are you an Indian?"

He looked up at that "sir," thinking she jested. But there was no sarcasm in her expression. "My mother was a *genizara*," he said, "an Indian stolen from her people to be a slave to Armando Morales. He gave her many children, and I"—he spread his hands—"am one of them."

"A slave," she echoed in her soft, dangerously husky voice. "Everywhere in this country, there are slaves." Her mouth tightened and she stilled, bowing her head.

She was a puzzle, this strange woman who cared for her slave as one would tend a sister. Perhaps she was afraid she would be left alone in such dangerous country with no one familiar, but he thought it was not so simple. These two had a deeper bond.

"Are there no slaves where you come from?" he asked.

She curled her arms around herself. "Only slaves to hunger."

St. John knelt nearby and took food from a pouch, hard bread that kept for weeks called pan, and dried meat. Joaquin wished fleetingly for something with blood in it, a rabbit or an antelope, and he looked forward to going home, where he might have fresh tortillas and green chili. He took a portion of the sturdier dried food and gave some to the woman.

"Did my friend here bother to introduce himself?" St. John asked.

Tess tore into the meat gustily, shaking her head.

"Allow me. I'm Roger St. John, late of the British Cavalry. I think I told you before that the man tending the horses is Raul Libre. I don't think that's the name he was born with, you understand." He gestured toward Joaquin. "That scary fellow is Joaquin Morales, of Taos."

The woman looked at each in turn. "I am Tess Fallon, and that is Sonia."

"Mrs. Fallon? Did you say your husband was Seamus McKenzie?"

Her lids flickered. She was lying about something,

Joaquin thought. "Fallon is my old family name."

"I see." Roger glanced at Joaquin. "Well, it won't be long till you're reunited with him, at any rate."

"How long will it take us to get to Taos?"

Joaquin shrugged. "A week, maybe two. Depends on the weather."

"I'll need more herbs for my woman, then."

"What kind of herbs?"

"It grows by the rivers. I don't know the name of it here, but we called it 'yarrow' in Ireland."

"Are you one of those witchy women?" Roger asked suspiciously.

Her eyes grew bright and hard, and she drew her small body up. "So some say." Joaquin was pleased by the arrogance in the tilt of her chin. "I'm a healer, as my mother and grandmother were before me."

"A medicine woman," Raul said in his gruff voice, joining them.

Tess looked up, meeting his gaze steadily and without fear in spite of his obvious hatred. "I am."

Raul dropped to sit on a flat rock and took a hank of jerky from the box. "Plenty of need for healers on them plantations, ain't there?"

Again, she did not waver. "Aye."

In the softly spoken word, Joaquin heard a world of knowledge, of fury and sorrow. It whispered into some long-forgotten place of compassion in him and settled, the way a dog comfortably settled upon the feet of a beloved person. He looked at the small, fierce woman with her untamed hair. A surprising tingle tightened his loins.

Abruptly, he stood. "Your gift will be welcome in Taos, then," he said.

He thought he felt her gaze on him, but did not look back. She was not his kind. And she was married.

A few more days, and they would be in Taos once again. There he would find willing partners among the women of his class, and even a few of the *ricos* lustful wives, who called to him to do small jobs when their husbands were away, and gave him tall cool drinks on their patios. He flirted with them, sometimes more. Not often. Generally, he kept to women like himself, mixed-blood and free. Perhaps he would even choose one to make a house for him soon, if profits stayed strong. He was of an age when the thought of children and a warm woman in his bed were more appealing than all the pulque and dice and whores in the world.

These sensible thoughts in his mind, he settled himself on the ground, wrapped in his serape and a warm blanket, and settled in to sleep.

As the camp settled down, Tess curled her body around Sonia's. She'd grown used to sleeping like this, out in the open, with only Sonia close by to make her feel secure, but it was different tonight. Tonight, she strained her ears for the sound of that terrifying battle cry—that wild high whoop she heard over and over again in her mind. Like banshees, warning of death.

And no banshee could be more terrible than those beautiful warriors, fierce as her famed ancestor Cuchulainn when they descended upon the wagons.

By the fire, the black man kept watch. He smoked a thin cigar, a rifle over his knees, and listened to the night. From time to time, she saw him look at her—or perhaps at Sonia. She had not missed the lingering way his hands moved on Sonia's body, as careful as if he tended a babe.

To her relief, neither the Brit nor Raul had seemed to think anything odd about an Irishwoman who traveled with a slave. Raul continued to look at her with hatred, for he probably believed what the rich clothes said about her. Tess would make sure he continued to believe that until both she and Sonia were safe.

Tess had no doubt that Seamus McKenzie would be on her trail, and although they'd been careful, there was a trail to follow. She had not realized what an oddity two women alone would be, nor what a struggle they would face trying to find escort to Santa Fe. Everyone in Independence would remember her and her beautiful slave.

Tess knew her husband well enough to know he would not give up until he had found her. And punished her.

Overhead, the wind whipped up a whirling dervish that spun sand and small rocks over the nearby ground. Tess jumped and then pressed closer to Sonia, taking comfort in the easy sound of her breathing.

A vast wave of homesickness overtook her. *Ireland.* The memory of it made her soft. There it was never hot as wretched Arkansas was, nor snake-infested, nor filled with every manner of crawling or flying insect God ever created.

But she'd been starving in Ireland. In Arkansas, she'd at least been able to eat her fill when she sat down to a table. Last winter in Ireland, food had grown so scarce her teeth had grown loose in her mouth. Fevers swept their small village, preying on the weakened number. Many died, her father among them.

As the last of winter chilled her bones, as all hope seemed lost, then had Tess's fortune turned. Or seemed to. Seamus came home to his village, flashing his wealth around in the way the villagers best understood: he bore food with him. Hams and hearty beef and stout bread. Tess, along with the rest of the village, cared little that he'd gained his spoils by piracy and murder. The dead mattered less to them than their hunger.

And starvation was a slow death. A little at a time, then a little more. The days were filled with a yawning, yearning need that put all else to dimness. Tess admitted to herself that she had cared not at all from whence those hams and cakes had come.

When she'd found Seamus himself—bluff and ruddy-faced—feasting his eyes on her body, she was willing enough to do what she could to save herself and her brother Liam.

For Liam, just gone seventeen and a big youth, bright

as the dark nights were long, she gave herself in marriage to Seamus McKenzie. Seamus had been cruel as a child, and had grown crueler still as a man. These things Tess knew, and thought she could manage—what worse thing could there be than the slow, certain starvation she faced?

That was before she'd seen the slaves.

On the soft sand of the arroyo, Tess shifted. She'd known sorrows in her days, but none like that of the slaves. No, none like those sorrows. And there, as overseer on the plantation, had Seamus McKenzie honed his cruelty, even upon his own wife when she dared interfere.

So Tess, and Sonia with her, had run.

Run to the West—where it was said a slave could disappear and never be found again. West, where a woman might have a chance to build a life for herself.

She had believed they would be safe in Taos, a town that was a little out of the way, and by all accounts thriving, though smaller than its cousin Santa Fe. They would find work as seamstresses or weavers, or perhaps as cooks or nannies. There was never a dearth of honest work.

Now, Tess wasn't sure. There was a new language to learn, and Indians, and Seamus surely trailing them. In one way, the Indian attack was good. Perhaps Seamus would learn of it and think Tess and Sonia dead. Or perhaps Indians would find him before he found her.

But what if they didn't?

Both women were exhausted, and now winter was setting in. She was sure it snowed here, and did not know what that would be like. Further travel would be difficult, that much she knew. And she had little knowledge of where else to go.

Wearily, she closed her eyes. Perhaps they would have a little time in Taos to learn what the next opportunity would be.

On one point, Tess was thoroughly clear—she would not return to Seamus McKenzie. She would sooner kill him herself.

*   *   *

In the morning, Tess wakened before the others. Or so she thought until she came back from a private place and found Señor Morales pouring water from his canteen into the coffee pot. She halted uncertainly.

He frightened her. Against the thick, gray fog, he stood out dark as an elm. Beads of moisture clung to his long black hair, tied with that scrap of red cloth that made her think of the red hands painted on the Indians' horses. There was stealth—or maybe only quiet—in his movements.

Clutching her skirts, Tess watched him as he tucked a bleached arm of cottonwood more deeply into the flames. Her gaze caught on his hands, lean and dark and somehow beautiful in their sure, easy movements. His legs were very long, his shoulders broad below the serape.

But it was his face that snared her. In the cool, gray light, she saw it was a face of no small beauty, carved with sharp angles and high slopes that were unlike any she'd seen before. The strong lines and uncommon tilts gave her an odd pleasure, and she felt she could contentedly look at him for a long time.

He seemed not to notice her, so she did not call attention to herself, and gave in to the rare sense of quiet his smooth movements kindled in her. Even as she felt it, she wondered what made it so. Perhaps it was only that he seemed to fit this vast land, as if he belonged here. As she hoped she might learn to belong.

Last night, he'd taken pains to make her comfortable with him, as if he accepted terror as his due. Now she thought of the way he had looked when he smiled over the Brit's teasing. It was an easy, bright sort of smile, one that hid little. Surely no man who could so easily smile over a bit of silliness was dangerous.

Holding the serape he'd given her close to shut out the cold, she moved toward him and held her chilled hands out to the fire. "Good morning, Señor Morales," she said softly.

He did not look up, and Tess realized he'd known she

was there all along. "*Buenos dias*." A glitter shone in his eye when he did raise his face. Somehow the cheerful light reassured her.

"Is there some task you would have me do?" she asked.

Again she had the feeling she had surprised him, for a faintly quizzical expression painted his brow. His eyes were a fathomless black, with an exotic cast she found beautiful. A quickening moved through her, and she looked away. "I've yet to learn the culture here," she said. "If I've given offense, you must tell me."

"Ladies are not usually so willing to dirty their hands."

As Tess well knew. But she could not protest his assumption, not when she was so desperate to maintain his belief in her story. She shifted the serape on her shoulders and shrugged. "'Tis not so common one must thank another for her life, either." She paused. "I'm grateful to all of you."

"*De nada*." He gave her a strip of the jerky they had eaten the night before, and a square of the hard, black-ened bread. "We ride long today. Perhaps we can find rabbits or an antelope before tonight."

"If you find a rabbit, I'll gladly cook it."

"You cook?"

Tess lifted a brow. "Aye—and what kind of woman doesn't cook?"

He shrugged, smiling carelessly. "A lady."

A twitch of nervousness reminded her she should be careful. Aloud, however, she said, "Not Irish ladies." She changed the subject. "Will we ride by the river soon? I'll need more herbs for my woman."

"We're only a little way from it now. I can take you there." He stood.

"Now?" Tess didn't know why it so alarmed her, but suddenly her terror rushed back. He towered over her, loose-limbed and calm, but Tess had the feeling there wasn't a single nerve in his body that was not utterly alert.

"*Sí*. While the others yet sleep."

How could she gracefully refuse? Quelling her reluctance she stood, brushing her skirt of the worst of the grime that clung to it. She could do nothing about the bloodstains, and was grateful for the long covering fall of the serape.

He moved ahead of her, leading her down the arroyo beyond a turn in the little canyon. Tess hurried to keep up, afraid she'd be lost in the dense fog. His soft leather boots made no sound, but she saw his footprints in the sand carried an indentation for toes. The sight gave her a sharp, strange vision of his bare feet, and she quickly looked away.

They ascended the wall at a small, sloped break. Tess paused at the top to look around her. Only pale mist could be seen, punctured at intervals by the slim green swords of a fan-shaped plant. She leaned over one, as she had several times since first spying them, and touched the leaves cautiously. Leathery, with a faint scent. From the middle grew a thick cluster of flowers on a tall stalk, the pods dry and cracked open now. Curiously, she broke one of the pods off and smelled it.

Señor Morales waited beside her. She fingered the plant, and held out the pod. "What is this called?" she asked.

"Yucca. We use the root for soap—very good for the hair, and clothes." He said the last word, "cloth-es," as if it were two syllables.

Tess nodded, pleased by her sense that the plant must be useful had proved true. "Perhaps there are women in Taos who will teach me the ways of these new plants."

"Perhaps my sister. She is a healer, like you."

"Is she now?" Tess smiled. "The plants here are very different than the ones I know. I look forward to learning." Carrying the pod with her, she shifted her skirts and walked along with him. The fog made her vaguely homesick for a land as lush as this one was spare. "Everything is different here," she said.

"You're brave to come so far."

Brave. The word gave her a bitter smile. She'd run

from Ireland and hunger, now she ran from Seamus McKenzie who claimed her as wife. "Brave I am not," she said firmly. "Practical, perhaps."

To her surprise, he smiled, and the expression gentled the hard, dark planes of his face. "As you wish."

A fluttering noise of many birds disturbed the almost eerie stillness. As the fog parted, Tess saw a line of trees that indicated the river, and to her right, a wide marsh, its edge lost in the mist. Dried cattails covered it like a thick, miniature forest. Perched on the tips, like some odd plump fruit, were dozens of blackbirds, chuttering softly, taking wing and simply sitting. Tess paused to admire the scene. "How do you say their name in Spanish?"

"*Los mirlos*," he said. "Ah, and look." He moved close to the edge of the marsh, sending birds scattering in alarm. He plucked a bract of leaves and held it up. "Sage. Do you know this one?"

His fingers were extraordinarily graceful and long, aristocratic hands on another man. The plant he held was silvery-gray, with slightly furry foliage. "No," she said. "Is it for healing?"

"Yes. And it is very common here." He put the clip in her hands. "You should remember it."

"Thank you." Tess smelled it. "I will."

They walked to the edge of the river, where Tess searched once more for yarrow. Perhaps it didn't grow here. She frowned, wondering what she might be able to use in place of it. So few of these plants had any meaning for her.

The river clucked along, dark-colored against the cold mist. Tess knelt on the bank and formed a cup with her hands, then drank deeply of the cold, fresh water. Next to her, Señor Morales also drank. Tess rocked back on her knees, very aware of some pleasurable link between them in the primitive act of drinking from a river in the close fog, with few civilized humans for hundreds of miles.

Across the water, a magpie screeched, its long tail

flashing black, and a second rose up behind it. Tess looked up to watch them. She pointed. "They fly to the right—a good omen for our journey today."

He grinned. The tilt of his eyes made her think of the enchanted creatures of the forest, elves and fairies. He could easily be of their number. "I do not know this omen," he said.

"If they'd flown to our left, it would not be so good."

He lifted his eyes toward the birds. "I'll remember."

Suddenly, Tess was quite profoundly glad to be alive, on the bank of this river, watching a magpie fly, the sweet taste of cold water in her mouth. She took a breath and that was a pleasure, too, the dry, cold air in her throat and her chest, the sting of morning on her cheeks.

"The land is different here, but it has its own beauty, no?" he asked.

"Yes. And I have you to thank for the fact I am seeing it at all."

His rich smile flashed again, giving a light to his eyes, a somehow endearing crook to his well-cut mouth. For a fleeting second, it seemed his gaze touched on her lips. "I'm glad you are no longer afraid of me."

Tess shook her head, but looked away for fear her face would betray her. She spotted a patch of onion tops a little way up the bank and cried out, "Look! Find a rabbit and a good stew I'll cook tonight!"

He lent her his knife again, and she dug up the small, wild bulbs, a little soft but not yet ruined by frost. Their pungent scent pleased her, and as they walked back to camp, she felt very happy. It was only as they reached the arroyo that she identified the strange emotion.

Hope.

3

Joaquin went down the steep incline into the arroyo first, then turned to hold out a hand to Tess. Her skirt was filled with onions, her hem and shoes muddy, her light brown hair loose and curling around her shoulders. The brightly striped serape, in combination with her fairness, made her look exotic. And strangely attainable.

She hesitated, turning her feet sideways on the slope, and only when she skidded a little did she grasp his outstretched hand. Her fingers were cold, and chapped from her long journey. He noticed her nails were chipped and broken, as if she had worked hard with them.

She jumped down the last bit of the hill, but Joaquin, absorbed in his study of her hands, didn't immediately let go. She stood beside him, slight as a willow whip, a tendril of hair blowing across her face. Her cheeks were red with the same cold.

Beautiful, he thought and his mind gave forth a beguiling vision of his mouth on hers, that playful strand of hair touching his cheek.

Hastily, he let her go, disturbed at the strong response she brought out in him. It was not like him to be bothered by a woman—any woman. Women came to *him*.

He stole a glance over his shoulder at her. She walked

steadfastly in the uncertain sand below their feet, her hands clutched to her skirt and its burden of onions. Very different she was from the women he'd known, with her fair skin and golden-brown hair. What colors did a woman have when she was so fair as this? Would her breasts be tipped with cocoa, or perhaps the pink of a new-born rose?

He scowled at the vision. It was only the difference that made him so curious, so interested in a woman with hardly more curves than a boy. He called up a memory of Elena, vividly colored and lushly rounded. There was a real woman. Not long now till he would be able to taste of her fruits.

As they came around the last turn by their camp, Tess gave a small, soft gasp, and started to run forward. Alarmed, Joaquin scanned the bluffs and the camp below, but saw nothing immediately amiss.

Ah, there. The slave woman was sitting up, propped by a solicitous Raul, who held a cup to her lips. Joaquin grinned. Raul was smitten. It was his way to fall in love like this—fast and hard upon sight. Sometimes it lasted a few days, sometimes a month, once even an entire year. But it did not last.

Joaquin watched Tess drop to one knee next to the woman. Raul stiffened visibly, and by his expression, Joaquin knew to move quickly to intervene. Too late. Raul said something Joaquin couldn't quite catch, and he pushed at Tess's outstretched hand.

Joining them, Joaquin said with a fake bluster, "Looks like the sleeping one awakes."

The woman looked up, utterly expressionless, and he decided Raul might last a little longer with this one. High cheekbones centerpieced a face as elegantly formed as that of a china cat he'd seen in his stepmother's house.

Tess looked at Joaquin, and angrily pointed at Raul. "Tell him to let me tend her wounds."

"He ain't my bossman, lady, and neither are you."

"Raul, my friend," Joaquin said gently. "Give them a little time, eh?"

Raul straightened, his hands still on the slave woman's shoulders. "She's pregnant," he said baldly. "And this—"

Joaquin jerked his head for Raul to follow him. Before he could move, Tess pushed Raul's hands away from Sonia. "Go tend your horses. A woman tends women."

"Ain't nothin' a *lady* like you got to do with a woman like this but make her your pack horse. How could you bring her on the Trail, knowin' she had a babe in her?"

With a shrug, Joaquin stepped back. They might as well get this over with. It was yet a long ride to Taos.

Tess ignored Raul, as if he hadn't spoken. Deliberately, she took the onions from her skirt, and with muddy fingers took the herbs from her pocket and set them aside. With the clean back of her hand, she felt Sonia's face, and murmured a question Joaquin couldn't quite hear. Sonia answered in the same quiet way. Below the spoken words, a wealth of communication passed between the two women, hands gripping and releasing, eyes snagging and darting.

Yes, Joaquin thought, the bond was far deeper than that of slave and lady. It was not so strange—had not his own father fallen in love with a slave? How much easier for two women to become friends?

"If you want to see her live," Tess said to Raul, "you might help me instead of blustering about. I need water to tend her wound, if you'd be so kind to fetch it."

That little chin went forward, not quite arrogant, but determined. Joaquin winked at Roger when Raul did as he was bidden.

"Some woman," Roger said, eyeing the line of Tess's back appreciatively.

Joaquin quelled a rumbling annoyance at the comment. With a dismissive tsk, he said, "The Anglos have no color to them." He turned away, to get the camp moving. There was a scent of snow in the air.

* * *

When Raul stomped off, Tess bent over Sonia and lifted the old patch of leaves, mud and herbs from her wound. As she did so, she whispered urgently, "Our story stands."

Sonia answered ironically, "Yes'm."

Tess lifted her head and smiled. "You must feel better."

"I reckon I'll live now." She touched her slightly swollen belly, not near big enough for the six-month babe within her. "Don't know about this one."

"Nor do I. Has it moved?"

Sonia nodded. "Wild for such a wee one."

A crunch of sand told Tess Raul was back. He put a bucket of water nearby her leg. "Mind yourself," he said gruffly, "I already put it on the fire when she woke up."

"Thank you." Aware of his intent and disapproving gaze, Tess dipped her hands first in the steaming water, gasping at the heat of it, and then the blistering cold that met her wet fingers when she withdrew. It stung near enough to put tears in her eyes.

She gave Raul a pointed look, but he didn't move. Tess looked at Sonia, and saw the spark of amusement there in her dark eyes. She was used to such protective gestures from men.

"She'll not die of her wound," Tess said, for his hearing. "And well I've delivered many a babe, so this one is not so different. When it comes, I will be ready."

"Can she ride?" He touched his nose. "I mean, with me? Without hurting her?"

"That I can't answer."

He frowned. "Thought all you folks kept them fancy horses for your pleasure."

"Perhaps there are things of which you know little, then," Tess replied calmly. The wound looked good. Clean and healthily red.

"I doubt it." Abruptly, he stood. "Roger," he called, "help me rig up a travois for this one. She'll likely lose the babe anyway, but we can try."

"We can't take a travois over Raton."

Raul looked at the sky, and Tess watched curiously as he lifted his head and seemed to smell the air. "We ain't gonna make Raton anyhow. What you think, Joaquin? The fort?"

Joaquin looked at the sky and nodded.

Tess paused. "We're not going to Taos?"

"Not today, we ain't," Raul said. "And if we don't get moving real soon, we ain't gonna make the fort, either."

The men moved off, to do their business. "They'll be kind enough to us, I think," Tess said to Sonia in a low voice. "Do you feel safe here?"

"That one looks like an Indian." Sonia's dark gaze touched Joaquin, then flitted away. "Ain't you afraid of him?"

"No." Tess wanted to add more, but the words seemed lost somewhere in her throat. Or perhaps she only understood now how ridiculous they sounded: *I trust him because his face is kinder and more beautiful than any face I've looked upon till now. I didn't know such faces were in the world.*

No, that wouldn't do.

Instead she said, "He is the one who found us. He could have killed us while we were alone there."

Sonia gasped as Tess washed her wound. As if to distract herself she whispered, "Is the black one a free man?"

"No," Tess said with low chuckle, "I rather think he's your slave." She glanced over her shoulder. "And he thinks none too highly of milady, I can tell you."

"That was plain enough."

Tess crushed herbs to make a poultice with water, and packed the mixture on Sonia's wound. "Let it dry now." With a frown she rocked back on her heels. "You feel better, though? How much pain in the wound? Any heat to it?"

"You don't act too sure o' yourself, sister."

"I don't know these plants well. I'm only making do."

"Tell me some other time." Sonia shifted until she was

sitting upright. "It feels good, to tell you the truth. Not like a whip. Musta been a clean wound."

"Aye. The arrow was smooth as steel—that helped."

Sonia jumped, making a grunting sound. Her hand flew to the small, round lump in her belly.

"What?" Tess inquired sharply. "Tell me!"

"Just a good kick." She smiled and once again, Tess was overwhelmed with gratitude and relief. She wanted to hug the woman close to her, but it would be unseemly, even for a healer, to hug her slave.

As if any healer worthy of the name could claim to own another human being.

Tess took Sonia's strong hand into her own. "I'm very glad you'll be all right," she whispered. "I was afraid you would die."

Sonia squeezed her fingers. "Can't kill me that easy."

Raul appeared once again, a looming, disapproving shadow. "Got the travois ready. Whyn't you come on over here and see if you think it'll work out? We gotta get moving."

The skies remained heavy and dark as they continued their journey over the prairie. Sometimes it seemed impossible to Tess that these men could find their way in the patchy fog. It obscured the horizon and all landmarks. To her, it all looked the same—rolling land carpeted with coarse, yellowed grass, dotted with yucca and patches of cactus. Only the river stood out, protected as it was by unending sentinels of cottonwood trees and scrub oak.

Tess rode with the Brit for most of the day, and he kept up a good-humored commentary on all that they passed. He was a small man in comparison to the other two, not much taller than Sonia, and Tess found that fact, along with his relentless cheerfulness, reassuring. When she did not ride with Mr. St. John, she rode the great black beast that belonged to Señor Morales, who led the gelding as he walked on the open ground.

Their going was slow, because of the travois Raul pulled behind him. Sonia lay on it, covered with a buffalo hide, appearing to sleep. When they paused to eat at mid-day, she roused enough to take a cup of water, but she ate nothing.

The weather provided an odd sort of blessing. The low, still clouds seemed to hush the wind, and the party traveled in relative comfort. It was the first time in weeks the wind had not blown, and Tess was thankful for it. She sometimes thought she'd never wash all the dust from her body, fearing the wind had implanted it upon her skin forever.

Toward late afternoon, Tess felt spots of wet on her face, and looked up. Instead of rain, snow filled the air. The flakes twirled and twisted and drifted, silently catching on the horse's mane, on Tess's sleeve, and on her curls. She examined them in wonder, amazed that each one was different, like tiny, intricate jewels sparkling with iridescent color in the low light. She'd never seen anything so beautiful in all her life.

"Sonia," she called over shoulder. "Look! Snow!"

Sonia opened her eyes and flakes caught in her lashes. She held her hands palm up, to catch some, and put her tongue out. " 'Sakes alive," she said, and gave Tess a smile.

But at the first glimpse of the fort, nestled close by the river, Tess forgot her wonder over the snow. Against the low dark sky, the mud walls rose to turrets on all four corners like those on a medieval castle. Tess glimpsed an armed man atop one of them, silhouetted against the deepening twilight. From within came the faint sounds of voices, and laughter, carrying easily in the windless air. Ribbons of shimmering heat from fires bent the horizon.

Beyond the fort itself, spread like a small city around the walls, were teepees. A deep, squeezing terror gathered around Tess's heart when she saw them. The Indians who lived in them moved around easily in buckskin and blankets, bending over cookfires or knotted in small, quiet groups. It looked like any village at dusk, but for the strange dwellings. There were no decorations on the canvas and hide-made walls. Smoke rose from holes at the tops. Tess smelled meat.

As if he sensed her terror, Señor Morales dropped back a pace. He put his hand on Tess's knee. "They are camped here in peace," he said in a low voice. "None will harm you."

Tess couldn't speak. Some of the women in the camp looked up curiously at the group, then went back to their evening tasks. Children ran in a circle around the perimeter, caught sight of the horses, and ran toward them. Even the small ones frightened her, and on the travois, Sonia made a low, keening noise. Raul turned to comfort her.

"Who are they?" Tess asked. Instinctively, she put her hand on Joaquin's and gripped it. He didn't seem to notice.

"Cheyenne," he said. With a quick tug on the horse's reins, he stopped them, and looked up at Tess with a grave expression. "Listen closely to me now, señora. This is very important."

Tess nodded, though she kept looking over his shoulder at the teepees, where now a few men appeared, unpainted, but no less terrifying in their robes, blankets and leggings, hair wild all around them. She thought she saw the leader of the Indians who had attacked their party—but no, it was impossible. It was only fear that made her think it. She forced herself to pay attention to Joaquin.

"The others, at the gate, do you see them?"

Tess nodded.

"They are Arapaho, and they may even be the same men who attacked your party."

She clutched the saddle horn until her fingers ached, trying to bite back her fear. A cold sweat broke down her back as she peered through the snow to the men at the gate.

Señor Morales gripped her hand. "Listen, señora. There is a man in Nuevo Mexico who is greedy for power. You know those kind?"

Tess nodded again.

"Armijo wants everything for himself—land, slaves, money, all of it. He would not give these people back some children that were stolen from them." He paused, and Tess noticed with some distantly reasonable part of her mind that his eyes reflected the shadows of trees against the gray sky like a mirror. "They asked politely, and when the children were not returned, the Arapaho took it as an act of war."

"Then these are the—" she began, her voice shrill.

"Listen," he said again, touching his ear as if to illustrate the act. "Think. What would you do if your child was stolen and made a slave. Would you fight?"

Tess looked over his head at the camp. A woman snagged the arm of a boy who was running by, and the boy playfully struggled against her hold. Woman and child laughed, and the boy ran off.

"Yes," Tess said at last. "I would fight."

"The Cheyenne are no danger, but we will take care with these Arapaho warriors. I will see that you are protected."

"Yes."

He patted her leg again. It occurred to her that in the other world, in the worlds she'd left behind, this would be an overly familiar gesture. In this world—or perhaps only because it was from this man—it seemed only meant to comfort. He stepped away from the horse, and said something to St. John, then to Raul. He gestured, and they all followed him to the gates.

Tess looked at Sonia. Fear showed in her dark eyes, but not panic. Tess wondered suddenly if the man who had almost scalped her would be here—if he would recognize them, and if he did, would he want to avenge his honor? Tess had hurt him, she knew she had. Did such men as these take umbrage at a woman's blows?

She wanted to ask Señor Morales, but he strode toward the busy gate, moving in that loose-limbed way. For so tall a man, he was extraordinarily graceful. She liked the look of his long, long legs and wondered—

A scandalous thought. She turned her face away.

The other two riders flanked her closely as they approached the gates. Raul got down and gave the reins of his horse to Roger, then leaned over Sonia, murmuring words Tess couldn't hear. He touched the wound on Sonia's brow in some concern, then took the red scarf from around his neck and tied it over Sonia's head as a kerchief. The edge of the fabric hid the wound.

At the gates was an open window, around which milled a half dozen Indians—a boy and two women, the rest men. As their party approached, three of the men took something from the window and disappeared inside. Señor Morales turned and gave a nod. All was well.

Tess let out a breath. Her hands still trembled, but she found herself staring at the remaining Indians. She let her hair fall forward so she could look at them from beneath it.

All of the Indians clasped buffalo hides or blankets around their bodies—the blankets in rich tones of red or green or blue, with black stripes adorning the edges. The colors blazed in the foggy light, almost unbearably bright.

Perhaps in contrast, their hair was very black, and dressed with small braids and soft leather wraps and feathers and beads. A boy had bells on his ankle and Tess could hear the faint ringing below the general hubbub.

It took her a moment to realize they were staring at her with as much curiosity as she regarded them. A sharp, echoing terror cut through her, and she nearly bolted in panic before she realized there was no hostility in their gazes, only frank interest.

Taking in a slow, deep breath, she looked up at the armed men on the ramparts. It was all so strange, so different, so unlike anything she had ever even imagined existed. A small burst of wonder touched her. She'd never thought to dream of things beyond her village—that had been the realm of her brother, Liam. It had been he who'd told her of exotic places, and strange peoples. Indulgently, she had listened.

And now, here she was, a simple girl from a poor village, upon a great adventure. Ah, Liam would love it so!

For him, she would quell her terror at all the strangeness. For him, she would not pass judgments, or bolt in terror over every new thing. She would take it in, and remember the details. Perhaps she might even write them in a letter to Liam, who'd gone to Dublin with her departure to seek a better life for himself.

Squaring her shoulders and lifting her chin, she rode into the fort, her eyes eager for the new things there were to see.

4

In spite of his words to Tess, Joaquin was concerned to see the Arapaho warriors. He was almost certain it had been members of this band who'd taken the scalps of the Spanish traders that Tess and her woman had traveled with.

He braced himself, too, for the stir such a pretty pair of women would cause among the men at the fort. There were women here at times, but never had he seen an Anglo, nor any woman quite as stunning as Tess.

And his worry on this was not unfounded. As they passed below the arched gate, there was a great commotion. Soldiers lined the upper gallery, nudging each other. Traders and trappers stood up from their fire in the square. The Indians stared. Joaquin glanced over his shoulder to see how Tess was taking it.

Her face showed no strain. Her enormous gray-green eyes were calm, unafraid as she looked back at all of them. There was dust in her hair and on her smooth oval face, but Joaquin knew the men would find her beautiful, desirable. Perversely, he was glad she was married.

William Bent himself, who with his brothers had built the fort as a trading post, showed them to a room on the upper gallery. It was two rooms, actually, with a bed and a small table, and one small, shuttered window looking toward the prairie, another looking to the plaza within the fort. Tess insisted her woman should lie on the bed. Raul dutifully carried her there.

Joaquin lingered. "I'll bring you some food," he said. "Do you need anything else?"

"Water for washing." She looked at Bent. "Are there other women here?"

He nodded. "My wife. A few others."

"Might someone come to us?"

"Yes, ma'am. Right away."

Tess turned back to Sonia, obviously putting the men from her mind. Raul stood by the door, as if he were loathe to leave. Joaquin inclined his head toward the door, and reluctantly, Raul moved outside. Bent went out with him.

Joaquin paused a moment, watching as Tess shed the serape she'd been wearing since the night before. Her hair moved to one side, tumbling over one shoulder, and the nape of her neck showed, white and smooth. The sight was almost unbearably feminine, and he felt a swift urge to press his mouth to her collarbone. Scowling, he shifted his gaze, and saw the bloodstains on her skirt. "You will be wanting clean clothes. I'll find dresses, for both of you," he said.

"Oh, please, don't go to any trouble," Tess protested. "We'll wash these."

He shook his head slowly. "Those marks will never come out. And I do not wish for the Indians to see that blood."

"I see." She swallowed, and inclined her head. "Then, we will be glad to accept whatever you may find."

Her formality made him smile. "I'll have someone bring water, too." He nodded toward Sonia and went outside, latching the door behind him.

Raul had already gone down to the plaza but Bent waited for Joaquin at the top of the stairs. "I have something to show you."

Joaquin followed him to a small room off the trading

post. A mesquite fire burned on the hearth, and Joaquin put his cold hands close to the flame.

Bent reached into a drawer. "Two days ago, a war party came off the plains with several scalps they said they took from Spanish traders," he said, lifting the gruesome trophies. "Armijo would not release the captives, so they'll send these scalps as a message to him."

"And the war party is out there now?"

Bent nodded. "I reckon those women are survivors of the raid?"

"Yes," Joaquin said with a rueful expression. "We found them by the river. The slave was wounded, but the other was unhurt."

"If the warriors catch sight of the pair of them, they could be in danger. Warn them to be careful."

"There will be no trouble from them."

Bent gave him an ironic grin. "No trouble? There's a score of horny men out there, and I'd wager it's been years since any of 'em have seen a white woman. She'd best keep to herself as much as she can."

"She's married."

"But there's no husband here, is there?"

"No."

For a moment, Bent was silent, pursing his lips in thought. "Make her your wife. A make-believe wife, to protect her. Will she allow it?"

The idea tempted him, and just as quickly warned him it would be unwise. "St. John would be a better choice as her husband."

Bent chuckled. "Except he's already flirting with the women outside, making himself at home in the teepees. He's not the marrying kind."

That was true enough, and Bent had a good point. At best, Tess would be forced to fend off amorous advances while they stayed here. At worst—well, at worst, she would suffer far more. Joaquin was known, and the men would not bother her if she was thought to be his wife. "I'll ask her."

"Good."

Joaquin stepped into the plaza and simply stood there for a moment, gathering himself. The smell of cooking meat teased his empty belly, and he made for the kitchen first. The room was warm and dry, scented with the stew bubbling in a big iron pot over the fire. Herbs and chili *ristras* hung from the ceiling.

Two women tended the enormous hearth, a grandmotherly Spanish woman, Juana, and a younger black woman, Marguerite, who had been rescued much the same way Tess and Sonia had. This was one of the women with whom fickle Raul had been besotted, but Marguerite bore him no ill will, for she'd married a trapper soon after, who kept her in good style.

She saw him first and gave a little cry of welcome. "Joaquin! *Como esta?*" She bustled forward and kissed his cheek. "We heard you caused no end of excitement just now—brought a white woman into the fort!"

He hugged her, chuckling. "I could not leave her on the prairie to die. There's a black woman, too." He moved his hand over his belly, rounding the air to indicate pregnancy.

Marguerite nodded, her mouth tightening ever so slightly. "I saw her. A slave, by the look of her."

"By the look of her," he repeated noncommittally. The puzzle had not yet been solved, and it was safer for all if the story stayed much as it was. All the same, he found himself adding a defense of the lovely Tess. "Her mistress is kind, and is not used to slaves or servants, I think."

Marguerite lifted an eyebrow. "That or you're just thinking with something besides your head."

He allowed a small grin in response. "Juana," he said, moving forward to hug the old woman and swing her in a little circle. "Will you marry me today?"

She laughed and slapped his chest. "Put me down, you big randy boy!" she said in Spanish, and tsked as she smoothed her hair. "What do you want?"

"Ah, do I always have to want something?" He plucked a slice of bread from a basket lined with blue gingham.

"*Sí,*" she said, slapping his hand, but not hard enough to force him to put the bread back. "I suppose you want food for those women."

"Ah, that's why I want to marry you!" he exclaimed. "Because you are so wise!"

She shook her head good-naturedly, but she smiled as she waved him toward the storeroom. "Get me a crock," she said. "I'll send some good chili to warm their frail bones."

Joaquin winked at Marguerite as he bent to kiss Juana's cheek. "*Gracias,*" he said. "Oh, I almost forgot," he added, and pulled a small bundle from his pocket.

"What's this?" Juana asked.

"For you, all the way from Taos. I remembered you this time."

Juana untied the tiny canvas bundle and unrolled it. Within it were a pair of hammered silver earrings in the shape of crosses. "Oh, *h'ito!*" she cried, and reached up to pat his cheek. "They're like the ones I lost! What a good boy you are!"

"Anything for you, Juana." He squeezed her ample arm and went to fetch the crock for stew.

A young soldier brought two jugs of water and clean bandages to Sonia and Tess. He also brought a bar of lavender soap, still wrapped in its paper, and a bottle of Florida Water cologne. Tess thanked him profusely, delighted at the prospect of actually smelling like a woman again.

Blushing and stammering, the soldier managed, "Señor Morales sent the sweet stuff—he's known for such things."

Tess grinned. "Well, do thank him for me."

"Yes, ma'am." He backed away so quickly he nearly tumbled off the gallery.

Tess shook her head with a smile and closed the door. "You'd think he'd never seen a woman in his life," she said to Sonia.

"Probably been a while since he seen one like you."

"Perhaps." Tess uncovered the wound high on Sonia's thigh. "It's healing very well. If you put no weight on it for a day or two more, I expect you'll be hobbling around nicely."

Sonia gave her a wry smile. "Yes'm, I reckon I will."

Tess put her hands on the mound of Sonia's babe. "Have you been feeling him today?"

"All day. I reckon he's as hungry as I am."

A soft knock sounded at the door, and under Tess's hand, the babe kicked. Both women laughed. "Startled him."

"Or made him mad, more like."

Tess rose and opened the door to reveal a slim, strong-looking Indian woman. Tess froze, taking in the buckskin dress, worked with beads along the bodice, the black hair, oiled and braided, the expressionless face with big dark eyes. "I am Owl Woman," she said, her voice lilting. "My husband said to come to you."

Her husband. Tess thought of the warrior who had nearly scalped Sonia, and sweat broke out on her lips, and between her breasts. She felt cold and uncomfortable. "I—that is. . . ."

"My husband is William Bent."

Tess flushed. "I'm sorry." She stepped back and motioned the woman inside. Owl Woman. Did that mean she was wise?

The woman entered silently, her feet clad in the soft leather boots Tess had heard called moccasins. Her dress swayed gracefully around her. She saw Sonia on the bed, and moved closer. "Ah," she said, smiling. "*El niño.*"

"I worry she will lose it, and do not know the plants here to prevent it," Tess said. "I use yarrow at home, but have not seen it growing here. Can you help me?"

"You wish to stop the baby coming too soon?"

Tess nodded.

"I know not this yarrow, but I know what will help. I'll bring it to you."

"Thank you."

As soon as the woman left, Tess poured fresh water into a bowl and stripped off her dress, which she hung by the fire to allow the smoke to purify it a little. Frowning, she brushed at the bloodstains. "What I'd give for a clean dress," she said. "But even washing my face seems a fine luxury."

"It does at that." Sonia used a wide-tooth comb to work free the braids she wore in a circlet around her head. "I wonder if I can find some oil for my hair."

"Ask Raul," Tess said with a grin.

Sonia smiled secretively. "He's a fine-lookin' man. Where do you reckon he got a name like that? You think he's a free man?"

"It isn't a slave name that I've heard. He's free now, whether he was or not in the past."

"He got some gentle hands."

Tess chuckled. "Unless he were to put them about my neck!" She plunged a scrap of rag into the water and bathed her face, her neck, her arms, first with plain water, then with the sweetly scented soap. She breathed in the smell, closing her eyes. Tired senses stretched and eased.

The grit of three days had made her skin feel dead and dusty. With a clean hand she touched her cheeks and sighed happily. "Much better."

She carried the bowl to Sonia and turned her back to give her some measure of privacy. Sitting in her chemise in front of the small, odd-looking fireplace, Tess brushed her tangled curls and reveled in the feeling of life returning to her skin.

A scratching noise at the door startled her a little. "Who is it?" she called.

"I have come with herbs," Owl Woman said.

Tess carefully opened the door, halfway hiding behind it, giving the Indian woman entrance. Owl Woman carried a small pot that gave off steam in the cold air. "I bring

tea and herbs," she said. "And Señor Morales sent these
things for you to wear." She held up a simple white blouse
and a blue skirt, and a bigger dress, slightly faded, sewn of
yellow and green calico.

"Thank heaven!" Tess cried as she accepted the clothing. It smelled of woodsmoke, but the crispness of the fabric told her it had been laundered not too long before.

Owl Woman poured a tisane into a cup for Sonia. Tess
bent her head to smell it, scenting raspberry and a hint of
something she couldn't identify.

She looked at the dry herbs Owl Woman had given her,
and noticed the tight, multiflowered head of yarrow. She
held it up with a crowing sound. "Yes! This is what I
sought. What do you call it?"

"The Spanish word is *plumajillo*. It grows everywhere.
You will see it in the fields by the road."

Tess smiled. "Thank you."

Owl Woman nodded and Tess saw her gaze catch on
the high, shiny rope of scar tissue on Tess's arm and
breast. She lifted her dark eyes soberly to Tess's face.

Tess lifted a hand to cover the ugly marks. Owl
Woman shook her head. "Scars are the marks of a warrior. A woman's scars are not like those of a man, but you
should never be ashamed."

From her place on the bed, Sonia gave a low, husky
chuckle. "We're mighty brave warriors then, aren't we,
Miz Fallon?"

Tess laughed. "Yes, ma'am."

Even the Indian woman smiled, her dark eyes glittering
at the irony. Nonetheless, Tess put the blouse on and buttoned it to the neck, to hide the marks Seamus McKenzie
had left upon her body. The skirt was a mite large in the
waist, but not too much. When she'd brushed and braided
her hair into one long rope that hung down her back, Tess
felt almost new.

Owl Woman said, "I must return to my son, who needs
feeding. If you need to know more, tell Joaquin and he will
find me."

"Thank you again," Tess said, seeing her to the door. As Owl Woman left, Señor Morales was coming up the stairs. He stopped to say a few words of greeting, and Owl Woman murmured quietly in return. A quick smile flashed over his dark face, and Tess heard Owl Woman laugh, the sound light as it rang into the darkening night. Tess inclined her head, watching him as he climbed the rest of the stairs, his black hair shining, even in the darkness. What an unusual man he was, she thought. He made everyone calm.

He was still smiling as he came to the door, carrying a small, covered iron pot and a basket. "I see you've met Owl Woman," he said. "Did she help you with everything you needed?"

"*Sí*," Tess said with a smile, taking the basket from him.

She peeked inside and saw a stack of thin pancakes, very dark blue, glistening with oil. Señor Morales put the pot on the table and lifted the lid, releasing a rich aroma of pork and unfamiliar spices. There were wooden bowls, but no spoons. "What do we eat with?"

He winked. "Tortillas. I will show you." Deftly, he poured portions of stew into each of the bowls.

Her mouth watered. It had been days since she'd eaten anything hot, and her stomach growled in anticipation. Embarrassed, she laughed a little. "I'm so hungry!"

"Good." Señor Morales took one of the pancakes and tore off a piece, which he fashioned into a kind of spoon he used to capture the stew. He popped it into his mouth. "You try."

First Tess carried food to Sonia and helped her sit up, covered with the warm quilt that lay on the bed, a shawl around her shoulders. "Did you see how he did that?"

"Sure. Like soppin' up gravy with a biscuit."

Tess settled at the table, feeling somehow shy next to the tall, good-looking trader. He pushed the bowl toward her, and the scent wafted upward. "A tortilla, too."

"Tortilla?" Tess repeated, trying the word on her tongue as she took one of the small pancakes from the basket. Imitating him, she folded a piece, dipped it, and scooped stew into it. She saw bits of onion, and tomato, and the strips of some green vegetable she didn't recognize.

She was starving, and the food was hot, and it hit her mouth with a rich explosion. Spicy, as if made with a lot of pepper, but also savory with the pork and onions and fat. Immediately, she scooped another bite, and another, licking her fingers. Her mouth burned a little, and her nose started to run, but it was delicious. The tortillas were soft and fresh, as much like real bread as anything she'd eaten since they'd left Independence.

Behind her, Sonia groaned in pleasure. "Have mercy."

Tess nodded, and some of the chili in her tortilla dripped down her chin. With a quick laugh, she wiped it away, licking the stew from her fingers. "I'm making a pig of myself."

Señor Morales smiled at her. With one finger he pointed to his chin. Tess lifted her hand and discovered she'd missed a little. "What is it?" she asked.

"Only green chili. It is good you like it. You will eat it often."

Blinking the heat-tears from her eyes, Tess poured a cupful of water from one of the jugs and drank deeply. She thought for a moment. "It is—how do you say it?— *muy bueno.*"

He laughed. "Yes."

It was the first time she'd heard him laugh. The sound, low, warm and real, melted something in her heart. Laughter transformed his face, making his eyes tilt and his irises shine. Her gaze caught on his dark throat, moving with the sound, and on his wide mouth, filled with such strong, white teeth.

And once again, she felt overcome by his unusual and powerful beauty. She stared at him even though she knew she should not—stared at the way the fire shone on his black hair—stared at the wings of his dark brows on the broad, intelligent brow.

He noticed the way she looked at him, too, for the laughter slowed, and his expression sobered, and in his eyes she read things she should not see.

She looked away, taking another tortilla from the basket. A pulse of shame beat in her throat. She seemed to be forgetting that she was a married woman. Married, eternally bound to another man. Whether that husband was a man she wanted did not matter—she had confessed in holy Church to be his wife. The thought gave her a small, distant ache.

"Can you walk with me for a moment?" Señor Morales asked into the sudden awkward quiet.

Tess looked up, afraid. *Walk with him?* "Where?"

"Bent asked me to do something. I must have your agreement before I do."

Even his voice was beautiful, Tess thought sadly. She liked the quiet in it and the musical lilt his accent lent his words. She should not walk with him, should not be alone with him.

And yet, how could she refuse so simple a request after he'd saved their lives, fed them, clothed them? She turned to Sonia. "Will you be all right?"

Sonia smiled, a very slow, amused smile. "I'll be fine, ma'am."

Tess rolled her eyes at her, then turned back to Joaquin. "All right, then."

Joaquin held the serape he'd given her, and he moved forward to drape it around her shoulders with a courtly gesture she hadn't expected. Lifting her hair, she let him put it on her. His hands did not linger on her shoulders.

"Thank you," she said quietly, and pulled the warm cloak closed around her as if it were a shield.

He gestured toward the door, and Tess followed him out.

5

Full dark had fallen, and Tess found it made everything different. In the courtyard below the gallery on which she walked with Señor Morales, men crouched around fires. The bright flames cast sharp light and darker shadows over the figures of trappers in furs, with their unkempt hair and long beards, and the soldiers in their uniforms.

And Indians. Tess tried not to look at them, at the bare limbs and glimpses of chests she could see at the opening of blankets. Curiosity and fear warred in equal measures. She had never seen men with so much hair on their heads and none on their bodies, or with such a penchant for adornment. The feathers and beads and bells intrigued her.

And yet, she had seen firsthand the savagery of which they were capable. She admired them as one might a wolf—beautiful and dangerous—best kept at a distance.

Someone played music in the courtyard—she picked out the notes of flute and fiddle—haunting and pleasant against the darkness. A voice sang indistinctly and the sound made her smile—she'd missed singing these many months. She paused to listen, recognizing an old ballad of lost love. Softly, she picked up the refrain, singing along, moving her head in time.

"You like singing?" Joaquin asked next to her.

"Aye. The Irish are great singers, you know." She grinned up at him, something in her easing with the music. "Keeps our minds off our bellies."

"Were you so hungry?"

She felt his gaze, steady and curious on her face. "I would not wish on my worst enemy such hunger."

He said nothing, only looked at her steadily, his dark eyes catching pinpoints of dancing light from the fires. Tess could not bear the depth of that gaze. She shifted her gaze back to the men in the courtyard. It was only then that she realized how many of the men were looking up at her. A trapper with a wild, grizzled beard stared with peculiar intensity, lifting a bottle of whiskey to his lips and wiping his mouth with his sleeve without ever looking away. She backed up a step, seeking to hide herself in the shadows. "Why are they staring at me?"

Señor Morales made a tsking sound and gestured for her to walk. "They have been without women for a long time. That is what we came out to speak of."

In silence they walked to the end of the gallery, and behind a small room alive with the sound of men's voices, shouts and laughter, and the sound of much drunkenness. "In there," Señor Morales said, "is a billiards table, and a lot of drinking goes on. You should never come by here alone."

Peering through the unshuttered window, Tess saw a cloud of smoke and smelled the acrid scent of cigars. Rough-looking men played cards, smoked and drank glasses of amber whiskey. In her curiosity, she didn't see a step and stumbled. Señor Morales caught her arm with a strong grip to keep her from falling.

"Careful," he said.

"Sorry." She smoothed her hair in embarrassment. She followed him to a secluded place behind the tower. He leaned on the waist-high wall, folding his arms in front of him. Tess joined him, gingerly putting her hands on the adobe. It was cold, and wet from the snow. A murky darkness lay over the plain.

But closer in, just beyond the fort, stood the village of teepees. Fires within glowed orange and yellow, and shadows moved against the walls—the shadows of the families who lived in the lodges. Airy snow began to drift out of the sky, giving the village a look of a magical kingdom lost somewhere in an enchanted forest.

"It's beautiful," she said.

"Yes." Against the low, gray clouds, his profile was clean and sharp, and Tess didn't think he was simply being agreeable. He liked it, too.

She spread her hands and let snow catch on her fingers. The wide, fluffy flakes melted into tiny drops of water on her fingertips. "So many new things for a day. It makes me dizzy."

He settled on the wall more comfortably, leaning on his elbows so he did not tower so far above her. "What new things? What do you think of them?"

Snowflakes caught in the blackness of his hair. "The snow is like falling stars," she said quietly, a quickening in her. "The food is good. The rest—I don't know." She admired the small village of teepees, glowing and warm against the night. "Some of it is so beautiful my heart catches, and some of it is so frightening I cannot breathe."

He simply nodded. A moment of quiet, filled only with the sound of the music behind them, fell and grew faintly awkward. Tess began to wonder why he had called her out there, wondered if he had some nefarious plan to—

She rubbed the rounded edge of the wall. Foolishness. He had shown no sign of attraction toward her, only the kindness she suspected he would offer any weary traveler he discovered.

"Bent spoke to me about you," he said abruptly.

"About me?"

He nodded. "The men here are not civilized gentlemen, what you might have been used to."

Tess quelled a most unladylike snort. She had never known any gentlemen. But she waited for the rest.

"He does not trust them to—" He sighed, and suddenly straightened, pulling himself to his full and somewhat intimidating height. "He asked me to act as your husband while you are here."

Tess stared at him blankly. "My husband?"

He glanced over her head, over to the teepees, down at his hands. "If I offend you, señora, I apologize. He asked me to ask you this. It was not my thought."

"I am not offended, Señor Morales. Quite the contrary."

His head came up. Tess realized how much she had revealed and hurried to make amends. "That is, I am flattered to be considered important enough to warrant such a heroic move."

"Ah." There was a wealth of amusement in the single syllable. "So you will not mind?"

She smoothed her serape. "I'll do what I must."

A slow, impossibly seductive chuckle rolled out of him. As if the notes carried some magic, Tess felt the sound flow down her spine and then over her nerves like warm brandy, intoxicating and dangerous. She swallowed but did not look at him. There was something about this place, about the smells and the snow and the sounds that was casting some queer spell over her.

"I asked if you would mind," he said, and there was still a teasing amusement in his voice.

It pricked her pride. She lifted her chin, meeting his gaze. "And I said I would do what I must."

The smile on his lips didn't ease. "Tell me about this husband of yours, señora. Is he handsome?"

"No," she bit out. She thought of Seamus, a big, fat Irishman with red hair and the skin of a dead carp. "But he is my husband and I am bound to him for as long as I live." She whirled away, afraid of what else she might reveal if she stood with him another moment.

"Señora," he called, and then he was behind her, his

hand light on her shoulder. "Forgive me. My mouth runs away without my brain sometimes. I was flirting with you. That's all."

She let go of a breath and turned. "'Tis I who should apologize." He was unexpectedly close. She had to tilt her head to look into his face, and the nearness gave her a new, unwelcome jolt. She took a step back, and nearly lost her footing.

Once again he caught her arm, laughing. "It is well you have me to protect you," he said. Unexpectedly, he touched the crown of her head. "Or your pretty head would twice be broken."

She closed her eyes against the dizziness that washed through her. No one had touched her with such casual warmth in all her life. Unnerved, she stepped sideways, slipping away from his hand.

For a minute, he didn't move. She sensed him standing where she'd left him. Then he said, "You say this husband of yours is in Taos?"

She pressed her lips together, afraid her mouth might speak the truth if she opened it again. She nodded.

"I know of no Irishman in Taos. Perhaps he is in Santa Fe?"

"Taos is where he wrote to me from," she said.

"I do not understand a man who would allow his wife to travel so far with only her slave for protection."

"No," she protested, turning. Now the lies came easily, for she had told them so often, she believed them herself. "He arranged for us to go with the traders who were killed."

Joaquin inclined his head and she thought he was going to say more. Instead, he gave a quick shrug. "Are we agreed, then, señora? You will not mind"—he grinned, tongue in cheek— "pretending to be Señora Morales for the few days we stay here?"

"Not if Mr. Bent has deemed it necessary."

"*Bueno*. We'll go down and walk a little, so they see you are with me." He moved close and took her arm lightly in his hand.

"How will I say I met you?"

"I met you through the mail. An immigrant bride looking for a husband. Then we do not need to show much affection." He looked down at her, his eyes dancing. "Unless you wish for a more affectionate story."

"I believe you're flirting again, Señor Morales."

His grin was swift. "So I am, Señora Morales. It's not so large a sin, hmmm?"

"No," she said, smiling in spite of herself. "I think it a very small sin indeed."

"I think, señora," he said, "you will have to learn to call me Joaquin."

Tess balked at the notion. It was too intimate, too dangerous. "I cannot, sir."

"What wife calls her husband by his title?"

"Many do, in public."

He chuckled. "Very well."

Five miles beyond Pawnee Rock, Seamus McKenzie was forced to take shelter. The storm that had begun innocently enough now whirled in a mad, spitting frenzy. He could not see three feet beyond his horse for the blowing, blinding snow, and the cold wind seared through his warm coat as if it were only a lady's gauze gown.

When he caught sight of the small abandoned shelter in a copse of trees, he made for it with gratitude. Wind howled through the cracks between boards, and snow drifted in little spills inside, but he managed to get a fire going with wood left behind by previous occupants. When it was well-established, he moved outside and kicked around in the snow to find more wood to feed it later. His horse was protected somewhat by the trees, but after some thought, Seamus brought the beast in with him. Not out of any great love for the stupid creature, but without the gelding, Seamus would be forced to walk.

He no longer nursed any doubts about where he'd find his errant wife. Traders at Cow Creek remembered her well—a white woman and her nigger slave were hardly the most common sight on the Trail. The bitch had thought herself so clever, but Seamus would find her. And punish her.

He lived for it. He'd saved her life, taken her from Ireland where she was slowly starving to death, and given her comfort in the heart of America.

And how had she repaid him? By stealing a slave and running away from him. Seamus had been fired on the spot from the position he'd attained.

He'd been besotted with her, with her sweet young body and innocent eyes. He had dreamed of bedding her, only to find her cold and missish, whimpering if he were even a tiny bit aggressive. She whined over the slaves from the moment they arrived in Arkansas, and over their food and the whippings. It disgusted him. He continued to lie with her only to plant himself a son. The rest of the time, he slaked his lust with the slaves who could not say him nay, no matter what he asked.

Oh, yes, he'd find Tess Fallon and that uppity slave, Sonia. If not for Sonia's arrogance, Seamus would be awaiting the birth of his babe, living in comfort in the overseer's house with its big bed. But Sonia had defied him, and Tess had interfered, and everything Seamus had worked for was gone.

Grimly, he stared at the flickering fire, smelling horse and wet wool, hearing the wind howl beyond the rickety walls of the shelter. His dreams of revenge kept him warm.

6

Tess awakened slowly the next morning, feeling an odd sense of comfort. The first thing she became aware of was the warmth of her bed—it had been many weeks since she had been warm when she awoke. She luxuriated in the feeling for a long moment, and slowly became aware of a second pleasantry. She smelled lavender instead of horse and plains. The scent was on her hands, and she remembered washing with it the evening before.

Then she remembered the walk on the gallery with Joaquin. Señor Morales, more properly, but she'd come to think of him by his Christian name. It was beautiful, and it suited him.

She poked her head out of the piles of robes. The light in the room was dim and cool, not yet dawn. The fire burned low on the grate, but it was enough to keep the room warm. Sonia snored lightly from the bed.

Joaquin sat on the bench by the wall, putting on his shoes. They had agreed he should sleep within their rooms to give weight to their marriage claim, but Tess was startled to see him there anyway. His unbound hair—as straight and black as the pelt of a seal—tumbled over his shoulder. It hid his face and Tess allowed herself to admire him in the quiet. She liked the lean elegance of those brown hands deftly moving upward as he buttoned his shirt.

He caught sight of her and smiled. "*Buenos dias*," he whispered. "I was going to get coffee before you both woke up."

Tess sat up, gathering her loose hair. "Have they any tea here? I'm longing for some. We never drank coffee at home, and I must admit I am not terribly fond of it."

"Tea, then," he said. "If you will build up the fire, I will be back in a little."

Tess washed her face and combed her hair, weaving it back into its neat braid. By the time Joaquin returned, she had the fire blazing. He shivered and moved close to it. "We will be here a few days, I think." From under his serape, he brought a square package wrapped in yellow paper. "China tea, my lady."

She smelled it. "Heavenly. How much do I owe you?"

"Nothing."

"I insist. You mustn't spend money on us. We have saved a little, and planned carefully. We have no lack."

He looked at her for a moment, and Tess caught something measuring in that even gaze. "Keep it. You will need it when you go to Taos."

There was truth enough in that, Tess knew. But he didn't. "Nonsense," she protested. "My husband will care for us."

"What if he has been killed by Indians—or a fever? What will you do then?"

Tess sighed. "Very well. But I insist you not feed and pamper us any more. We're quite capable."

He smiled but didn't answer, busying himself with the coffee. Tess, following his lead, shaved tea into her cup, her mouth nearly watering at the prospect of real tea after so many months without. It had never occurred to her that not everyone drank tea as she did, and she'd missed it. "So you do not think we'll be leaving soon?"

"The weather is very poor—I doubt we can leave before the end of the week."

"What do people do here?"

He shrugged. "Play dice and cards. Drink." A twinkle grew in his eyes. "Tell lies of the women they've known, or the animals they've caught."

She chuckled. "And you, señor, what lies do you tell?"

"Oh, I do not lie." He sat on the bench and stretched his legs before him. The coffee began to boil, filling the room with a tantalizing scent. "I have no need to lie, for I have seen many wondrous things."

"Have you now?" Her tea began to steep, turning a nice deep shade of brown, as she stirred a lump of sugar into it. "Such as?"

He inclined his head, the barest hint of a smile at the corners of his eyes. "A white buffalo, big as the sun, leading a herd over a river."

"Is that all? Why, I've seen a white elephant, strolling o'er the meadows at Killean."

"Well," he said, leaning forward, "I have seen a dragon, in the cliffs nearby Taos. An ancient creature, with wings as wide as this fort."

"What color was he?"

"It wasn't a he, it was a she. And she was blue, the color of a robin's egg, but bright and shinier."

"Everyone knows dragons are not blue, but red." She sipped her tea to hide her smile. "And the ladies among them have yellow stripes." She gestured to her belly. "Right across their stomachs."

The hint of laughter now grew stronger, tilting the corners of his long eyes, beginning to print tiny lines in the sun-taut skin over his broad cheekbones. "What you saw is not a dragon, but a sea monster."

Tess laughed. She couldn't help it. "And when, señor, have you ever been to the sea?"

"I didn't say I'd seen one. But everyone knows dragons are blue."

"I never heard such silliness in all my life," Sonia put in, sitting up in bed. "If y'all wanna tell tall tales, you gonna have to have to do better than that."

"Good morning!" Tess said, her spirits unaccountably buoyed by the wild tales. Or perhaps it wasn't so much the wild tales themselves as the pleasure of feeling comfortable enough to tell them again. It seemed she'd been on her guard forever.

It was only then that she realized she'd let it down at all. Somehow, this laughing man with the gleam in his dark eyes had made her trust him.

He stood. "I must go. There is work for men to do in such weather." He put his cup on the table. "Do you have what you need?"

Tess nodded. "As I told you, we'll be fine, señor. Thank you."

"Do you know," Sonia commented as the door closed heavily behind Joaquin, "I've never heard you laugh in all the time I've known you."

"Until now," Tess said, slowly, "there was little to laugh about."

The snow continued for three days. It fell sporadically, at times simply drifting out of a leaden sky, the flakes like shreds of torn cotton. At other times, it came with fierce, wailing winds, and spun into a blinding blizzard that obscured everything.

Tess found it thrilling. She sat with Sonia one cold, bleak afternoon, listening to the wind howl beyond the walls as they sewed. For the moment, there was no snow, only the cold wind and a low, gray sky, and some of the men had gone out to hunt.

In the cozy rooms at the top of the fort, Tess and Sonia sat by the fire, drinking tea. Joaquin had given them each a length of fabric to fashion into new dresses. Although she protested, he would not take the coins Tess withdrew from her hiding place. He insisted she should keep the money for her arrival in Taos. With his quick smile, he said, "I'm rich enough."

In truth, Tess was glad of the work to keep her busy,

and they'd both worn the same clothes since leaving Arkansas. Although she had tried every method she or any of the other women knew, the blood would not come out of the old clothes.

Using her travel dress as a rough pattern, Tess and Sonia had cut the fabric the day before. Today they began sewing. Her own was a beautiful green calico, with tiny white and teal flowers. It made her think of an Irish spring, when the emerald landscape was dotted with the first wildflowers.

"That color's gonna make you look like a queen," Sonia said, breaking a bit of thread with her teeth. "Señor Morales has a good eye for what suits a woman." She smiled. "Or maybe he just has a good eye for one particular woman."

Tess waved away the comment. "He's a good observer, that's all. He chose equally well for you." Sonia's fabric was a simple red cotton, peppered with tiny black dots. "I still think you should put a little white lace around that collar."

"Nah, I don't go in for all that froufrou. This'll be just fine like it is." Carefully, Sonia tied a tiny knot and then with a groan, put it aside. With one hand to the small of her back, she said, "This child is kicking me to death today."

"Maybe you should lie down for a while."

Carefully testing the weight of her body against the wound in her leg, Sonia stood. "I'm tired of lying around."

"Walk, then." Tess smoothed the seam of what would become the full skirt of her new dress with a feeling of pride in her neat, tiny stitches. "Surely 'twouldn't hurt you to stroll along the gallery."

Rubbing the round of her belly, Sonia looked toward the door and pursed her lips. "I ain't been out there atall."

Tess put the skirt on the table. "Shall I walk with you? So you might have someone to lean on?"

"No." Sonia waved her back down. "I'll limp along all right by myself." A mischievous smile tugged her mouth.

"I know you have reason to finish that pretty dress just as quick as you can."

A prickle of heat rose in Tess's cheeks, and she bent her head to hide it. "I don't take your meaning."

Sonia chuckled. "Honey, those eyes light up like mornin' when that man comes around. You think I can't see?"

Soberly, Tess raised her head. "I am bound by my vows, Sonia. I am already married, as well you know."

"To a man, God willin', we'll never lay eyes on again."

"God willing," she repeated fervently. "All the same, to him I am wed—and wed I must stay."

"You can't mean to give up men the whole rest of your life."

"I do."

"Not all men are like your husband."

"That I know well," Tess said, taking another tiny, perfect stitch. "But I did not promise Seamus McKenzie. I promised God."

"The good Lord never meant for a man to be as mean as that one."

Tess looked at her friend silently.

Sonia sighed and shook her head. She grasped the ladder-backed chair with one hand and rested the other on her belly. "What about children?"

The thought stung. There was a whisper of sorrow in her whenever she thought of the future, stretching ahead endlessly without the comfort of a child of her own. "Please," Tess said quietly. "I'll not speak of this if you insist upon torturing me so. Isn't it enough to be free of him?"

To her surprise, Sonia laughed. "A good man would give you the answer to that question."

In spite of herself, Tess longed to know more. Sonia had loved another slave for many years, before Tess came to the plantation. The man had died of a snakebite in the fields, and when Sonia spoke his name, Tess heard the grief that would never entirely disappear. But there was also laughter and heat and love in the word—Moses. It was the way Tess's dad had spoken of her mother.

Needle poised and forgotten in her hand, Tess found her thoughts straying toward the quickening she felt in Joaquin's presence, when he looked at her with those laughing eyes, when his lips quirked into that irresistible smile.

She pushed the images away firmly. "Perhaps 'tis well that I've never known such things," she said. "One cannot miss what one has never known."

There was a knock at the door and both women looked up. Sonia limped over to open it. Raul stood there, holding a pot of stew. When he saw it was Sonia at the door, a fierce gladness blazed over his face. "Good day to you," he said with a nod. "I brung you some stew."

Sonia laughed, the sound as bright as a blue butterfly against the still day. "I'm gonna be fat as a hog if you don't stop feeding me every hour."

"You could use some fattening up."

Tess watched the exchange with a close curiosity, noticing the way they spoke with far more than their mouths. Their eyes talked, and their bodies. Raul leaned forward ever so slightly, and his gaze fluttered all over her, now a shoulder, now a hand, now the swell of her belly and breasts, and the sleek oiled hair.

Nor was Sonia still. Her elegant head tilted to one side in a coyly engaging slant. Her body softened at the shoulder, and one hip cocked out against the soft cotton of her old, worn skirt. Tess couldn't see her face, but she knew the secretive little smile Sonia was wearing.

With a smile of her own, Tess tucked her needle into the seam for safekeeping. After folding the fabric neatly, she put it in a basket nearby the hearth and took her cloak from a hook on the wall. She flung it around her shoulders. "I'm so sleepy from sewing, I think I'll take a walk."

Raul glanced up, startled as if he'd just realized she was there. "They're fixin' to serve supper in the dining room," he said. "Joaquin told me to send you on down so you can eat with him." He inclined his head toward the courtyard. "He's waitin' for you."

"Thank you." Tess pulled the cloak around her, passing Raul as he came in the room. He spared her not even a glance. At the door, she could not help sneaking a peek at the pair over her shoulder. Raul put the pot on the table and reached for Sonia's hand. Sonia moved as if she had no feet—she floated forward and melted into him. Both were tall and strong, and their bodies seemed like two pieces of a single sculpture, wrapping, pressing, fitting together.

Tess bowed her head and latched the door firmly behind her. But the fleeting glimpse of passion lingered as she walked down to meet Joaquin.

7

Joaquin watched from the foot of the stairs as Tess came out of the room on the upper gallery, her swirling cloak a bright splash of color amid the duns, browns, and grays of the fort. He wasn't alone in his admiration as she descended the steps, mindful of the snow covering them. Men all around him caught the movement of her skirts and stopped what they were doing to watch her. Joaquin thought of geraniums blooming on the patios of Taos—there was something about Tess that had the same strong and delicate beauty. Geraniums were chosen for their strength to withstand the fierce sun and drought that marked the Taos landscape, and for their ability to bloom with delirious color in spite of it all.

"*Buenos tardes,*" he said when she joined him. Her cheeks were pink—with cold or happiness, he couldn't have said, but she'd been outside only a moment.

"*Buenos tardes,*" she repeated haltingly, a question in her wide, gray-green eyes. Snowflakes caught on her lashes, giving her the look of a beautiful child. "Is that 'good night'?"

He shook his head. "More like 'good evening.' 'Good night' would be '*buenos noches.*'"

She smiled. "And how do I say, 'I'm hungry as a bear'?"

"'*Lo hambriento a de oso*.'" Aware of the men watching them, he took her hand. She jumped a little, but he didn't let go. Her small fingers were cold. With the easy familiarity of a man with his wife, Joaquin held her cold fingers between his two hands and brought them to his mouth, blowing hot air on them. "You must have gloves," he said, rubbing and blowing gently, watching her face.

Her great eyes gave nothing away, but he saw her swallow, as if there were a lump in her throat. Hope stirred in him, hope and a leap of desire. How simple it would be to continue the ruse, and kiss her quickly before she had time to protest. Would she like it?

It was the trust in her eyes that decided for him. He could not betray her so. "Come. Juana has made her beans for supper tonight. It is a treat you'll not want to miss."

They ate in the small dining room, with cloudy glass in the windows and a good, warm fire in the hearth. There were only a few of them for this meal—the rest would either eat later, or outside with the rest of the soldiers. An officer Joaquin had never met watched Tess through the meal with narrowed eyes. Joaquin saw that it made her uncomfortable, and wondered if she understood the man disapproved of an Anglo woman taking a mixed-blood husband. Joaquin could see the jealousy in the officer's eyes, and it pleased him perversely.

At last the officer spoke. "Where'd you find such a pretty bride, Señor Morales?" he asked, lifting a slim glass of wine to his lips. His nose twitched, as if he smelled something he couldn't quite identify.

"Through the mail," Joaquin returned calmly. "Lucky me, eh?" He winked at Tess, but her taut expression did not ease.

"Is that right?" The officer focused on Tess. "Must have been some surprise to come out here and find yourself wed to such a big, dark fella."

"Aye," she said lightly. "And doubly so to find a husband so handsome."

Warmth rose in Joaquin, both at her assessment of his attractiveness, and her ability to stand up to the insinuations.

The officer looked from Tess to Joaquin and back. "Does your daddy know?"

"I'm afraid he is dead," Tess returned. "I'm sure he'd be pleased to find me well-cared for."

"I don't quite recognize your accent, madam. Where are you from?"

She fisted her hands in her lap. From the corner of his eye, Joaquin saw that her knuckles were white. "Ireland, sir."

The officer's expression eased all at once. "Is that right?" he said in a bored tone, and turned to the man next to him. In a voice he pretended to lower, a voice that carried exactly as he wished it to, he said with a snicker, "That explains a lot, doesn't it?"

The men laughed.

Joaquin narrowed his eyes and looked back to Tess, who stared at her plate as if it were full of writhing snakes. Her ears were red.

With his elbow, he nudged her discreetly. She looked up and he smiled, then lifted his chin toward the plate. "Eat," he said quietly. "Juana's beans are not to be wasted on dogs like them."

She picked up her fork. He heard her take a long breath and let it go, and she began to eat once again. He touched her leg below the table, and when she looked up, he winked.

When they had finished and gone back out to the courtyard, he said, "The Anglos confuse me sometimes," tucking her arm into the crook of his elbow. "He made you very angry. Why did he say that about the Irish?"

"Don't you know the Irish are only dogs?" Her cheeks were pink with anger, and he could see it took great effort for her to control her voice at all. It came out with exaggeratedly rolling syllables, the brogue lilting. "They'll let us all starve before they'll change their bloody laws, see us all in our graves before they're through."

"Who starves you? I don't understand."

She took a breath and blew it out, but her fingers were like a vise on his arm. "The English landlords. They leave us nothing, and the soil is exhausted and won't grow anything anymore, and the fevers come through, taking all the weak and hungry."

"Is that what happened to your family?"

"Some of them. My brother and I still live."

"You are here now. There are hardships, but you will not starve here." He smiled and patted her hand.

She looked at him, and again he was reminded of the shallow edge of a hot springs pool. But those waters were still, and these roiled with a bitter anger. "I came here because I had no choice, señor. I *miss* my home. I miss Ireland and my brother and my little garden, where I grew my herbs."

He stopped and turned to her. "I know. But now you are here." He gestured to the snow beginning to fall again, to the Indians huddled at the door of the trading post in their blankets and hides, at the soldiers and the traders. "Think what you would have missed."

She looked around her, the taut expression easing away from her mouth.

"And there is more, waiting for you. There is Taos, and the mountains—oh, the mountains are beautiful. And the little church where our priest says the Mass, and the trees in the summertime." He saw that his words had captured her attention, and started to walk again. "Come—let us go up and look at the prairie, so you remember how beautiful you thought it was."

The smallest of smiles touched her mouth then, and her fingers eased their sharp grip against his arm.

She let go to ascend the steps in front of him. When they reached the gallery, he captured her hand in his own. She looked up at him in question, and with a lift of his chin toward the soldiers still watching them, Joaquin said, "So they will not think there is trouble between us and bother you."

For a moment, she continued to look at him, but then nodded. "Very well."

It seemed a very large thing, the close press of their fingers. He walked beside her as if it made no difference, but he could not seem to keep himself from moving his thumb to explore the small ridges of her knuckles. He stroked the finely made bones and the edge of her index finger and her thumb, and it gave him a strange, buoyant feeling, as if he weighed nothing and could swirl into the sky like a snowflake.

They walked around the upper gallery slowly, and ended up on a high, narrow walk overlooking the corrals. Only a single bored soldier on the bastion was nearby, and he was far enough away that he would pay them no attention.

Below, in the walled corral, horses and cattle shifted restlessly. A cow lowed softly at a chicken skittering through the dangerous forest of hooves. A blackbird perched on the fence, whistling.

Joaquin reluctantly let go of her hand to gesture toward the vista. Under the cloak of clouds and flurries of snow, the land was covered in blue and purple shadows that crept out from the cottonwoods along the river, and were echoed in the faint, faraway mountains on the horizon. "There," he said. "Remember?"

Her face showed nothing as she stared out at the gloaming. "Yes," she said quietly, and her pretty red mouth quirked into something like a smile. "My brother would love this so. I wish he could see it. I must write to him soon, and tell him what I'm seeing. He was the adventurer, not I."

"Tell me about him."

Her smile now was genuine, and indulgent. "He's younger than I by five years. A big, strapping boy—though I suppose he's now a man. His name is Liam. And there is"—she looked over her shoulder— "a soldier here who favors him." She gestured toward a knot of young men squatting around a small fire. "There he is—the one with the hair."

Joaquin picked out the boy she meant. About seventeen, he had a thick, chestnut pelt of hair that spilled over a raw-boned face with a wide, full mouth. The boy had not yet finished his growing—there was that coltish awkwardness in the wrists that hung below his uniform, and clumsy, too-large feet. Joaquin smiled. "Ah. You should write to him and tell him to come to Taos and share your adventure."

"Perhaps I will." She lifted a shoulder. "Do you have brothers and sisters?"

"I have many. Most of them live with my mother, but one sister is very close. Juanita." He grinned down at Tess. "Very beautiful—all the men in Taos want her, even though she is only the daughter of a slave. You will like her—she's bright like a brand-new coin, full of laughing."

"No others live with you?"

A stab of fresh sorrow rippled through him. "No more," he said, and swallowed. "My brother Miguel died two months ago. Gored by a bull."

"Oh, I am sorry."

"He was a good man, gentle and kind. He was to be married in the summer." Joaquin sighed, rubbing the cold adobe as he remembered his father Armando, weeping, as he carried the still, bloody body into the house. The grief was still new and piercing. "I think he was our favorite, all of us. Born late to his mother, younger than my sister and I—we miss him." He shrugged lightly. "His mother, though, she's gone loco with missing him. He was her only child, and he nearly died when he was born."

"Your mothers are not the same?"

He shook his head. "My mother is Cheyenne. Miguel's mother is my father's wife."

Her mouth tightened. "Like the plantations. The slaves'

children look like the master and the overseer more than the children in the house."

"It makes you angry," he said.

A flicker of something he couldn't quite catch moved in her eyes, then was gone. "It is immoral."

"Slaves or bastards?"

"Bastards cannot bear the blame for the sins of their fathers, now can they?"

"No."

Looking down at her, Joaquin felt heat rise in him and fill his chest. It seemed he could see nothing but the unsettled waters of her eyes, the smooth curve of her white cheek. He leaned a little closer, letting his arm brush hers.

"My father and mother love each other," he said. "They met when they were very young, when he was a boy. He vowed to marry her, and his father beat him until he just gave up, you know?"

He could smell Tess now, the faintest hint of spice from the beans on her mouth, lavender in her hair. And something deeper, too; he thought it might be her skin. It was not sweet, as the flesh of many women, but darker, like the shadows of a mountain grove. It made him dizzy.

"That does not make it right," she said, and he thought there was a faint breathlessness in her words, as if she were not as unaffected by him as she seemed.

He smiled. "But he stayed with her. He married Doña Dorotea, but it is Sleeping Bird that he loves."

"Sleeping Bird?" she echoed. "What an enchanting name."

"She is an enchanting woman."

"And she loves your father? She does not mind being a slave?"

He straightened. "She is no slave, no more. Her tribe took her back when I was eight, the year Doña Dorotea finally bore a son." He cast a single glance at her. "My mother sneaks down from the mountains every few months to see my father, and they run away for a week or two."

Tess laughed. "I think you're telling me stories again."

"No." With a smile, he raised a hand in oath. "I swear it is all true."

"Well, then it is romantic, even if I feel pity for Doña Dorotea."

"Don't waste your pity. She was a mean woman long before she met my father. She made my sister's life a misery. And you see I am a comanchero, even though my father wishes me to help him with his ranch."

A sharp wind blew up, cutting through their clothes. "Come, it's cold," he said. "Let's go to the rooms now."

Tess folded her arms over her chest. "Raul and Sonia" she broke off, and he would have sworn there was a blush on her face.

"You want to stay here a little while longer, then?"

She shivered, but nodded bravely. If she were his true woman, Joaquin would have taken her into his embrace to warm her. He would have put his arms around hers and pulled her body close to his and put his chin on the top of her head, so they could watch the new snow fall. And for a longing moment, he wished it were true.

As if she caught the direction of his thoughts, she looked up suddenly. Snow fell between them, light and airy, as if in contrast to the dark attraction growing between them by the hour. He glimpsed it in her eyes, a reflection of the wide emotion he felt.

And as they stared silently at each other, he wondered how he could ever have thought Anglos had no color. She was painted of a thousand shades, the faint rose in her cheeks and lips, the shifting hues of her eyes, the tangles of color in her hair. He stepped closer, only realizing after he'd done it. When she didn't move away, he stepped again, and put his hands on her shoulders, feeling the faint brush of her body against his own. "The soldier is watching," he said, looking over her head at the man who leaned against wall, his back to them. "Put your hands on my waist."

They stood there a moment, touching lightly. Joaquin

lifted a hand and brushed a lock of hair from her face. Remembering her words at dinner, he said wickedly, "So you think me handsome, hmmm?"

"You already knew that. I'm sure all women find you handsome—and charming, too."

Pleased, he chuckled. "'Charming, too?'"

She smiled. "Perhaps a little conceited, as well."

Her hands rested lightly against his sides, and his were on her shoulders, and there were layers and layers of clothes between them, but all at once the intimacy seemed very powerful. "Maybe," he admitted. "Men are vain creatures."

She shivered, and Joaquin pulled her closer. "Just pretend for a minute," he said quietly. "Pretend so they will think I truly am your husband." Knowing he was cheating, he bent to put his mouth near her ear. "Just pretend to be pleased."

Her earlobe brushed his mouth, and a lock of hair fell against his forehead, making a tingling place between his eyebrows. He closed his eyes as the scent of her enfolded him, rising from her pores in warm, intoxicating waves. Shadow and light, forest and stream—he smelled them all. It took every shred of restraint he had to make his hands be still on her slim shoulders, to keep his mouth where it was, without turning to take that small, round lobe into his mouth. His flesh grew turgid as he stood there, doing nothing but smelling her.

And then, into his ear came the sound of her breath—quick and shallow. Her fingers were gripped fiercely against his waist, almost painful, and he knew he could turn and kiss her and hear a little cry of surprise and yearning. She longed to touch him, too. He felt it.

But he was mainly an honorable man. He swallowed and forced himself to straighten, to put her away from him. "Let's get out of this cold," he said.

Tess only nodded, and accepted his hand.

8

Tess tried to keep her expression neutral as she walked back to the room she shared with Sonia and Joaquin. Until now, she had not been concerned about his proximity. He simply came in very late, laid next to the fire in his bedroll, and went to sleep. He slept easily—the mark, her father had always told her, of a man with a clear conscience.

She had lost much of her trained missishness on the long journey from Ireland, and even more across the plains. It no longer seemed strange to her that men and women should share the same small space for sleeping, or eating, or even washing, though she still liked privacy for that, as much as possible.

So, as they returned to their room in the cold dark of a snowy evening, just as they had these three nights since she'd come to the fort, Tess tried to remind herself nothing had changed.

But something had. Since meeting the comanchero, she'd been aware of a stirring in her blood, and fought against it. Tonight, there was more. Tess didn't know if her emotions had been stirred by Sonia's teasing, or her own curiosity—that kindled by the beauty of Raul and Sonia melting around each other—but tonight she had been unable to keep herself calm and detached in Joaquin's presence.

As they walked along the gallery, she was aware of his long, lean form next to hers, aware of his hand, hanging close. She could reach out and clasp it in her own, if she wished, for no one would be the wiser. He had done it.

She didn't because Joaquin would be wiser. He would know she—

What? Her heart thudded uncomfortably as she thought of it, thought of his breath on the edge of her ear, the feel of his hands, warm and broad and strong, on her shoulders. She had closed her eyes—oh, shameless!—to smell the damp wool on his back and the mesquite smoke in his hair. To smell his flesh next to her own.

Endless, that moment, him hovering so close, only breathing softly against her neck, the air rustling her hair. Even now, she felt the ghostly presence of it, and shivered.

"Are you cold, señora?" he asked.

"A little," Tess lied. Afraid to look at him for even a moment, afraid to glimpse again that deep, searching gaze he'd turned on her, she looked over the wall at the warm triangular shapes of the inner-lit teepees.

With that courtliness that seemed so much a part of him, he reached for the clasp on the door and opened it, then gestured for her to enter before him. As she ducked in, shaking snow from her braid, she had to think about that again. The men here, in general, were not a polished lot. They had the rough manners and bawdy mouths of peasant men everywhere. In contrast, Joaquin had very pretty manners. Someone had taught him. His father?

Sonia and Raul sat before the fire, not quite touching. "Brrr," Sonia said, pulling her shawl close around her shoulders. "It's gettin' right cold out there."

"That it is," Tess murmured. She shook her cloak and hung it on a hook, then sat at the table and took up her sewing without ever looking at Joaquin. If she could keep from looking at him, perhaps her muddled senses would clear.

"There's coffee," Sonia said.

Tess shook her head. "Thank you, but no." She lit the small oil lamp on the table, settled her old woolen shawl around her shoulders, and spread the newly stitched seam of her dress on her lap to find her needle.

She could feel Joaquin moving, easily, as he did everything. From the corner of her eye, she saw the striped serape, and his long-fingered brown hand, all lean elegance in spite of the work he did. She saw a flash of his simple, full-sleeved white shirt as he knelt by the fire to pour himself some coffee. Sonia made some low comment, and all three of them laughed. Tess, head bent fiercely over her work, stabbed her finger with the needle. The unexpected sting nearly brought tears to her eyes, and she wondered if she were losing her mind.

A wooden cup made a noise on the table, the chair scraped on the floor, and Joaquin sat down. His knee was crooked close to her own, nearly touching her skirt, and he tipped back comfortably in his chair, completely at ease.

"How much longer you reckon we'll be stuck here?" Raul asked.

"A few more days, perhaps. The snow looks as if it will stop soon," Joaquin answered. "Are you in a hurry, amigo? The permit is already expired."

"I ain't in no hurry."

"But the ladies are. Or at least one lady," Joaquin said, and he nudged her with his knee. "Eh, señora? You're in a hurry to get to your husband?"

Tess glanced up at him, knowing he baited her. It was a mistake, as she must have known it would be. Light from the round fireplace shone in his black hair, and gilded his nutmeg flesh, highlighting the sweep of cheekbone and brow.

But it was his eyes that spoke to her. His lips smiled, but in his eyes she saw heat and a rich promise. For one searing moment, she had a vision of them entangled, his mouth raining kisses on her throat.

Quickly, she bent her head. "As much hurry as any wife to get to her husband."

He laughed, the sound low and indulgent. "And how much is that, I wonder?"

Sonia, content as a cat by the warm fire, one hand resting on her rounded belly, laughed. Tess heard that knowing sound again, undercut with the bitterness both knew. "That would depend upon the husband, now wouldn't it?"

Tess shot her a warning glance. Sonia saw it, but her smile did not falter.

"This wife speaks very little of her husband," Joaquin said, and again she heard the challenge in his words.

Tess felt a plucking sting of regret. There *were* women who longed to be reunited with the men they had married, women who could clasp such men to their breasts with joy with a glad cry. That joy would never be hers.

Quietly, with her attention on her work, she said, "Some marriages are made for love, others for duty. All are equally binding."

Joaquin asked, "Are they, señora?"

She remembered what he had said about his mother and father, that they loved and made children, and had a life in all but sanctioned name. "Perhaps it is not so here," she said. "But I am bound by God and church to honor my vows." Those she could, anyway. She did not think God would require her to stay in the home of a man who beat her, who made her lose her child, who had unnatural and painful tastes in the dark night.

But wed him she had, and she was bound to take no other man as long as Seamus McKenzie walked the earth.

"God and church are not always one and the same," Joaquin said, inclining his head in that way that he had. It somehow loosened Tess whenever he did it, making him seem friendlier, more approachable.

She frowned. "I am no theologian, to make such distinctions. 'Tis the priests who tell us what God will say."

"Ah." He smiled. "The priests."

Her cheeks grew hot. "A woman might think you wished her to become an adulteress," she said sharply.

Again, he laughed, the sound genuine and rich in the small warm room. "But what sort of man would I be if I did not cajole a beautiful woman?"

"An honorable one."

Raul snorted, the first sound he'd made in quite some time. "A man without *huevos*."

Tess had heard this phrase. She was not sure of the actual meaning, but thought it was crude by the way the traders had grabbed their crotches when they said it. "One thing is true, I see. Men do not change from one land to another."

"Is that so terrible?" Joaquin asked, his eyes glittering. "What man would not admire beauty?"

Tess silently vowed to halt this flattery and flirting before she misspoke. "Which only proves my point—one husband is very like another." She put her sewing on the table. "Only a woman with holes in her head would be eager to be in the company of any of them."

She knew she'd lost the moment she stood, her face burning with low-lying fury and a hunger for Joaquin she only vaguely admitted to herself. As she started to move off, intending to remove herself from his presence by going to the other room, he grabbed her hand.

Even the simple warmth of those long fingers made her hips soften as if in readiness for him. She tugged, but he held her fast. To her great alarm, he bent his great glossy head, with the too-long hair and the red cloth catching it all back, and pressed his lips to her fingers. Against the rise of her knuckles, she felt his lips move, full and seductive. She stared down at him, unable to move, and saw the fan of black lashes lying upon his cheeks.

"Forgive me," he said, and Tess thought he would finish it now, that he would let her go. Instead he held her hand, his head bent over the back of it. "A woman who had been properly tended by a man would eagerly seek that lover," he said, and there was a strange gravity to the words.

Tess did not move. Her heart ached as he moved his mouth over her hand, a firm but somehow giving mouth. This time, there was the faintest presence of his tongue behind the lips. She stared at the crown of his head, from whence the hair grew in such abundance, and wanted to put her hand against the part. Welcoming him.

A tingling rushed through her body, and gathered in her breasts. Against her clothes, she felt the press of the aroused points and shame filled her. She wanted so much, too much, to taste of him, to allow him the cajolery and flattery and gentle loving at which he seemed he would be so adept. He probably smiled when he made love, and talked, and made silly jokes.

She tore her hand from his grip and turned away, moving into the dark corner to lie on the narrow bed that she would vacate when Sonia came in. She closed her eyes, and began to pray for strength. It would be a terrible sin to break her vows. The thought of it filled her with dread—she would bring disaster upon them all if she allowed herself to slip. People at home had often told stories of women who'd broken their vows—sometimes nuns, sometimes wives—and brought famine and drought and plague upon their villages.

From the other room, the sound of Joaquin's laughter floated in to her, low and warm and so full of life. Why did such punishments only fall to women? she wondered fiercely, pulling the pillow over her head. Joaquin's father had broken his vows, and had he suffered? Had his ranch dried up and blown away? Had his children suffered mysterious illnesses?

No. Perhaps it was only superstition, then.

With a low cry of dismay, she pushed the traitorous thought away. Superstition or not, could she bear to take the chance?

She drifted into a doze with the sound of Joaquin laughing, feeling tempted and conflicted, and oddly, safe.

*   *   *

It was quite early the next morning when Tess awakened. For a long minute, she only lay in her warm bedroll, listening. No sounds yet of men, but there was something else: birdsong. A lot of birds. She tried to pick out which were which. The magpies were easy, and the melodious whistle of blackbirds. There was another she didn't know—a whirring note, long and unusual.

She and her brother had often played a game as children, a contest to see who could name a bird most quickly. Hearing now the sound of the strange exotic call, she missed him. How much he would love these adventures!

Finally, she stuck her head out and opened her eyes. It was not yet full dawn, but Tess felt the difference in the light immediately—there would be no clouds or snow today. A sense of excitement touched her, a buoyant, invigorating pleasure in simply being alive. It was an emotion she'd not felt often in many years.

The room around her was silent, but for the sound of breathing, slow and deep. Quietly, Tess emerged from her pile of blankets and skins, and took the top layer to wrap around her, a thick, soft buffalo robe that she put against her so she could revel in the softness of the fur. The animals looked as if they would have coarse, scratchy coats, like sheep, but it was soft as eiderdown.

She glanced at Sonia, who slept deeply, and Joaquin, his face buried in his blankets. Only a slice of forehead and the tumble of black hair showed. Again, she felt a strange urge to touch his head, and resisting, turned away. She stirred the fire and put on new wood, then bent over the tin bucket of clean water that stood in the corner. After breaking the thin layer of ice covering it, she dipped the coffee pot in it and put it by the fire to heat.

Drinking tea had been one of the great luxuries of the fort. This morning, she shaved a measure from a hard block printed with an elaborate design into a cup and waited for the water to boil.

On a small table in the corner were ink and paper. Tess retrieved the small bottle and quill, and moved once more by the sleeping Joaquin to sit at the main table. Her robe brushed the crown of his head, tousling a lock of hair, and she paused, hoping she hadn't awakened him. He didn't move.

When the water was hot, she made her cup of tea, then put coffee in the pot for the others. She settled in to write to her brother, sharing glimpses of the wonders she'd seen, and the journey she now made. She told him that she'd left Seamus, and that she was going to Taos. Smiling, she signed her name and leaned back to let the ink dry before folding the page for mailing. Then she leaned forward again and added a postscript: *Please join me here.*

A stirring caught her attention and she looked over to see Joaquin moving, tossing the covers aside to sit up. As the blankets fell away, she stared, a fist tight in her belly. His hair was tousled. With a sleepy hand, he pushed it off his face and blinked. The buttons at his throat and chest were undone a little, and Tess glimpsed an impossibly smooth slice of skin that made her think again of touching him, open palmed. It was intimate, watching him awaken, so unguarded, and she wanted this picture to last a long, long time—the bright yellow light coming in, the smooth adobe walls behind him, and the tangle of blankets and buffalo skins at his feet. Even so early in the morning, there was a look of energy and cheerfulness about him.

After a moment, he looked up at her and his smile was warm, giving light to the dark brown eyes. "*Buenos dias,*" he said. "Is that coffee I smell?"

Tess could only nod. He unfolded his long, lean limbs and stood up, wearing only a white shirt with full sleeves and a pair of close-fitting breeches. His feet, long and brown, were bare. He went to the door like that and gave Tess a wink as he slipped out.

She smiled to herself, too content this morning to allow herself to be dragged into the depths she'd gone the night before. He was a beautiful, charming man, and his company pleased her. Was that so great a sin?

It was not. She was to be around him for at least a few weeks longer—would it not be more pleasant to enjoy his good-natured flirting, his teasing and jokes, than to fight it? Perhaps if she accepted her attraction instead of fighting it so fiercely, it would not be so difficult. Surely, he teased all women this way. There was no danger but the temptation in her mind.

When he came back in, she said, " 'Tis a beautiful morning."

He crossed to the fire and poured coffee into a tin cup. "It is. We'll be able to leave in a day or two—depending upon the mud."

Tess nodded, and folded her letter. "The rest has been good for Sonia."

He joined her at the table. "When is *el niño* due?"

"Not for a couple of months, I'd guess. Before Christmas."

"And will the child be your slave, too?"

It felt unfair, but Tess had brought it on herself. She lowered her head, wondering how to answer him without giving herself away.

Before she could form a reply, Joaquin reached over the table and took her hand. It startled her, and she jumped, but he caught her fingers closely in his own. "It is plain, señora, that you are not a slave-mistress. Perhaps you can tell me your story. Perhaps I might help you."

For a moment, Tess was sorely tempted. She dared not look at him, but focused instead on his long hand, gripping her own, lending her strength.

But already she was dangerously drawn to him, relying upon his good nature to see them safely to Taos, thinking of him in ways she should not. And she did not wish to draw him into the dangerous coil of her problems.

"You are a kind man, Señor Morales," she said at last.

"But you will not tell your story."

"There is no story to tell," she said lightly, removing her hand. "I am only a simple Irish woman, unaccustomed to the ways of slavery or even servants. Sonia has been my only friend in this land and for that, I will care for her as if she were my own sister." She forced a smile. "Not so strange."

He inclined his head, taking her measure. Then he stood. "Very well."

A sting of rejection touched her. Had she done the right thing? She watched him putting on his clothes, first stockings that covered his feet, then his high-laced moccasins and the striped serape. He rolled his blankets into a neat, tight bundle he stowed in a corner, and all the while, Tess drank in his black, shiny hair, his angled face, his graceful movements. When he left, he only gave her a nod and ducked out, leaving Tess with an ache inside.

Yes, she'd done the right thing.

But his questions served to remind her of the long journey that lay ahead, and the lies she would yet have to tell when they came to Taos and the husband who supposedly waited for her. What would they do then?

"I can see by your face you're frettin' again," Sonia said from the bed. "Don't worry so much, woman. The good Lord has looked after us so far. He'll see us the rest of the way safe enough. You'll see."

Tess nodded. "I hope so."

9

Tess and Sonia spent the day sewing, then went outside to walk late in the afternoon. The warm sun had begun to melt the snow very quickly. It dripped from the branches laid over vigas overhead, and made enormous puddles of mud before the doors and in the yard. In the corral, the earth was churned into a muddy sea, and all the men were coated in the muck up to their knees.

Out of boredom, the women wandered into the fort's store and admired the pink-and-rose china, rolls of satin ribbon in many colors, sewing kits and spices of all kinds. It was quiet there this morning, and they leaned on the counter, dreaming.

"I'd like to have china one day," Tess said. "With a gravy boat and silver ladles."

"And a big fancy house to go with it, so's you could have parties?"

Tess smiled. "Why, yes. And glittering women in beautiful gowns dancing all over the rooms, and the men in handsome suits with gold buttons." She pointed. "Perhaps even epaulets."

"I just want me a nice stretch of garden for my own, to grow greens and carrots, fresh. Maybe a cow for some milk, and a couple of good hogs." Sonia put her chin on her hand, her eyes sparkling. "One o' them nice lace table-cloths and some good pans."

"Well, now that sounds very fine." Tess chuckled. "And more likely than my dream of china."

"You don't want that fancy life any more than I do, Tess Fallon," Sonia said. "You ain't got the heart to be a rich lady, passin' out orders and makin' folks' lives miserable. First time some poor folks need anythin', you'll be givin' away all you got."

"You overestimate my good nature," Tess said, thinking of the rough cottage in which she'd lived with her brother. Everything in it had been gray—gray with age, or overuse, or the mists. She thought of empty pots, with a few cabbage leaves to boil, and a single poor potato. "I'd be ready enough to try it."

"And how you reckon to get all that without giving up yo' vows that you think are so precious?"

Tess shook her head slowly, looking at the pristine china with its delicate, pink roses and edgings of gold. "I don't suppose I will," she said wistfully.

Sonia glanced over her shoulder to make sure they were alone. The storekeeper stood in the middle of the muddy yard, smoking a pipeful of tobacco. "You're pretty enough, you can catch a rich man, if you'll only do it."

"Oh, no—and find myself with another Seamus McKenzie? I'd rather starve."

"And you might, you don't let go of those silly notions of yours. What you gonna do? Go back to Ireland? Get old doing needlework for rich folks?"

Tess rubbed the buffalo hide tossed over the counter. "I haven't thought so far ahead as that," she admitted. " 'Twas first my wish to save my brother and me from starvation, thus I took Seamus McKenzie for my husband. Then it was my wish to leave him, and I've done so. Whatever my next step shall be, I imagine will be revealed."

"That ain't no way to live a life."

"Well, then, what is your plan?"

"I'm gonna find me a fur trader or a Mexican. I'll raise and sell hogs and good sausage. And grow vegetables of my own in a garden I planted for my family." She touched the swell of her babe below her dress. "And I'll watch my child grow up free."

Tess smiled. "A fine plan it is."

"And you need one, too."

"I'll think on it, then."

But as they wandered back outside, to walk the gallery in order to build the strength in Sonia's leg, Tess felt a cloud of loneliness descend over her. She had no doubt Sonia would find the life of which she dreamed. Perhaps even the smitten Raul would be her husband.

And Tess would be essentially alone in a land she knew nothing of, far from anyone who knew her, without husband or child, or particular skills. She dreamed of riches and china because she knew nothing else to dream of. All her life had been spent going from one crisis to the next. She'd never had the luxury of dreams.

But then, neither had Sonia, and now she imagined a whole new life for herself. In Sonia, there was no conflict about what or who or how. For Sonia, freedom for her child was dream enough.

Freedom. Tess had sought freedom, too, had she not? Freedom from hunger, freedom from a cruel man. And she had, by luck and her wits, managed to attain both. Why not strive for the life she wished to have?

They paused at the wall, looking toward the cottonwood trees that edged the river. From the earth rose wisps of fog, hanging like a magic blanket over the muddy ground. "If I might have all I wished," Tess said quietly to her friend, "I would ask for naught more than a man who is kind and good, and a handful of children and food for all their mouths." She paused. "I'd like to grow flowers in the summertime, and make quilts by the winter fires, and tell my children the stories of my ancestors who rode so proudly over Ireland so long ago."

"Ah! That's it."

"But I see no way to have what I wish, Sonia. You may find it foolish that I believe so, but my soul will be blackened if I disregard the holy vows I took to be wife to Seamus."

Sonia opened her mouth, then closed it. "It ain't foolish," she said at last. "Faith is a mighty thing, and not to be taken lightly. I'm sorry for sayin' otherwise." She lifted her face toward the sky. "But I reckon a good prayer can do a lot. You keep that dream in your head, and maybe the good Lord can find a way to make it true for you."

Tess smiled. "That I will do."

Joaquin stomped through his day, put out of temper by the buzzing on his nerves that Tess had kindled. To ease his tension, he sought hard work, and now stood splitting logs in the warming afternoon, aware of the dripping, melting snow that made mudfields of the desert. It would be two days at most before they could leave the fort, since they had no wagon to worry about. Raton might already have snow—a misery he'd preferred not to contemplate. If it were only he and his men, it would be different, for they were used to hardship. Escorting two women would make the difficulties far greater.

The work brought heat to his muscles, and eased some of the tightness in his shoulders, but he could not shake some images from his relentless imagination. Tess, this morning, looking tousled from sleep, her cheeks flushed with health and youth, her hair a tumble of long, corkscrew curls around her shoulders, her lips as red as—

What a fool he was. He told himself again it was only the novelty of her that made him so hungry. He'd never seen eyes of that color, or hair of such wild abandon. And unlike many women he knew, she listened when he spoke, as if his words carried weight, as if she wanted to hear his thoughts. Until now, the women he'd known were more interested by far in his listening to their thoughts.

He also knew she didn't prattle on about herself because she hid secrets. He wondered for the thousandth time what they were.

There was no doubt in his mind that she was married. There was too much resignation in her voice when she spoke of her husband for it to be otherwise. A woman feigning to be married would not think to include such a telling emotion.

Resigned then, to a loveless marriage, and vows she would not break. He admired her for that, especially when he sensed she was not only resigned, but fearful, too. Was he cruel, this husband?

Joaquin could not bear the thought, and pushed it away, going again through the possible list of men who might claim the honor of being her husband. Neither Taos nor Santa Fe were large enough for a man to hide in—and Joaquin could think of no man who could be the husband she supposedly was going to meet.

He placed a thick chunk of wood on the stump and swung his ax. In the distance, he heard men calling out as they herded cattle to the river. He paused momentarily to look at them, wiping his brow. The sky, washed by the storm, was a blazing shade of blue, almost achingly bright in contrast with the patches of brilliant snow. His breath made clouds in the air.

There was no doubt she had a husband, but he also felt in his gut that she was lying about something. More than once, he'd seen silent signals pass between Tess and Sonia, so Sonia, too, was part of the deception.

He swung the ax forcefully, taking pleasure in the splintering chop that split the log neatly in two. What had Sonia said last night by the fire? *That would depend upon the husband, now wouldn't it?*

A cruel husband, he thought now, grimly splitting another log. So why did she go to him willingly? And what part did Sonia play?

Raul said they were what they appeared, a slave and her mistress, traveling out west. And in truth, the clothes

Tess wore when they found the women seemed to uphold that.

But Tess herself did not fit the mold of a grand lady. She was too fearful of unspoken things, and too wise to the matters of hunger, and too kind to her servant. She willingly worked, and her skill told him the habit was not new.

He frowned—and suddenly wondered if she was not traveling *toward* her husband, but instead, was fleeing away from him—and Sonia with her.

Straightening, he looked toward the fort, narrowing his eyes against the glare. He considered the way that solution fit the pieces. Her fear, the odd sympathy between the women, the perplexing mystery of why a man would allow his wife to travel so far in such dangerous circumstances alone.

Yes, that might very well be the truth.

He tried to quell the small spark of hope the thought lit in him. Whether she fled the man or went to him, she'd made plain her feelings toward her vows. Such honor was the mark of a virtuous woman, and he could not fault her. Nor, in good conscience, could he tempt her.

There were women enough in the world that he did not have to have just this one. He wanted this one, that much was true, but he did not wish to harm her, or give her more to bear than she carried already. If she truly fled a cruel husband, the last thing in the world she needed was another man in pursuit of her.

So he would quell his lust in her presence, and try to think of Elena with the sultry eyes, who would be warm and waiting when they reached Taos. And to Tess Fallon, he would be only a friend.

But it was not as simple as he believed it would be to put this woman from his thoughts. He avoided her all through the day, and into evening. After supper, he went to the billiards room. It was dark and smoky, dominated by the exquisite table. In one corner, between windows with their shutters flung open to air the musty stench of men too long unbathed, stretched a small counter, with pale, green bottles of whiskey on the wall behind it. A length of painstakingly painted canvas covered the floor.

Joaquin ordered whiskey and stood at the bar. A pair of trappers played a game of checkers, the board open on top of a whiskey barrel. At the end of the counter, a Cheyenne, a trapper, and two soldiers played a game of monte. The trapper offered to deal Joaquin in, but he shook his head.

The whiskey moved through his limbs, sending ease and warmth through the muscles he'd held tight these last few days. The growl of men's voices, punctuated with ragged laughter, was familiar, too. Here, he was comfortable, unlike he was with Tess Fallon.

He took another swallow, holding the liquid in his mouth for a moment as he thought of her hair. Tess of Ireland, with her musical accent, and the glimmer of mischief in her eye—but only when she forgot to be worried. He swallowed and relished the heat in his throat, echoed by a heat in his loins.

"If I had me a woman like Morales, I shore wouldn't be hangin' out with a bunch of men." The voice was rough, belonging to one of the trappers playing checkers.

Knowing snickers met his words, and Joaquin felt an edge of tension in the room. He kept his face expressionless. In his haste to avoid her, he'd forgotten the bogus marriage. Now he looked at the trapper and smiled slowly. "Sometimes a little seasoning makes sweet flesh all the more delicious, eh?"

"Long as you can rise to the occasion," another man called out. "But you have any trouble, we'll tend that sweet flesh for ye."

"Only a dead man couldn't rise for that *bizcocho*, eh?" came the answer, and more laughter.

With effort, Joaquin tamped down his anger at the vulgarity. He straightened. "She is my wife," he said simply.

The trapper at the bar clapped a hand on his shoulder.

"Don't pay 'em no mind, hombre. Just a horny bunch of bastards."

Joaquin put his glass on the bar and motioned for a refill. No one said anything else. He drank his whiskey and made for the door. The man who made the vulgar comment bent over the table to make a shot and Joaquin deliberately jostled him. "*Lo siento mucho*," he said, smiling.

The man straightened with a furious movement. Confronted with Joaquin's far superior height and considerable reputation, he backed down.

"*Buenos noches*," Joaquin said, and left.

10

Tess bent over her sewing. Already, she had a crick in her neck, and her eyes were weary from the close work, but she'd made good progress on the dress. She couldn't wait to have something new and pretty to wear.

But in truth, that was not the reason she worked with such dedication. If she kept her attention on the dress, her mind would not wander toward other things with such frustrating regularity. But despite the task, bird-voices chattered in her head—was Seamus following them? What would they do when they got to Taos? Would this worry never cease? And the one she tried to ignore more than all of them—not a voice, but a picture—Señor Morales awakening this morning.

With a sigh, she put the sewing down. She stood up and stretched her tight back and shoulders, then put the pot of water on the fire. Raul and Sonia had wandered off more than an hour ago, and Tess felt a little lonely. If no one returned soon, she supposed she ought to simply go to bed.

From beyond the door came the night sounds of the fort and the village of Cheyenne beyond. Men's voices and pipes from one, the low thud of drums and high-pitched singing from the other.

Restlessly, she wandered to the door, pulling her shawl close around her, and opened it. Fires burned against the night, and the sound of laughter spilled into the darkness from somewhere. A pair of soldiers coming up the stairs nodded at her, tipping their hats politely. She wished they would stop and chat, but knew it was futile. As they made their way to the common barracks room a few doors down, she watched their backs. They were so young. They opened their door, letting out a cascade of yellow light and a rain of greetings.

Another man approached along the gallery, and seeing the lean, graceful silhouette, Tess felt her heart catch. Joaquin. His shadow was imposing, taller by far than most of the men here, with shoulders broad as a buffalo. Beautifully made, he was. What woman could fail to notice?

He reached her place at the door and stopped. "*Buenos noches*, señora," he said in that resonant voice. "Are you all alone?"

She smelled whiskey on his breath and wondered fleetingly if he were dangerous when he drank, like many of the men she'd known. Like Seamus. "I am," she answered, crossing her arms.

Lazily, he leaned on the wall nearby her, so close she caught the scent of mesquite smoke in his hair. "Do you wish to play cards or checkers? I might find some somewhere, if you like."

There was more of a lilt to his words tonight, a longer roll of the Spanish tongue on the r's, a lingering on the i's. Yes, he'd been drinking. "No, thank you," she said.

He turned his head, and he was so close Tess felt the warmth of his lips near her temple. "Are you frightened of me, señora? I swear I am a cheerful man, even drunk."

"Are you drunk?"

"I'm afraid I am. *Un poco*." To her surprise, he lifted his hand and displayed a bottle. Not whiskey, but one of finely bottled wine. "Would you like to join me?"

"Ladies don't get drunk," she said primly, but her smile betrayed her.

"No, no. You needn't get drunk. Only share a little wine with me."

She considered. She had no head for spirits, but surely one glass would not hurt. Perhaps it would help her sleep. And he did not seem dangerously drunk, only a little in his cups. "All right," she said, and stepped back into the room.

He followed, his movements as seemingly effortless as always. It was rare that such a tall man could move so easily, without clumsiness. Liam had stumbled and lumbered through his adolescence, but perhaps that was only a boyhood trait. By now, he might have learned to manage his long, long legs and big hands.

Joaquin sat at the table, and worked on the cork in the wine. Tess took the pot off the fire and joined him, self-consciously smoothing her blue skirt over her knees.

The cork came loose with a little pop. Joaquin smiled as he filled a wooden cup. "Doña Dorotea would screech to see us drink fine wine this way."

"Doña Dorotea is your father's wife, am I right?"

"*Si*. A very fine lady, from Mexico City. She brought six trunks and seven servants when she married my father. Everything all the best." He made his voice nasal and faintly falsetto: " 'All the best things are *de Espana*.' "

Tess smiled. "I can see how fond you must be of the woman."

He poured himself a generous measure of wine and put the bottle on the table between them. "I almost did not make this trip, for fear she would make my sister's life more miserable than ever once I left. But my father, he said he would look out for her."

" 'Tis a lucky thing for Sonia and I that you did."

"I think, señora, you might have found a way to make it, with or without us."

"Perhaps." The wine was rich and she drank again, liking the feel of it in her blood. "You were worried about your sister because Doña Dorotea was distraught over her son's death?"

"I don't know distraught," he said with a slight frown. "Crazy weeping, day and night? This is distraught?"

"Yes."

Joaquin's mouth, so often shaped to smiling, was now sober. It gave him another look entirely. "She was distraught."

"I miss my brother, too," she said impulsively. "But I can write him a letter, and he can send me one back."

"Is that who you wrote this morning?"

She nodded.

He leaned back in his chair, kicking his long legs out in front of him. "I thought it might be your husband."

There was in the seemingly casual comment a hint of something deeper. "What point would there be to that, señor, since we are the only ones going on to Taos? Who would deliver the letter?"

He lifted his brows. "Let's not talk of husbands tonight. Sing me a song."

Tess laughed, startled. "A song?"

He grinned. Light once more brightened his dark eyes, and made of his face an array of slants. She liked the crookedness of his mouth in such an otherwise perfect alignment of features. The curious low stirring in her blood moved once more.

Perhaps it was the wine, or the night, or simply being alone with no witnesses, but Tess found she did not feel the need to tamp down the pleasant arousal this time. She let it be, let it move in her as it would.

"Yes," he said. "You give me an Irish song, and I will give you a Mexican one."

"But if you sing in Spanish, how will I know what you're singing?"

"I will tell you," he said with a somewhat wicked smile.

"Perhaps I should not hear it, if it puts that look on your face."

"I promise it will be a song you like."

She narrowed her eyes mockingly. "I am somehow not reassured."

He laughed. "Please. Sing for me, señora."

The man was utterly irresistible, even more so in this rash and teasing mood. With a smile, Tess thought for a moment, sorting through the ballads she knew. She never minded singing—her voice was clear and strong, if not particularly beautiful. She chose a simple tale of a lost suitor who returned to his lover many years later, and married her. Joaquin listened, sipping his wine, and clapped when she finished.

"Now your turn," Tess said, and raised her cup. To her surprise, it was nearly empty. Joaquin immediately lifted the bottle. "No," Tess said quickly, aware of a breathless, light-headed feeling. "I think I've had enough."

"There is not so much wine in a single bottle to make us both drunk," he said. "Have just a little more."

Candlelight played over his glossy hair, and edged his long beautiful fingers on the bottle. Tess found herself looking at his mouth again, at the dip on the upper lip, and the firm, full lower one. "I am not used to spirits," she said, almost in a whisper.

"It has put color in your cheeks," he said, leaning over the table. She jumped when his fingers brushed her skin, faintly, then moved away. "It makes you even more beautiful."

"Oh, do not flatter me, Señor Morales."

"Just for tonight, can you not call me Joaquin?"

"I . . . I think—no, I could not."

"Maybe you'll let me call you, Tess, though, eh?"

A sudden loud crash sounded from beyond the room, and before Tess could blink, Joaquin was on his feet, running for the door. Tess ran behind him to see what was the matter. For a minute, she could not tell for all the rushing and shouting, but then the noise came again, and she saw it was a trapper with a rifle, obviously drunk and wild. Even as they stood there, two soldiers wrested the weapon out of his hands.

Joaquin lifted his chin. "The old man does it everytime he's here."

Standing next to him, Tess clutched her shawl closer to her against the cold air. "Why don't they take his gun when he comes in?"

"They do, but he always gets it back." He turned, and Tess realized they stood very close. To her alarm, he didn't back away as he ordinarily did, but instead braced one arm against the doorway on one side of her. "The men in the bar made sport of me, tonight, Tessita."

"Made sport?" He was so close she could see the fine sun lines traced below the uptilted corners of his eyes and the feathery hairs of his brows.

With his free hand, he lifted a curl from her shoulder. "They said a husband who would spend his time drinking with men when there was a beautiful woman waiting for him was not much of a man." He fingered the tendril of hair slowly. "So I came back."

Tess clutched her shawl in her hands, feeling the wool compress against her somehow sweaty palms.

"They're watching now, you know," he said. "Down there, to see what I'll do with my beautiful wife."

Her breath felt lost, far away. "Surely they do not expect public displays."

"Oh, but they do." He eased ever so slightly closer, until Tess could feel the merest brush of his body against her own. "Will you pretend with me, just this once, and restore my good standing?"

Tess had to swallow before she could answer. Against her breasts his chest was an excruciatingly light pressure, and some wanton urge made her wish she could arch against him, feel that weight against her more firmly. She did not. "Pretend how?" she whispered.

"Pretend to kiss me." He leaned closer, so close now she could not see any details of his face. A lock of his thick hair, loosened from the queue, fell against her cheek, cool and silky at once.

"Just pretend," he murmured, and gently pressed his body against hers. Her breath caught at the welcome intimacy. "Put your hands on me."

With more eagerness than she would have admitted, Tess dropped her shawl and reached for him, putting her arms around his waist, touching the heat of his skin through his clothes. Against her belly, she felt the unmistakable rigidness of his arousal, and instead of the disgust it engendered in her before, it caused the heat in her blood to rise even more.

"Now, we just pretend," he whispered, and there was strain in his words. His breath touched her upper lip, and one hand skimmed her back. "From there, they can't see we are not really kissing."

"No," she managed. His mouth, that mouth she had so often admired, hovered above hers like a bee over the heart of a flower.

A swirling dizziness engulfed Tess. He smelled of mesquite and wine and wool, and his body was so lean and strong, and that mouth, hovering so close to where she might taste it—

She tipped her head an inch, no more, as if by accident. Their lips touched. A rush of something wild washed through her at the contact, and she pressed closer, fitting her mouth to his. He made a sound of pain or need, low in his throat, and his fingers tightened on her side.

She was unprepared for the way he responded. His head came down more, and his lips grew hot, and Tess found herself opening her mouth to his tongue.

Until now, the only kisses she had known were those of Seamus, who groped her as his mouth smothered hers. This was not like that. Not at all.

No, Joaquin kissed the way he laughed, with relish and enjoyment and awareness of her. It was true his hips moved a little against her, so she felt the need he had of her, and his hand roved restlessly over her back, up her side, but there was more. His lips moved gently, teasing and playing, and his tongue led a dance with her own, and there was a nectar deeper, deeper—

She wanted to drift forever in the dark sweetness of his taste, in the fierce passion she felt lurking just beyond his control. He made a sound, and suckled her lip, and plunged his tongue in her mouth again, and Tess felt a deep, delicious heat rise in her loins.

He broke away suddenly, and Tess made a protesting sound. He gripped her shoulders and lifted his head. "Señora," he said in a rush, "I'm sorry. I can't think why—" With visible effort, he stepped backward and removed his hands. "Forgive me," he said, and turned away.

11

Tess followed Joaquin silently back into the room. She felt disoriented and dizzy and foolish. Her cheeks burned.

Joaquin did not look at her, but went to his bedroll and began to lay it out near the fire. Only the faint crackle of the fire disturbed the deep silence between them. Tess stood by the door, twisting her hands in her shawl.

Had she really kissed him? Humiliation stuck in her throat, and she had no words to ease the awkwardness between them. At last, she followed his lead and began to spread out her own bedroll. First, one thick buffalo hide to soften the hard floor. Next, two striped woolen blankets, and a second hide for warmth on top. She kept her back to Joaquin in the small space. Once they bumped—her elbow into his side, and both murmured hasty apologies. A second time, her bottom collided with his and she nearly pitched forward. Tess swiftly moved away, kneeling on her bedroll, ostensibly straightening the covers.

Behind her, Joaquin sat down and tugged off his boots. She felt his movements as he climbed into his bedding. Tess walked to the table, blew out the candle, and climbed into her own warm bed.

Still there was only the sound of the fire to break the silence. Tess lay on her back and stared at the ceiling, watching orange light flicker over the beams. Over and over she re-imagined the kiss—the feel of his full lips, giving and taking, the slide of his adept tongue, the tight heat of his body against her own, and the murmuring, wordless sounds he'd made. It made her breath come faster.

Only a half an arm's length away from her on the floor, he made a sound, something between a curse and a groan. Tess looked at him. He lay on his back. Firelight caught on the underside of his chin, gilding his jaw and throat. Abruptly, he turned to look at her.

Neither of them spoke. She stared, stricken by her wish to trace a finger along the places where the firelight washed over him. Soberly, he looked back at her.

If he had reached for her at that moment, if he had slipped his long-fingered hand from below the robes covering him, and stretched it over the small space, Tess would not have been able to resist him.

But he did not reach for her. At last, he spoke in a raw, hushed voice. "Good night, Tessita."

Tess swallowed. "Good night, Señor Morales."

On the fourth day of Seamus McKenzie's stay in the mud and sticks shelter on the plains, the snow at last stopped. All day, he endured the misery of dripping, melting snow, watching his dirt floor become a slime pit. He slept little in the muck, and when the fifth day dawned bright and clear, he was all too eager to resume his journey.

The going was slow. Mud clung to the hooves of his horse until the animal could barely move. Seamus dismounted and led the beast. After most of the morning spent struggling, he discovered there was a method to beating the mud. Instead of sticking to the trail worn by hundreds of wagons and horses over the years, he walked in the grass alongside it. By evening, he reckoned he'd managed a solid ten miles. Not bad, considering.

He took a peculiar pleasure in enduring the hardships of weather and travel. None of the fancy lords he'd known as a boy could have managed the trek. They'd've whined about the snow, the mud, and the slow going.

But Seamus McKenzie was no stranger to hardship. Too often as a child he had starved. Too often had he worked dawn to dusk on his father's wee patch of poor Irish soil, only to lose the crop to pests or weather or both, and a good portion of what was left went to the bloody English landlord. One by one, Seamus had seen his brothers fall to hunger or fevers, and one to a foolish rebellion against a trio of British soldiers intent on satisfying their hungers with Davey's young pretty wife. Davey had been shot, his wife taken anyway, and though the village clucked their tongues over it, all knew there was naught to be done about it.

So Seamus bided his time. He learned to steal, carefully and skillfully, so he'd not end his days on the gallows. He showed true talent for the art, and an uncanny sense of when to strike.

From thievery,'twas not so large a jump to killing. And for killing, too, he'd found a peculiar talent. The first kill had been an Irish landowner, surprised by the burglars in his house. Seamus had strangled him neatly and cleanly, without so much as a twinge of shame. It had left in him a kind of peace, in fact, draining away some of the poisonous hatred and anger that lived in him like a boil on his black soul. Not everyone could kill without remorse, and he counted himself lucky to be able to do it.

But he'd not kill Tess, though he had come West with that intent. Twice during the storm, he'd dreamed of her, and awakened to find his member in his hands. The dreams reminded him of her nubile flesh in ways he'd forgotten.

No, he'd not kill her. Tess was the wife he'd chosen, and wife she would be. Sons she would bear him. He'd been stunned when she fled—he'd not thought she had it

in her. It was more of a pleasure than a sorrow to learn
she had that much spirit.

Upon his return to their village last year, Seamus had
been smitten by the girl, who had grown to such astonishing beauty over the years. He'd been snared like a
foolish bear in the trap of her eyes and her fairy hair. She
was near starved to death when he found her. Pale and
bony, but for all of it, beautiful as few women were at
their best.

He'd been glad to feed her, and watched her eat, her
teeth tearing into the beef he brought with a savage and
stimulating gusto. He watched when she walked back to
her father's house, her breasts the only flesh upon her
body with weight enough to move. He thought, that first
night, to lure her to his bed with promises of good food.

But sometime in those weeks, Seamus had come to
another decision about Tess Fallon. Watching her move
about the village with her head up, her dignity intact in
spite of the bones sticking out the shabby elbows of her
dress, he had decided to marry her.

Oh, he'd had women aplenty, but more often than not,
they were whores, bought for a night, or women who were
rough and hard, like him. Never had he lain with a woman
so fresh and clean, or softly spoken, or schooled as Tess
was. Her mother had been gently born, and had pressed
upon her husband the need for her children to know how
to figure and read. Upon her death bed, she'd extracted a
promise from the village priest to teach them, who saw to
his promise with dedication.

So Tess carried herself like a lady of the manor, that spine
straight, that chin upheld, her manners as fine and dainty as
any Dublin miss. Watching her, Seamus McKenzie made up
his mind that he'd never have a better chance to take himself
a wife of some beauty and bearing.

Before the whole village, he'd wed her. And that night
he had taken her sweet flesh again and again. He'd heard
talk that ladies disliked the act, and so he bore her whimpering terror of it.

Crouched by the flickering fire, Seamus remembered with a haze of sensual pleasure the taste of those fine, taut breasts, the plushness of her lips, the tight clutch of her protesting body against his own. The familiar ache rose in his loins.

No, he'd not kill his wife.

Joaquin awakened before dawn. His mouth tasted like August, dry as the bones of a dead desert animal. He shifted and felt the protest in limbs growing too old for the unmoving sleep of a drunkard. A netting of painful veins clutched his head. He winced and sat up.

Tess slept deeply. Sonia's bed was empty, and the room was cold, for the fire had died to embers. He shivered. His serape lay at the foot of the bedroll and he put it on and quietly fed tinder to the fire, then a good chunk of pine. Moving soundlessly, he put on his boots and rolled his blankets, ever aware of the sleeping Tess beside him. Only when he'd finished his tasks, and the fire had begun to flicker again did he allow himself to look at her. He sank down on the bench and clasped his hands between his knees and watched her sleep. It hurt to do it, in some nameless, yearning way.

In the gloomy predawn light, she looked like a wraith, something ethereal and otherworldly. Her skin shone pale and smooth. In her haste and embarrassment last night, she had not braided her hair but left it tied back with ribbon, and while she slept, the ribbon had come undone, letting her hair spill in a tangle of wild golden-brown curls. He half-smiled, thinking she would face a struggle combing it out this morning. He wished he could brush it for her.

Last night. He took a breath and released it. Last night. Her tiny shifting in his arms, the gentle offering of her lips, the way she had lain near him, so silent and wounded. He had wanted to soothe her, but he could not speak of it. Not yet. Not while the taste of her was still on his mouth, when the shadows and light scent of her still clung to his hands.

One of her arms was flung out of the bedroll, and part of her chest. The blouse he'd found was too big for her, and gaped at the neckline, but regrettably, no skin showed. The cotton lay close against her form. Joaquin, his hands braced on his thighs, admired the round thrust of her small breasts. He imagined cupping the sweet plumpness in his hand, imagined tracing the rise with his fingers until the tips rose to his caress. From that thought, it was not difficult to imagine unbuttoning the placket down the front, and looking at the skin beneath, and putting his mouth, his tongue, his face against the softness.

Unwelcome heat rose in his loins. He could not halt the vision. He wanted her, very much, and he thought she had not known much pleasure with men. There had been in her kiss last night a hesitant innocence mixed with her desire that told him she had not been properly handled. He would like to be the man who gave her the pleasure she'd never had.

She shifted in sleep, as if sensing his perusal. Restlessly, she turned, pushing at the weight of blankets and hides, and he noticed her brow was damp with sweat. She kicked one leg out, and it was bare to the knee, her skirts tangled high on her leg. Light caught the straight, white length of her shin. He closed his eyes against temptation.

So beautiful. So sweet. So hungry. He wanted to take her hand, and kiss her, and tease her. He wanted to lie with her through a long, dark, cold night, just the two of them, and hold her in his arms.

He took a long breath and let it go, willing himself to stop thinking of it. She was married. Even if she weren't, there were many hardships for the woman of a mixed-blood trader. He could give her nothing, and she had had plenty of that already.

Gently, he moved forward and reached for the blanket she had kicked free. It was not yet warm enough for her to be uncovered so. But to make her more comfortable, he folded back the buffalo hide on top, then reached for the lighter blankets to pull over her shoulders. She sighed softly, and snuggled into the blanket.

Kneeling there next to her, Joaquin ached. Knowing he should not, he gave in to his wish and reached out. He touched the faintly blue temple, and traced the curve of her cheek. His fingers looked rough and brutish against her skin, and he wondered how anything human could be so unflawed as this cheek with the peach blush. There were no pores that he could see, no blemishes or wrinkles—only the unbroken expanse of skin.

His thumb brushed her mouth, and she stirred. She turned her face into his hand and put a kiss against the center of his palm.

Joaquin closed his eyes, willing himself to be still, to go away, to do anything but what he did. He caressed her face, and touched her neck, and waited until she opened her eyes. Hazy sleep clung to them. He slipped his other hand around her jaw, and bent over her, and kissed her.

She made a quiet sound, as if it hurt her. He straightened. "You were so beautiful lying there in your sleep," he said softly, "that I could not help but kiss you, Tessita."

She looked up at him. "I dreamed of you," she said. "And when I awoke, it wasn't a dream."

No man, he told himself, no man could resist such sweetness. "Ah, Tess," he murmured, and bent to kiss her again. This time, she disentangled her arms from the covers, and put them around his shoulders, drawing him down.

Gray light began to spill in through the small thick windows. Joaquin allowed himself to be drawn, and lay down next to her on the soft bed of buffalo robes. He gathered her close and pressed her body close to his, and kissed her and let her kiss him, for a long time. "I have dreamed of kissing you," he said, smoothing a lock of hair from her cheek.

"Did you?"

"A thousand times," he replied. "Ten thousand." He moved to touch his lips to hers. "Did you imagine kissing me, Tessita?"

"Yes." The word was a breathy whisper.

"Yes," he repeated, and kissed her deeply, drinking of the nectar of her mouth, tasting her giving lips and the eagerness of her small tongue. Her fingers combed through his hair and roved his neck, and he felt himself grow thick as a tree branch.

He tasted her chin, her throat, the hollow of her neck, breathing in the scent of her, that wild note that smelled of everything at once—of mountains and plains and lake and sky. He pressed his forehead, his cheek, his mouth against her skin, closing his eyes, caught in a place of no thought.

She grabbed him suddenly, pulling him up to put her hands on his face. She kissed him fiercely, kissed his mouth and opened herself to his tongue. Joaquin fell into her kiss, almost mad with need—not of any woman who would open her thighs for him, but this particular woman with her guarded eyes and secrets and heartbreaking need. No woman with so warm a heart should have had to wait so long to know a man could give her pleasure—and he sensed by her wildness that she had never known it. Gladly he returned her kiss. Gladly he touched her ears and neck, and rubbed one leg against hers, and kissed her again.

The sound of voices drifted into the private silence broken hitherto only by their soft moans and murmurings. Even through his haze, Joaquin recognized Raul's deep voice, and he identified the sound of footsteps on the stairs.

He pulled away urgently, yanking the blankets over Tess in a rush. Then he turned away, glad for the long drape of the serape. Quickly, he knelt by the fire.

Sonia and Raul came in. "Good morning!" Sonia sang out, and Joaquin could not help but smile at the glowing satisfaction in her voice.

"Good morning," he said.

Raul looked like a child who'd been given an unexpected present—happy, but bewildered. "I rounded up Roger a little while ago," he said. "I reckon we can take off today. Get to Taos before we get another snow."

"Good." Joaquin glanced quickly at Tess. She'd straightened her clothes and now sat up. A hard, pink stain burned on her cheeks, and combined with the loose tangled hair, it gave her away more fully than she would ever know, especially to these two, who had obviously spent the night together.

Raul winked at Joaquin, looking from the curtained room to the wine on the table and back. Joaquin shook his head with a frown, aware of a sharp discomfort.

He turned back to the fire, his jaw hard. As passion receded, he saw how foolish he'd been. He'd been wrong to seduce her so. When the moment faded, she would feel shame and sorrow over her actions. It was not fair to exploit her desire to his own ends, especially when he had nothing to offer her.

Abruptly, he stood and grabbed his bedroll. "I will see to the horses and our supplies. You help the women prepare," he said to Raul. "I want to be on the road in an hour."

12

The weather was dry and clear as they set out after breakfast, much to Joaquin's satisfaction. In the heat of the warm autumn sun, the muddy fields were drying, and by the time they crossed the river into Mexico at noon, he had shed his serape. As they rode, he was glad to be back out in the open, away from the cloistering walls of the fort, and the temptation of Tess sleeping next to him in a private place every night. Out here, he did not have to think about her so much. There were things for him to do.

He set a vigorous pace, hoping to cover at least twenty miles each day, even with the women. Although the sunlight was warm now, he knew how quickly the weather could turn deadly. Travel was hazardous at the best of times, especially with women along, but they had pushed the season too far.

Each morning, he scanned the sky, scented the wind, listened to the voice of the wind for signs of oncoming snow, and he always had plans for alternate routes and shelter should they need it. His dread was a snowstorm over Raton, a treacherous, rocky pass through the mountains. Once through the pass, there would be less concern.

The third night, they made camp at Rio Purgatorie, a

slim river that ran between two ranges of mountains. The women had taken on the task of building their fires each night, and seeing to the preparation of food while the men tended the horses and scouted hares or fish.

Tonight the women were weary. He saw it in the tautness of Tess's mouth, in the way Sonia held a hand to her back as she bent over the fire. A twinge of guilt touched him as he eyed the pregnant woman. Perhaps he was pushing too hard. She had been injured, after all, and the weight of that child could not be easy. In the weeks since he'd known her, her belly had fully doubled in size. Perhaps he should speak with Tess about it—she seemed very knowledgeable.

He frowned and made for the river. Kneeling, he washed his face and hands in the water. He did not particularly want to initiate a conversation with Tess, not for any reason. He'd stayed as far from her as possible on this trip, and kept his mind on other things.

Roger came up behind him. "Hey, hombre."

The Englishman's hair had grown long and ragged, and a woman in the Indian camp had made him a gift of leather breeches. Joaquin grinned at him. "Hey, English, you're lookin' like a wild man nowadays."

Roger chuckled. From his pocket he took a metal flask and pulled at it, then offered it to Joaquin.

Joaquin shook his head. Since the night with Tess and the wine, when his mind and purposes had become so muddied by drink, he had not touched it. As long as she was in his keeping, he would not.

Squatting back on his heels, Joaquin eyed the horizon expertly. From the plains they'd ridden steadily toward the mountains, and the camp tonight was darkened early by the shadows the jagged peaks cast from the west. Only thin wisps of clouds hung in the fading, yellow sky. A good sign.

"I smell rain," Roger said, pursing his lips.

Joaquin frowned and lifted his head to the cool evening air. He scented pine and the copper scent of the river and a faint whiff of smoke from the fire, but no weather. "I don't smell it yet."

"It's there. We oughta make camp in those trees, I reckon." He stood up and pointed to a copse of cottonwood and piñon. "Maybe it won't come tonight. Maybe tomorrow."

Joaquin nodded respectfully. The first night after Roger had joined Joaquin and Raul, the Englishman had smelled bear. Insisted upon it, in fact, but Raul and Joaquin had been derisive. When a hungry, black bear wandered into camp close to dawn, Roger shot it right through the heart. Ignoring the others, he'd sat in wait for the animal. "Told you I smelled bear," he said.

An odd talent, this ability to smell things, but Joaquin would stake his life on it. "I hope it stays rain," he said.

"Better to be stuck down here than up the pass."

"I'll tell the others."

"A moment, if you would, señor."

Joaquin grinned. "An hour if you like, señor."

Roger lowered his head, then looked up with a friendly expression. "I don't mean to meddle, but perhaps you could toss a kind word to Señora Fallon when you have a spare moment. I know we're in a hurry, but you haven't been very kind to the woman since we left the fort."

"You've been kind enough for both of us," Joaquin said, aware of a bitter heat in his chest.

"That sounds like jealousy, hombre." Roger cocked one red eyebrow. "You ain't falling for her, are you?"

"You Anglos have no color," he said. "I'm waiting for Elena."

"Ah, Elena." Roger lifted the flask and pulled again, coughing hoarsely. He looked over his shoulder toward the women. "Elena's a beauty, but she's no Tess Fallon."

Joaquin tried to resist, but he looked toward the fire himself. Tess handed a cup to Sonia, who sat wearily on a rock, and turned back to the fire. Her thick braid swung forward, and she caught hold of it to keep it from the flames. A hard rush of something almost painful moved over Joaquin's nerves and he looked away. "So take her if you think her such a beauty," he said harshly.

"Well, I'll be buggered," Roger said softly, his bright blue eyes gleaming. "You *are* jealous."

"I have work to do." Joaquin moved away, leaving Roger to his suspicions. He had the life of those women in his hands. Jealousy or the lack of it had no place in his concerns tonight.

Tess sighed as she sat down on a rock, a cup of strong sweet tea in her hands. Overhead the sky had gone gray with the lowering sun, and a chill touched the air. She clasped her shawl close around her.

After the journeys she had already made, she hadn't expected this one to be so much harder. But the comancheros were used to a brisk pace—Roger had told her they had to get permits from the governor each time they left Taos, and the permits ran only two months. They had adapted to the most efficient methods of travel and the quickest pace. Her back and thighs ached from being in the saddle all day, three days running, and there was such bone-deep weariness in her limbs that she thought she could sleep standing up.

Sonia, too, felt the strain. She tried to keep a brave face, but Tess saw the grimness around her mouth, the lines of exhaustion around her eyes. The babe had grown apace with the good food at the fort, and Sonia's wound was healing well, but however hard it was for Tess to keep this mad pace, it was doubly difficult for Sonia.

Raul joined the two women, coming to sit between them by the fire. "How y'all doing?" he asked in his deep voice. The question was loosely directed at both of them, but he looked at Sonia. Concern touched his large dark eyes, and Tess liked him for that.

"We're fine," Sonia lied. As if to give credence to her

words, she straightened her back. "It's been a rough ride, but we're tough. Ain't that right, Miss Tess?"

Tess found a slight smile curling her mouth and she nodded. "I may not ride a horse again as long as I live, but I'll survive for now."

Raul looked at Tess. It wasn't something he did very often. Mostly, he ignored her, as if she were some annoying pest, like a horse fly or a mosquito. His face was grave. "I want the truth, now. You two gonna be all right? Neither one of you look too well."

"We have no choice," Tess replied. "Isn't that right? We must get to Taos before more weather halts us in some dangerous place."

"Well," he said, looking off toward the mountains, where a bright ribbon of gold still clung to the jagged peaks, "if you thought it warranted, we might be able to weather over one night."

The unexpected solicitousness nearly made Tess, in her exhausted state, want to cry. Bending her head to hide the quick emotion, she said, "Perhaps once we are through the pass, we might be grateful for a day's rest."

Sonia stood with effort, her belly swaying out like a ball under her dress. "I'll be back shortly," she said, and moved away. Tess watched her carefully, alert to any sign of discomfort that might mean the babe was too soon to come, or might be giving undue stress to the woman who carried it.

"Is her baby gonna be all right?" Raul asked quietly when Sonia was out of earshot.

Tess nodded. "She's not a new mother, you know. She's borne six children—and all of them easy. You needn't worry."

"Six?"

"Aye. One only three years ago."

Raul looked at her steadily, and she thought she saw a sign of something real and human behind his hard mask— a flicker of sorrow or yearning. Not the usual fury. "I left four children of my own, back in Mississippi. I think about 'em all the time, but there wasn't a one old enough to take from their mamas when I left."

"Sonia left none of them behind. None that were not already taken from her through death or sale." It had been that last sale that had brought them here.

"None will take this one," he said fiercely.

Tess smiled at him. "No."

For a moment, there was a rare peace between them. Raul moved suddenly and headed off into the gloaming. Tess knew he sought Sonia.

Which left Tess alone again. She glanced around camp and saw Roger by the river, drinking from a silver flask, lost in his thoughts. She had seen Joaquin head toward the horses a few minutes before, but didn't look for him now.

Since the morning when she'd awakened to find him bent over her, with that rich hungry look in his eyes, Joaquin had barely spoken to her, except to give an order or direction. Even then, he didn't meet her eyes. It wounded her.

Those stolen moments in the fort lived in her like something magical. She'd been dreaming of him, and opened her eyes to find him leaning over her, his dark eyes alive with something she'd ached to see there. And oh, how sweet his touch, his kiss had been! In all her days on earth, no one had touched her like that, had made her feel such a wild and wanton yearning.

Both of them had known the moments to be stolen. It was wrong, even when they did it. Afterward, as she hastily gathered her meager belongings in preparation for their departure, Tess had told herself she could not allow it to happen again—she had to be true to her vows, or something terrible might happen. If it were only her own life she had to worry about, she might have risked the wrath of the heavens for one night in Joaquin's gentle arms, but there was Sonia to think of, and her baby. Their fortunes were inextricably bound. Tess would not risk those lives for a selfish pleasure of the flesh.

But she hadn't even had the chance. Joaquin not only

ignored her now, he seemed ashamed. And no wonder, Tess thought, standing with a sigh to stir the pot of rabbit stew on the fire. What a wanton she must have seemed, kissing him so boldly one night, then letting him come to her as he had the next morning. It was only the interruption of Raul and Sonia that had kept more from happening between them.

As she straightened, a feeling of heat on her face, an extraordinary blaze of light burst over the landscape. A second ago, the world had been bathed in the familiar grayish cast of twilight. Now, through some trick, long fingers of light caught the treetops and the edges of the river, setting them all ablaze in the most beautiful color of light Tess had ever seen.

She stared around her in wonder, filling her eyes with the sight of bared cottonwood branches, washed in the strange, uncommonly colored light, a shade blended of yellow and rose and white. The sky, already dark gray, provided almost ethereal contrast.

She looked over her shoulder to see what might have caused it—and there was Joaquin, looking at her, bathed in the same strange sunlight. Behind him, she saw that the sun had slipped into a low valley between mountains, and long fingers of the last dying rays had shot through the break to give the world this rose-and-yellow brilliance.

She forgot there was strain between them, or chose not to acknowledge it just then. In a hushed whisper, she said, "I've never seen anything so beautiful in all my life."

He stepped closer, a crooked smile on his mouth. "Nor have I, señora. You look like something the sun made."

It was impossible to mind such poetic compliments. Tess smiled back at him.

"Wait until you see Taos," he said. "There, every evening, the world is thus. Tipping the branches, washing the adobe in that color. They say there is nowhere else on earth where the light breaks this way."

"Nowhere I've seen."

He settled on a rock near the fire. "Roger says it will rain tonight."

"But there are no clouds."

"None we see." He touched his nose. "Roger smells the rain—that's his talent."

Tess chuckled. "He does remind me a bit of a great dog."

He laughed with her. "Faithful and cheerful, yes?"

"Yes." Tess smiled. "He seems a good man."

"He is."

Silence fell, taut with things they would not say. Tess found herself unable to keep from admiring him. The beautiful light gilded him, turning his skin an elegant copper, washing with affection over his black hair, and dancing with gold sparks on the end of his long lashes. Her chest tightened with the yearning she had vowed to put away. To distract herself, she bent over the stew, holding her braid so it would not fall in the fire.

"Tessita," he said quietly.

Tess closed her eyes. "Señor, I beg you do not address me so."

She heard the rustling of his clothes as he stood up, but she remained still, willing him to stay far away. He did not. When he spoke again, he was very close, so close his accented words fell in a low murmur to her ears.

"What else shall I call you, Tessita? It is the only name which suits you."

His breath brushed her neck, and the response of her body was instantaneous—her breasts grew heavy, and her thighs felt suddenly soft. "I am married, señor," she said. She'd intended to sound hard and firm, but instead the words soughed out of her on a broken sound of despair.

"Yes," he said, and smoothed a lock of hair from her face. His fingers barely touched her cheek, but Tess yanked away, aching.

"I am not free to flirt this way," she said harshly, swallowing the emotion in her heart. She stepped backward from him several paces. "I cannot betray my vows, señor. I cannot."

His jaw, highlighted by some capricious finger of light, tightened. "I know." He lifted a hand, and dropped it again. "Will you once say my name, señora? One time."

The word rose to her lips, infinitely soft and rich on her tongue. A thousand times in her mind she'd whispered it, sung it. *Joaquin.* But now she shook her head, afraid what would happen if she did, afraid it would somehow bind her to him. She crossed her arms. "Do not ask it," she said quietly.

"Very well." He stepped closer. "But I will tell you, Tessita, that you are the most beautiful woman I have ever seen. I think of you at night, when I'm lying alone by the fire, when I'm riding ahead." His dark eyes burned. "We are passionate men, my people, and once the fire is lit, it does not easily go out."

"Don't—"

"Don't? Why not?" He stepped closer, until their bodies were nearly touching, until she had to look up into his eyes. The mouth she longed to kiss hovered so close she had only to stand on her toes to take it. "Does it make you want me, too?"

"It doesn't matter if I want you, Señor Morales," she said, far more steadily than she would have believed possible. "I am not free."

Now he looked at her mouth, and lower to her breasts. "My hands remember the feel of you, Tessita. The softness, the eagerness. And I think you do not forget the burn of my fingers and my mouth."

Curse him, it was true. Even as he stood there talking, she was filled with the memory of his big hands on her face, in her hair, of his hot mouth, of his reverent gaze as he looked at her with yearning. Again she closed her eyes. "Please," she whispered. "Have you no honor?"

At last he backed away. "*Sí,*" he said and she heard in the word a fine disgust. "More than I wish, señora, or you would now be mine."

He stalked away, loose-limbed and unbearably beautiful, as the light faded once more, leaving only grayness upon the world.

Near dusk, Seamus found the bodies. His horse started skittering just past the break, and Seamus had been alert, his hand on his rifle in case of Indians. But nothing moved in the thick, gray light. He heard only the cluck of the river and the whistles of magpies. A low wind moaned.

And then he rounded the bend in the track and saw the destruction. Even for a man of his experience, it was a gruesome scene. The overturned wagon, the bodies with arrows sticking out of them, the bare heads—

He retched. Not even a Christian burial for the poor sods, now left to vultures and crows and the assault of the elements. In the gloom, he caught movement from the corner of his eye and whirled, his gun at the ready.

It was only a pair of pantaloons, caught on a yucca. They lifted on the wind, as if in a sigh, then settled back down.

A pair of blue ribbons in the garment caught his eye, and he frowned, riding closer. The pantaloons were made of fine white eyelet, and blue ribbons laced down the sides, weaving in and out of the pattern, to end in a tie that would lace around a woman's dainty leg. Below the ribbon tie was a cascade of finest lace.

Tess.

He stared at them, remembering well the shop in Dublin where he'd bought them, thinking they might bring a smile to her sober eyes. No woman he'd known could resist lacy underthings. But Tess had only accepted them with her usual demure nod, and thanked him in a whisper.

He swore aloud. It sickened him to do it, but he needed a better look at the bodies, and he rode close around them, examining them as well as he could bear. It was impossible to tell anything after the storm and time had done their damage. He could not even tell man from woman. He retched again.

Bent's Fort was only a day's ride. He'd go there, learn what he could. "Ah, Tess," he said aloud to the night. "Was it so much worse with me?"

13

That night, Tess and Sonia lay whispering side by side on beds made of buffalo hides over pine branches and stared at a sky sugared with stars. Raul had taken first watch; the other two men were sound asleep. Roger snored lightly. It made the women giggle.

Glancing toward the low-burning fire to be sure Raul was far enough away so he could not hear her, Tess whispered, "You haven't told him, have you?"

"No! Why would I?"

"I think you're falling in love with him, that's why. And you want him to think well of me."

"Honey, I'm not about to put you in that kind of danger. How can you even think such a thing?"

Tess sighed. "I don't. Just don't be tempted. I'd rather he hated me for the rest of my natural life than have him know there's no husband waiting in Taos. For all practical purposes, I'm a thief."

"We're in Mexico now." She gave the word its Spanish pronunciation and Tess smiled. "They ain't got no slaves around here."

"Oh, but they do. Señor Morales is the son of a slave. They call them *genizaros*."

"But they're Injuns, not black folks, so maybe the law won't matter here."

"What's the difference?" Tess protested as fiercely as she could in a whisper. "Thieves hang."

"Will you quit agitatin' so? I won't tell."

"Thank you." Tess settled back in her cocoon of thick hides and blankets and looked at the night sky. It was so beautiful here it nearly took her breath away, and Joaquin had told her it was even more so in Taos. "I wonder what it'll be like there," she whispered now.

Sonia's answering voice was thick with sleepiness. "Raul says it's beautiful. Says you can grow all kinds of things because the sun is so warm."

"The land is so fertile here," Tess whispered. The plentifulness had amazed her upon her arrival in Arkansas. The soil was so rich, it grew an abundance of foodstuffs they'd never have attempted in Ireland where the days were cool and the sun often hidden.

Sonia suddenly propped herself up on her elbow and leaned close. "What are you going to do about Señor Morales when we get to Taos and you ain't got no husband waitin'?"

Tess sighed. "I'll lie some more, I suppose, though I admit I'm weary of it."

"How long can you lie?"

"I don't know. I can only take each day as it comes, and do what seems best."

"It'll be all right," Sonia said quietly, as if willing Tess to believe it. "You'll see. We'll find work as dressmakers or maids."

"We've learned precious little Spanish thus far. Who will hire a woman who cannot speak the language?"

Sonia laughed softly. "And you cleanin' her floors? You'll learn fast enough."

Tess cradled her cheek on her arm. From far away came the sound of an owl, calling out in the still night, and as if in answer, a wolf cried, low and long. Once the sounds might have frightened her, but she heard them now with a sense of pleasure and wonder. What a vast, wild land this was! "I wish my brother could be with me," she said quietly.

"It's hard, breaking off with everything familiar like this, running away someplace so different."

"Is it for you, too?"

"I don't want to go back, you understand," Sonia said. "But I miss things, miss knowing everything about everything, the way the plants grow, the way the sky looks and what it means. It's hard to leave the only place you know. I was born right there on that plantation, and even with all the grief it gave me, there were times I was happy, too."

"Well then, 'tis harder for you than it is for me. I knew no joy at that place."

"But you knew it back home." Sonia turned her head to look at her. "Back in Ireland."

"Aye. Some." But for all her protests, she had come to like this wild landscape. It made her feel free somehow. "None like yours—I didn't bear and lose a child, nor love and lose a husband."

"Life brings with it a little joy and a lot of sorrow. I aim to take as much of the joy as I can find." In the darkness, Sonia reached out and took Tess's hand in a firm, warm clasp. "I aim to see you do the same."

Tess squeezed her fingers. "Thank you," she said, and yawned. "Having found a friend is joy enough."

Sonia laughed, low and earthy. "Oh, how I'm gonna love to see you take those words back."

Smiling, Tess drifted into sleep.

The weather held all night and into the next day, but as the small party neared the summit of the pass, a thick fog moved in. Joaquin cursed it, and pushed on as long as he was able, but soon Raul protested the danger, and Joaquin reluctantly agreed to make camp.

He could see the women were relieved. Sonia, in particular, had seemed tense today. He dismounted and crossed over to her. "Señorita, are you all right?" he asked.

"Now I am." Absently, she rubbed the mound of her

belly. "I didn't know I was afraid of being high till"—she gestured toward the vista that would be visible if the fog had not engulfed them— "we got up here. It makes me dizzy."

Joaquin nodded. "The mountains do that to some people," he said. "Perhaps you should ride with Raul till we descend, then." He paused, peering at her face for signs of illness, but there were none. Her dark skin gleamed with health, and her eyes were clear. She walked with a straight, even gait that accounted for her belly in the way he'd seen mothers of many children do. "You are well otherwise?"

"Oh, I'm fine. Both of us are. All this good food agrees with him."

He smiled and touched her arm. "Good."

As he began to move off, she said, "Señor Morales?"

He stopped, turning back.

Sonia glanced over her shoulder toward the others. Roger sat with Tess on a flat boulder, and Raul had disappeared into the trees. Quietly, Sonia asked, "Will you take Tess out to collect herbs? She needs a distraction. I think she's worryin' a whole lot."

Joaquin lifted a brow, sensing some scheme. "Did she tell you to ask me?"

"Lord, no! She'd as soon kill me if she knew." A mischievous glint touched her eyes and curled the edges of her mouth. "Don't tell her, hear?"

"As she has told me a dozen times, she is married."

Sonia put one hand on her hip. "Maybe I had you figured wrong, after all. Here I been thinking you were a silver-tongued devil who could talk your way into the heart of a bear."

Joaquin snorted. "A bear would be less dangerous."

Her face sobered, the glittering eyes going suddenly solemn with the weight of knowledge behind them. "Wounds make a bear dangerous, but gentle handling can tame one."

Her meaning was plain. For a moment, Joaquin looked down at Sonia, considering. "What have you to gain from this, señorita?"

"Nothing."

He gave her a slight lift of his shoulder, neither capitulation nor resistance. "I will see."

Although the others huddled by the fire in the thick, cold gloom, Tess felt enlivened by the weather, which was much like home. Wrapped in her shawl and the warm serape, she explored the edges of the camp. She never ambled too far from the path, so she wouldn't be lost—or worse, tumble over the edge of some precipice—but amble she did. In the high woods, she plucked samples of plants and smelled them, and tasted them. Under a squatty pine tree, she discovered a hoard of small brown nuts, and put some in the pocket of her skirt. She found withered wildflowers, which she crushed and smelled, examining the pods and seeds so she'd remember them later. Her instincts told her the bark of one tree might prove useful, and the berries of another. One heart-shaped leaf made her eyes itch, and she examined it closely. Such irritants always had uses.

On a flat rock, Tess sat down to examine her treasures, one by one. Fog enveloped her almost completely, casting over the world that strange hush of bad weather. A single unseen bird twittered in a tree nearby, its song mournful and sweet at once.

She spread the leaves, stems, and dried flowers over her skirt. It was daunting to think how much she would have to learn to become a healer again in these parts. The plants were very different from the ones she knew, and though she had little doubt there was a program of medicinal applications for all of them, it was impossible to know which was which. Perhaps she'd never practice her art again.

It made her feel sad. Through all of her trials, she had always at least had that single, unshakable vocation to believe in, to count on. Twirling a leaf by its stem between her finger and thumb, she wondered what she would become.

Behind her came the unmistakable sound of feet crunching over the dry needles and leaves on the ground. She tensed, looking over her shoulder. Joaquin emerged from the fog, all dark, long grace. The leaf between her fingers broke.

"You should not be out here alone," he said.

"But I am only a stone's throw from the camp!"

"We cannot see you." Without invitation, he sat down beside her, one leg flung comfortably out in front of him, elbows propped on his other knee. "I'll sit with you until you are ready to go back."

Tess glanced at him warily, wondering what trick he now had up his sleeve.

"You would not want to be alone if Indians came," he said.

Tess couldn't tell if he was teasing her or meant the words as serious warning. "Surely any who live in this hard place will be safely home right now."

"Perhaps. Better not to take chances."

He sat close but not too close. Tess decided perhaps she could rely on his honor after all. Holding out the small brown nuts she found, she asked, "What are these?"

"Piñon nuts." He plucked one from her hand and cracked the thin outer shell with his teeth. "Taste one. They're good." He plucked out the meat and popped it in his mouth.

Tess followed his example. "Not bad."

"Better roasted," he said. From her skirt, he took a frond of dried flowers. "Are you studying the plants?"

"Aye. But with little success. What is this one?"

He tsked, rolling it in his fingers. "This one I don't know. My sister can tell you." From the tangle of things in her lap, he plucked a single dried stalk. "This is a pretty blue flower. It grows in the mountains only, but I don't know what to call it."

"Your sister will teach me the plants here?" she asked.

"If you wish to learn, she will teach you." He leaned back on one elbow, taking another piñon nut from the small pile beside her. "You will like her, I think. And I think she will like you in return."

Tess felt a little bewildered by his sudden mood changes. At the fort he'd been teasing and playful until the kisses between them, then he'd turned silent and distant on the trip until last night, when he'd seemed to be angry with her for refusing him. Now back again was the easygoing Joaquin, who seemed to wish nothing more from her than a simple conversation. With a little frown, she said, "I'll look forward to it."

"Not very long now. Down the hill, over the rivers, and one more pass into Taos. If the weather does not prevent it, we will be home by Saturday."

Tess blinked. "Saturday." She couldn't prevent a small laugh coming from her throat. "Do you know I've lost track of what day it is today?"

"This is Tuesday. Only four days to Taos. Maybe, if we have very good weather, less than that even."

A knot of mingled anticipation and worry congealed in her throat. "Oh," she said quietly.

"You are worried," he said, and narrowed his eyes intently. "I wonder what could worry you so?"

"A new life," she said. "A new place, with a new language. I never thought I'd travel so far from home."

"But have you not had a wonderful adventure, señora?"

She smiled. "Aye, that I have. When I was a child, I knew a family who emigrated to America, and I had dreams about it for a long time."

"Did you see me in your dreams?" he asked.

With a sense of alarm, she looked at him. He had not moved, but the faintest ghost of a smile played in his eyes. "You?" she repeated.

She looked at his clothes and his long hair and his moccasined feet and shook her head. "I did not know of men like you, Señor Morales. I had never seen Spaniards or Indians or Mexicans then."

"But perhaps I was there in disguise, eh? A handsome

prince, riding on a big white horse, coming to rescue you from bandits?"

She laughed. "A young girl's dreams are ever filled with princes and big horses, señor. There is not much mystery to that."

"Big horses, eh?" He licked his lower lip quickly, and cocked one impish brow.

At first she didn't understand his meaning. Just as it dawned on her and a hot blush rose in her cheeks, she spied the grin he was trying to contain. "Señor!" she protested, ducking her head.

He laughed out loud. "Forgive me," he said and touched her hand briefly. "It was too easy."

Reluctantly, Tess smiled. Much as it embarrassed her, she'd often heard bawdy teasing like this among the women in her village—the old women who no longer worried what the Church might say of their evident enjoyment of the nighttime side of marriage.

He tossed the head of a flower toward her. It struck her cheek softly, and she tossed it back at him. "I think I dreamed of you when I was a boy," he said.

"Is that so?" she returned, half-pleased, half-braced for more teasing.

"*Sí.*"

Was it her imagination, or had he edged a little closer to her? She could feel the warmth of his body now. "Well, what did you dream?"

"I dreamed," he said quietly, "of a beautiful woman with hair the color of whiskey and eyes like the edge of a hot springs pool, who came to me from the arms of a devil."

Tess closed her eyes. It was not only the words themselves, but the way they were delivered that moved her. His voice seemed a tangible thing, a sun-drenched sound rolling down her spine. She could not breathe for a moment, thinking of how it might be to have that voice moving over her in the night, as his hands and lips and body moved.

Clenching her fingers together, she willed the vision away. When she'd attained a measure of control, she said briskly, "I think you've been a sore trial to the women of this land for a very long time, Señor Morales."

He laughed. "Those are not the exact words they use."

"Let me guess. Arrogant? Vain? Impossible?"

"Impossible, yes, that's one." His eyes glittered. "Impossible to resist."

Tess laughed.

"And," he continued, "there is no arrogance when a man delivers what he promises. Vain?" He paused, as if considering the trait. "No," he said firmly. "Not vain."

"Let me say it for them, then. You are arrogant, vain, and impossible."

His eyes danced. "But charming, no?"

He definitely was closer now. His forearm leaned against her hip, and his thigh lay close to her knee. Unalarmed, she shifted an inch from him, and lifted her brows when he grinned up at her.

A small but definite shift in the light caught her attention, and Tess glanced up to see what had caused the change. With a quick intake of breath, she cried, "Oh, Joaquin, look!"

He sat up. The clouds that enshrouded the mountain in such deep fog had lifted slightly, revealing a resplendent valley far below them, cut through with a ribbon of water that reflected the silver-gray of the clouds.

The rock on which they sat was only a few feet from a dramatic drop, and Tess, thinking how blithely she'd walked over the hills, felt suddenly very unstable. Instinctively, she grasped his arm. His hand, cold and large, covered hers.

"Easy," he said. "You won't fall."

Tess looked at him. All at once, she was struck with the wonder of it: that she ordinary Tess Fallon, should be sitting on a rock far above the earth in Mexico, touching the arm of the most beautiful man she'd ever seen.

"You said my name," he said quietly, moving his fingers over hers.

"So I did." She removed her hand and put it in her lap. "It's a beautiful name."

"*Gracias*." He shifted slightly, and now very much of his body came into contact with hers. His thigh against the outside of her own, his arm against her shoulder. Teasingly, he brushed her cheek with the flower in his hand. "Say it again," he said quietly. "So I can remember how it sounds falling from your lips."

Tess swallowed, feeling a surge of longing rise in her, a longing for his touch, for his hands, for his kiss. Her thoughts flew in a tangle as he shifted yet again and lifted a hand to tuck a lock of hair behind her ear.

"Joaquin," she whispered.

He smiled, and the expression gave his mouth the endearing crookedness she could never resist. Fog had misted the edges of his hair, covering the black locks beside his face with long strings of beaded, silver water, and his skin looked moist. Her heart began to thud uncomfortably, and an odd weakness settled in her elbows. Everywhere was silence.

He kissed her. Tilting his head, he blocked her view of the valley, and pressed his mouth to hers. Sweetly. His hands stayed where they were, bracing him against the rock, and Tess didn't feel the need to lift her own either. She only accepted the offering of his mouth, giving back softly as he molded his lips to the shape of hers, and then explored to one side of her mouth, and then the other. After a moment, he paused. In his dark eyes shone a steady, smiling light.

Tess just gazed back at him, too alight to even move a finger. He lifted a hand and cupped her cheek, and the expanse of that hand was so vast that while his thumb caressed the edge of her eye and her cheekbone, his pinky curled around her neck.

"You like me a little, Tessita." He pulled her to him, and claimed her mouth again before she could speak, his tongue ribboning the edge of her lips, asking for entrance. But even when she opened to him, his touch was seductive and sweet without a hint of invasiveness—just a lazy, glorious exploration that set her blood on fire.

"A little bit, anyway," he said over her mouth. "You like me to kiss you, and tease you." In the huskiness of the sound, Tess heard his restraint, and it touched her more than she could have imagined.

Oh yes, she liked him. She liked his sweetness and his humor. She liked the courage and sure confidence he exuded in this wilderness, and the way he seemed to know a thousand things she'd never thought of. She liked his voice, as melodious as the song of the wind moving through the branches of a hundred trees.

And she liked his mouth, his kiss, his beautiful face and his long-limbed form.

Oh, yes, she liked him very much.

He lifted his head again and smiled. Tracing a line along her face, he said, "Now, remember, you did not kiss me. I kissed you. What woman could fight off a man so intent on having his way with her?"

In a voice hushed with wonder and desire, she said, "I've never met a man like you."

"I think that's a very good thing for me." With a quick wink, he got to his feet and held out his hand. "Come. Before I am tempted to do more than kiss you."

With a laugh, Tess accepted his outstretched hand and allowed him to pull her to her feet. They stood face-to-face on the high precipice. "I've never met a woman like you, either," he said, then turned away, leading her back to camp.

14

In the billiards room of Bent's Fort, Seamus McKenzie shared a bottle of good whiskey with a trapper by the name of Horace. The trapper, getting drunker by the minute, expounded on the joys of a mountain man's life. Seamus, made expansive by the good time he'd made the past three days, nodded agreeably.

Behind them, men talked in low voices. Seamus tipped the bottle into his glass, then generously into the trapper's. "Only one thing about the life," Horace said with a sigh.

"What's that?"

"Women. No white women out here atall."

Seamus shrugged. "A woman's a woman, in the end."

"Well, that's what ye think when ye're out here a long time. Ye ferget how a white woman is till one comes along and reminds ye." He stared mournfully in his glass, stroking his beard. "There was one here last week mighta started a war if she hain't been married."

"A white woman?" Seamus narrowed his eyes. "Only last week? Was she travelin', by any chance, with a nigger woman?"

Horace looked up. "She was. Heard someone say she was Irish. A relation o' yours?"

Carefully, Seamus stilled the sudden surge of fury in his chest by lifting his glass and deliberately drinking the contents in a single gulp. "I've been looking for her for a friend. You say she was married?"

"Ayup. Newly wed by the look of them," Horace said with a snort. "If'n you know what I mean."

Seamus knew. He thought of Tess, whimpering in protest when he came to her. "Who was her husband?"

"I forget." He looked to the corner where two grizzled men played checkers. "Johnny, what was that comanchero's name, the Mexican that had the woman with him?"

"Joaquin Morales. Good man. Bastard half-breed, but his papa's got some big ranch outside Taos."

A bastard half-breed comanchero. Seamus felt a burn rise from his belly, through his chest, into his throat and ears, until he could not hear. His vision clouded with red light. The trapper's lips moved, and he guffawed, but Seamus could not hear him. He thought of the men outside, the savages with their leather and long hair and dark skin, thought of one of them pawing his wife—his wife—and her letting him.

Newly wed, by the look of them. The whore had taken a lover, when she had denied her husband. His fury nearly choked him. Abruptly, he strode out of the billiards room, his mind awhirl with images of Tess Fallon's passion with another man.

No, he would not kill her.

But for this, too, she would pay.

Friday morning, Tess sat in the sun, drinking tea. Around her, the men prepared for the last leg of the journey, and she half-listened to their easy jests and murmured comments with a sense of nostalgia. Today, they would arrive in Taos.

For the first time, Tess realized how much she would miss all of this. The breakfast fire crackled in its circle of stones, letting free a musky scent of mesquite, and the sunlight tumbling into the clearing between pines was clear and yellow, and felt warm on her shoulders and face. In the trees, birds twittered and whistled as if in celebration of such a grand day.

Tess sipped her hot tea from a tin cup, trying to catch the sounds, spirit, and feeling of the moment, so she could carry it with her forever. She'd been happier with these men, on this journey, than she'd ever been in her life. Strange it should be so, but it was. She had been free these past weeks—free of Seamus, and hunger, and worry. She had been free to admire the vast, breathtaking land that she knew had changed her, somewhere deep inside. She had spun small, harmless fantasies of a beautiful man unlike any other she had known. She'd kissed him a few times, too, and even that now seemed part of a pleasant dream.

She glanced over at him, at Joaquin, saddling his large black horse. He'd shed his serape in the warm morning, so he wore only his leggings, fitting close to his long, hard legs, and a simple cotton shirt, open at the neck. His glossy hair was caught back in the strip of red cloth, and tumbled down his back. He laughed at something Roger said, and over his face broke a light like morning.

Her heart pinched. Of everything, she would miss him most. Against all wishes, all warnings, she had fallen a little in love with this gentle, laughing man.

Cradling her chin in her hand, she watched him, a tiny smile on her mouth. Even now, he seemed to be more alive than anyone else around him, more fully in tune with his life, and his world. He loved being here on this mountain with his men and his horses on a sunny, late September morning. He had loved the trail, and the fort, and when they rode into Taos, Tess had no doubt he would love that, too.

And because he loved being wherever he was so easily, so zestfully, he made others glad, too. When he looked at Tess, and teased her, and kissed her, she had the feeling that his whole attention was focused entirely upon her. It was a very rare thing.

Sonia joined Tess, lifting her skirts to let her feet dry from her walk in the brook. "I've never tasted water like this in all my life," she said, offering a cupful she'd gathered from the stream. "It's colder than anything, sweet as pie."

Tess waved a hand. "No, thank you."

"They say we'll be in Taos before supper."

"Yes." Tess felt the roiling nerves in her stomach. "I don't suppose you've thought of any great plan?"

"I think the simpler, the better. We'll be so surprised that your husband ain't there. Distressed, even." She cut Tess a glance. "Don't suppose you could work up a tear or two—maybe a faint?"

Tess made a wry face.

"Na, I didn't think so."

Tess drank the last of her tea. "I've plenty of money left. We'll take a room in a boardinghouse, and set about looking for work, and a more permanent place to live. Surely there will be a boardinghouse for ladies, or some such thing."

"Raul said he reckons he can help me find something."

Tess said nothing, feeling again a strange sense of desertion, though she knew it was unfair of her. Sonia had every right to her own life—each had come West to have just that chance. But Tess didn't want to be alone until she had her sea legs in the new place. "You won't marry him too fast, will you?"

"Marry?" Sonia burst out laughing. "I don't aim to marry anybody, sugar. And Raul Libre is a footloose man, at that. He ain't gonna ask me, and I ain't gonna spend the rest of my life worrying over whether he's gonna come home at night." She took Tess's hand. "You ain't gettin' rid of me that easy."

Tess smiled gratefully. "We're almost there—can you believe it?"

"It's been quite a journey."

"You ladies about ready to head out?" Roger called.

"Ready." Tess got to her feet and quickly gathered the few utensils they'd used this morning, while Sonia ambled over to the horses.

"Señora."

Tess startled at the sound of Joaquin's voice, resonant as always, but with a soberness to it, too. Smoothing her skirt, she looked at him.

The laughter was gone from his face, replaced with gravity. For a moment, he only looked at her, and Tess thought she would carry this picture of him always—the sun gilding the edges of his head and his shoulders from behind, his luminous dark eyes full of unspoken thoughts. In one hand, he held his hat, as if he were one of the *campesiños* they'd seen on the way. The other hand he lifted toward her, and turned his hand over to reveal a small pink rock, shaped like a heart.

Tess looked at the stone, then back to Joaquin. He lifted his hand, urging her to take it. "So you will remember me."

She plucked the stone up. In the sun, it glittered with a thousand tiny flashes of light, and it seemed almost translucent. "It's beautiful," she said. "But I will not forget you, Joaquin. I could not."

He swallowed, then took her hand and pressed his lips to the backs of her fingers. "Be well, Tessita. I will be thinking of you."

Then he spun on his heel and mounted, and called for the others to ride down the mountains. Tess clutched the heart-shaped stone in her palm as she looked after him. All day, she held it in her hand, so it never cooled from his touch.

Taos was visible most of the day as they rode down out of the mountains. It looked small and plain in the bright light of day, the buildings made of adobe the same color as the earth surrounding it. But Joaquin knew how different it was at evening, when rose-gold light blazed over the walls and trees. At evening, it would come alive.

As always, he was glad to have it in sight. Another journey had been made safely, and his bags were full of the modest profit they had made. He was glad to be home, where things were familiar and comfortable, where he knew the names of everyone in the village. Wherever he rode, he was respected, but in Taos, he was known. That he was a bastard did not matter so much—his father was highly regarded, and men still told awed stories of his mother's beauty, even these long years after her people had stolen her back to them.

He had missed his sister Juanita, and his father, who would put aside whatever he was doing to hear of Joaquin's travels—who he had seen, and what news there was. By the fire in his father's house tonight, Joaquin would eat well and smoke, and tell his father the adventure of finding these women. Even Doña Dorotea, lurking with tight disapproval on her pinched mouth, could not spoil the pleasure of such evenings. Afterward, he might find Elena and ease his frustrated desires.

But in truth the last prospect held little appeal. As they rode, he found himself lagging behind so he could watch Tess without her knowing.

This journey had changed him, making this homecoming different. His reluctance to seek out Elena was part of it, but he also wished for a finer home than what he had— only two small rooms at the edge of town, with a courtyard where he grew chilies, squash, and corn in the summer. He had built it himself, and whitewashed the earthen walls once a year to keep it clean, but the floors were only packed earth, the windows small, the only furnishings a single wooden chair and a bed and a table. Benches were built into the walls, but the whitewash came off on the clothes of those who sat on them.

He would like to have better, he thought as they came at last to flat ground. Ahead, Tess sat high and straight on her horse, the long, golden-brown curls tied back in a deerskin thong. Sunlight blazed in the bends of the wild curls that bounced with the movements of the horse.

Looking at her, Joaquin ached a little. He thought of her laughing, reluctantly, and as if the sound surprised her; of the soft sound of her breath when she had awakened to find him bending over her at the fort; of the conflict he'd seen in her eyes this morning when she clutched the heart-shaped stone. He did not want to deliver her to her husband. He braced himself for the jealousy he would feel when he saw them together.

Perhaps it would be best if he planned another trip as soon as possible. The weather would turn, so he would have to be quick about it. Perhaps he could winter at El Pueblo, a small Mexican settlement on the Arkansas River. It was a friendly place, and they would welcome him if he brought trade goods to share.

He eyed Tess once more, and let the longing for her fill him. Even the sight of her back stirred him, straight and small, as if braced against the future that awaited her. Sonia hovered close, as if she, too, worried about the woman, and he'd seen them in murmured, secret conversation off-and-on all day.

He worried about her, about this husband for whom she had no love. But he worried more that whatever had been born between them on this trip might not stay safely contained. He feared he would not be able to maintain his distance, that he might be tempted to seek her out, and that his passion would cause her sorrow.

She had Sonia to help keep her safe, and Roger, and even Raul, who had come to some private conclusions about Tess which he did not share. They would look out for her, and none of them would cause the pain Joaquin might cause for her if he stayed. Yes, to El Pueblo he would go, as soon as he'd rested.

To remove even the small temptation of watching her, he spurred his horse ahead of the small band. Coming from Taos, there were three men on horseback, riding out as if to meet them. Curiously, Joaquin watched them come closer, wondering what news they carried that would not wait until they got to town. When they were close enough, he whistled and waved.

The men did not wave back. One of them was Carlos Pineda, who dispensed what small justice the town required, and ran the jail.

Joaquin frowned. He looked over his shoulder at Raul, who put his hand on the rifle in front of him. Joaquin shook his head, and raised a hand to forestall him. Whatever it was that gave these men such grim faces could be managed without violence.

He turned back to watch their approach, his mind racing with possibilities. Had there been an Indian attack? Had Governor Armijo done something foolish again? Was there some plague in the village?

And then he thought of the women, of Tess and Sonia, and wondered if they had done something to warrant arrest. Could Tess have stolen Sonia from someone? Were they thieves or whores or murderesses? He looked at Tess and saw her face was tight and drained of all color. A sick worry rose in his belly, and he reached for his gun. They would not take her. He would not let them.

The men rode within shouting distance, and warily, Joaquin called out, "Greetings, mi amigos!"

None returned the greeting, but rode directly to Joaquin. "Señor Morales," said Carlos, "we must arrest you for the murder of your father."

"My father?" Joaquin repeated stupidly. As the knowledge sunk in, a virulent burst of pain washed through him. "My father is dead?"

15

Icy terror made Tess shiver. The men surrounded Joaquin with fierce intent, as if afraid he would bolt. But Joaquin appeared stunned. His face was devoid of expression as he dismounted and held out his hands to be bound at the wrists.

"What's happening?" Tess asked Roger.

"They're arresting him for the murder of his father."

"What?"

"I don't know what happened," he said, "but I can tell you we left the man standing in a field, waving. If Joaquin killed him, he's a magician." He spurred his horse. "See here, men, there's been a mistake."

"I'm sorry, señor, there is no mistake," said Pineda. "Doña Dorotea saw it happen."

"He's been with us for two months. I'm telling you it's impossible."

Sadly, Pineda shook his head. "I am sorry," he repeated. "I mean to cast no mark against your character, but it is not uncommon for one friend to lie for another." Dismissing them, he began to lead Joaquin away.

"Wait!" Tess cried. "Roger! Raul! Don't let them do this."

Raul rode close to her. "We can't do anything just now.

Let them take him. Roger and I will find out what happened." He put his big hand on hers. "Don't worry," he said with a wink. "We won't let him hang."

Tess nodded, her heart frozen in her throat, her eyes fixed on Joaquin, who walked away with his head bowed, his black hair gleaming down his back. As if he felt her gaze, he glanced over his shoulder, and their eyes locked across the grass-strewn prairie.

Then he turned and allowed himself to be led away. Tess stared after them, a hole in her soul. Under her breath she whispered a prayer, "Mother Mary, protect him!"

"Come on," Roger said. "Let's get into town and get these ladies settled so we can find out what happened." He looked at Tess. "Do you have a particular place you're supposed to go?"

Her face flamed suddenly. Now the lies would begin anew. "He said only Taos."

Roger narrowed his eyes, and for a moment, he remained silent. The silence of the high desert seemed to echo with accusation, but Tess met his gaze unflinchingly, as if she hid nothing.

Finally, Roger gave a nod. "All right. I doubt it'll take long to find him. I reckon you can eat and get cleaned up at Magdalena's boardinghouse. She'll take good care of you."

"Thank you," Tess returned with as much dignity as she could muster. She cast a sidelong glance at Sonia, who nodded almost imperceptibly.

And so it was that she and Sonia, after months of planning, and even longer months of travel, arrived in Taos. In spite of the terror of the past few minutes, and the worry she felt over her lying, Tess felt a wild surge of excitement.

The town lay against the shoulders of the mountains, blue in the clean, piercing light. The sky stretched endlessly above, arching over the wide, yellow plain that ended in the hazy distance with another line of mountains. Trees gathered in clumps of two or three, widely spaced across the valley, more thickly along a creek that chuckled through town. Cows and horses grazed behind a fence of sticks, and small houses dotted the fields.

As they crossed the creek and emerged on the other side, Tess felt a queer, exuberant joy well up inside of her, as if the land itself had given a shout of welcome. It was powerful enough that she nearly wept. It eased some of her worry over Joaquin. Surely all would be well now.

In wonder, she looked at Sonia, who turned to her and smiled. "It's beautiful!" she exclaimed.

Dazzled, Tess looked around once more, lifting her face to the benevolent sun, breathing in the fresh, dry air. Home at last, she thought, and was only a little startled by the emotion.

Home. Happily, she filled her eyes with the light, the scent, and the welcome of Taos. It was for this she had traveled thousands of miles, suffered these trails. This place had called her, and now she was here, and everything would be all right. She felt it in her bones.

Home.

Tess and Sonia were safely stowed in the small hotel belonging to Señora Magdalena Ortiz de Mascarenas, a plump, middle-aged woman with black hair showing only the faintest silver threading. She tsked over Sonia's swollen belly, and chattered in Spanish to the comancheros, then led the women to a room.

The hotel sat on the square that formed the center of town, and unlike its neighbors, rose two stories. The lower front room was given over to a cantina, which Raul assured them served the finest food in Nuevo Mexico. At the mid-afternoon hour, there were no customers, save the two old Mexicans who sat on wooden chairs outside, smoking and chatting quietly. Tess heard one give out a wheezy laugh.

Señora Ortiz led them upstairs to a small room at the front of the building, overlooking the square. One double bed sat below a window hung with lace curtains, and the window was open to a warm breeze that lifted calico curtains over the wide sill. Tess went to stand there and cool her face. Listening with half an ear to Raul and Señora Ortiz trade conversation in Spanish, she stared down at the small square, and at the mountains that rose all around like great blue soldiers. Lowering sunlight cast long fingers of gold light into the square, shadowing deep-set doors, and glinting on windows, and caressing the dust with a glow of copper.

Raul said finally, "I reckon you two will be just fine here. Roger and I'll go find out what's going on. We'll be back later with news."

Tess nodded and turned. "Thank you."

"*De nada*," he said dismissively. At the door, he paused. "Your husband, he's a white man, like you?"

"Yes." The word tasted like ashes in her throat, and Tess had to force herself to unball her fists. "Seamus McKenzie. A big man with red hair. An Irishman." To save herself more worry, she and Sonia had agreed to stick to the truth as much as possible.

Raul dipped his head. "A man like that can't be too hard to find around here. Y'all rest now, and get some supper. Just go on down when you're hungry. Magdalena will feed you."

He closed the door, and they heard his booted feet going down the stairs. When he was out of earshot, Sonia sprung up from her chair against the far wall, and gave Tess an exuberant hug. "We did it! We're here!"

Tess embraced her in return, feeling gratitude counter her worry. "Yes," she whispered. "We're here."

Sonia pulled back and took Tess's arms in a firm grip. "Don't you be frettin' about nothin' now, you hear me? Seamus McKenzie is back in Arkansas, stewing in his own meanness if there's any justice at all. He's long forgotten about you." She gave Tess a small shake. "We're free, Tess."

Free. Then why did she not feel free? Why did this knot

of dread still burn in her chest? Restlessly, she wandered toward the window. Below, Raul and Roger emerged and crossed to the small building she had not noticed before. Bars on the window bespoke its purpose, a purpose she knew with certainty when the comancheros ducked inside. "I don't feel free," she said quietly. "And our rescuer is certainly not free."

For a moment, Sonia's beautiful full lips tightened to a hard line. "True enough. But you and I both know the man didn't kill his father."

"What will it matter, if they believe he has?"

"You really are kinda sweet on him, ain't you?"

Tess sighed. "He is . . . a most unusual man."

"He's a good man. My papa was like that. A big man who laughed all the time, always had a joke for everybody."

In surprise, Tess turned from her post. "You knew your father, then? I've never heard you speak of him before."

Sonia shrugged, settling on the side of the bed, her hand bracing the swollen belly as if to hold it in place. "Master wasn't a real rich man back in those days. My folks and two others were the only slaves he had, and he took reasonable care of them, cuz he couldn't afford to lose 'em." She smiled in fond remembrance. "My papa was a fine man. He did his best for all us children."

"Where is he now?"

"His heart gave out on him when I was about fifteen or thereabouts. Came in from the fields one night, sat down, closed his eyes, and died." She smiled at Tess. "Hard to mourn such a peaceful death."

"Indeed," Tess said, and gazed off toward the mountains. "I once feared I'd starve to death. A terrible way to die—a little more and a little more and a little more. You can't think, or plan, or dream of anything but a good meal." She rubbed her arms. "I thought I could bear anything if my belly was full."

"I ain't never been hungry a day in my life," Sonia said quietly.

"I'll count it a lucky thing to die with a full belly," Tess returned, and gave her friend a rueful smile.

"And I'm gonna die a free woman, with a child who is free—thank you, Jesus!" Sonia flung her arms open on the bed, and groaned in pleasure. "It's gonna be sweet to sleep in a soft warm place tonight." She looked at Tess, sobering suddenly. "That is, if you don't mind me and my baby boy sharing your bed."

"Of course not." With a lift in spirits, she moved and flung herself down next to Sonia. "You seem very sure it's a boy."

"I done had me six children—I reckon I can tell by how I carry 'em. This one is low and forward, like my other boy. All the girls were up under my ribs the whole time."

"What will you name him?" Tess asked sleepily. The bed cradled her weary body with a comforting hand. She closed her eyes in reverent enjoyment.

"I don't know. I don't even have a name to give him, not a real name. I'll be damned if he carries a slave master's name."

Tess turned her head. "Take mine, if you like. No Fallon's ever been rich enough to have a slave." She grinned.

Sonia's face grew very still. "You mean it?"

"You're my closest friend," Tess said shyly. "I'd be honored."

Sonia lowered her eyes, and Tess grew afraid that she'd made some terrible error. But when Sonia looked up again, Tess saw a betraying shimmer of tears. "The honor would be mine, Tess Fallon, for then we'd be sisters."

Unable to bear the moment, Tess jumped up from the bed and dashed for the pitcher of water on a small table near the door. She carried it back to the bed, dipped her hand in quickly, and sprinkled Sonia with it. "Then," she said in a voice edged with laughter, "in the name of the Father, the Son, and the Holy Spirit, I christen thee Sonia Fallon."

Sonia screeched and held up her hands to ward off the drips of cold water.

Laughing, Tess put the water aside and fell back on the bed, curling up on a pillow. "To be a proper Irishwoman, you'll have to add Mary to your name, but that'll do for now."

Sonia squeezed her hand. "Thank you."

Tess closed her eyes, smiling. "This bed is soft," she said, and yawned.

"Mmmm."

Within minutes, they were both sound asleep.

Joaquin sat on a cot in his jail cell, and ate chili from a tin bowl. Darkness had fallen, and through the window he heard the stirrings of people in the square, laughter and a furious spate of Spanish, and someone plucking the strings of a guitar experimentally. There would be a fandango tonight.

The chili was made by the jailer's sister, and it was the first food he'd had since his breakfast on the mountain this morning. He ladled it up with blue corn tortillas, buttery and fresh, but barely tasted it. He was too numb.

Something had happened to his mind when the soldiers had told him his father was dead. Everything stopped—time, thought, feeling. He felt hollow, like a dry arroyo at the height of noon.

He lifted his head at the sound of voices. Raul and Roger, who had not changed their clothes yet, came to the bars. They pushed open the unlocked grill. Raul leaned on the wall while Roger perched on a small sturdy table.

"What did you learn?" Joaquin asked without emotion.

"Your sister is nowhere to be found. She disappeared the same day your father died," Roger said. His reddish hair, uncut for many months, hung in limp dusty hanks on his shoulders, and he shook it out of his face. "José Borrego says he thinks he saw her riding for the mountains that night, but she didn't stop when he called her name."

Joaquin stared at the stew in his bowl. "And my father? How did he die?"

"Shot through the chest, out in the pasture," Raul said.

"And Doña Dorotea says it was me?"

Raul scratched his scraggly beard. "Yep. She came into town, hysterical, 'bout suppertime the day we left, and said you and your pa had a furious fight, and you shot him, then rode out."

His father dead. The news was too huge to be real. He kept expecting someone to burst through the door, maybe with a big bottle of pulque, and tell him it was only a practical joke. "Did you see his grave, as I asked?"

"We did," Roger said.

Heavily, Joaquin nodded. "Thank you."

"They want to hang you," Raul said. "Doña Dorotea is insisting on it. Nobody much wants to do it, but she's written Governor Armijo. If he writes back with execution orders, you'll be dead at dawn the next morning."

"I see."

"We'll find out what happened, hombre," Roger said. "Don't worry."

The food turned to stones in his belly, and Joaquin put the bowl aside, feeling suddenly as if the air in the room had been sucked out. His father was dead. "Who would kill my father? He had no enemies, not Indian or Mexican. None. I don't understand."

Raul pursed his lips. "My money's on Doña Dorotea herself."

Joaquin rejected the idea. "No. She has a cruel heart, and she is crazy with sorrow, but she loved Armando. She would not kill him."

"What if Armando was going to name his bastard son Joaquin heir to his land and cattle?"

"What?"

Raul said, "Ignacio Lujan said your father told him he changed his will after your brother died, to make you heir.

Doña Dorotea was there when he signed it, and she was so mad, she fainted."

"But why did my father not tell me?"

"Maybe he just hadn't gotten to it yet."

"The thing is," Roger put in, "that new will ain't nowhere to be found. Doña Dorotea brought the old one out, and it names Miguel, then Doña Dorotea as heirs."

Joaquin's head spun. The ranch, his father, the plots. He closed his eyes. "I cannot think of this now, or I'll go mad. Go. We'll talk tomorrow."

The men headed for the open door. "Oh, one more thing," Roger said. "We looked and talked to damn everybody in town, and not one of them has ever heard of Seamus McKenzie."

"Seamus McKenzie?"

"Tess's husband."

"Ah." Even this did not penetrate the muffling cloud surrounding his emotions.

Raul lifted a brow, but said nothing. "You want anything? A bottle? A woman?"

Joaquin shook his head. "No." He wanted nothing. Except perhaps the joke to be ended, and things to be as they were.

"Go," he said roughly. "I wish to be alone."

16

Just past dark, Tess awakened. The last colors of day lingered over the mountains. Rubbing her face, Tess got up, careful not to disturb Sonia, who still slept very deeply, curled in a ball. Gently, Tess took the quilt from the bottom of the bed and covered her friend. Now that she slept, and the natural animation of her personality was dormant, Tess could see exhaustion around her mouth and eyes. The travel had been hard on her.

Pouring water into the basin, Tess washed. It felt so good to erase the dust of the ride that she stripped off her blouse and chemise and washed her arms, stomach, and breasts as well, rubbing until her skin tingled. What she wouldn't give for a full bath! She would ask Señora Mascarenas about it tonight. In the meantime, she shook the worst of the dust from her blouse and put it back on.

From outside came the sound of music and voices, and Tess, unbraiding her hair, wandered over to the window to look out. In the square there was dancing. Torches burned on sconces, a trio played music, and women dressed in colorful skirts danced. Absently brushing her hair, Tess watched them and felt a yearning to be a part of the music and the dance, to be a woman who would wear such bright things, and be so happy.

Her gaze strayed to the jail. What was Joaquin doing now? How must he be feeling? What would happen to him? She wondered if he were allowed visitors. And if he were allowed, would he welcome her, or would he feel shamed?

She worried about him. He had looked stunned and wounded when the soldiers led him away, and she could not bear to think of him alone in a cell, brooding.

A light knock sounded on the door, and Tess ran over to open it before a second knock awakened Sonia. It was Roger.

Tess held a finger to her lips and pointed to Sonia. Without bothering to rebraid her hair, she grabbed her shawl and went into the hallway. "How is Señor Morales?" she asked, closing the door behind her.

"I've seen him better. But that's not what I came to tell you. Your husband—"

Quick as lightning, Tess realized she'd made a foolish error, asking not of the husband who supposedly awaited her, but Joaquin. As if eager for news, she interrupted him. "You found him?" She clutched his arm. "Is he coming to get me?"

"Well," Roger scratched his nose. "Not exactly."

"What do you mean?"

"I mean he's not here. He doesn't live her. Nobody's ever even heard of him."

"Oh." Her mind spun. What would a woman who really believed her husband awaited her say now? She frowned, and remembered how Joaquin had reacted when given the news about his father. "I don't understand," she said at last.

"Have you eaten, señora?"

"Eaten?" she echoed.

"Let's get some supper and we'll talk about this a little more. Maybe we can figure out some answers."

Tess accepted the elbow he offered. "Very well."

Below, Señora Mascarenas settled them at a gleaming table in a room made warm with the light of flickering candles in hammered tin sconces on the walls. A tapestry covered one adobe wall, and the dishes were not the wooden cups and tin platters Tess had grown used to on her travels, but fine crystal glassware and handpainted china. Awed, she fingered the edge of a dinner plate. "I've never seen such beautiful dishes in my life," she said to Roger.

"The señora comes from an old Spanish family. Her husband was killed by Comanches years ago, but she stayed on to run this place because Taos was her home."

Tess smiled. "It seems a magical place, Taos."

"It is that," he said, slowly nodding. He put a white linen napkin on his lap. "I never intended to stay, myself, but I can't quite seem to go, either." His smile was boyish and rueful at once.

The food was a rich concoction of chilies and tomatoes and tortillas combined with a shredded meat and cheese, served by a young girl in a skirt so short Tess was scandalized. It revealed her entire ankle. Tess averted her eyes quickly, so as not to stare, but found herself marveling that the girl could serve the food so deftly while clinging to a long wide shawl Sonia had said was called a rebozo. When the girl moved away, her body swaying sinuously as if she were aware of Roger's appreciative attention, Tess couldn't help another glimpse at her skirt. Her whole ankle *and* part of her leg!

Roger chuckled. "I reckon you ain't seen women dressed like that before, but you'll get used to it."

Tess blushed. "It isn't seemly for you to comment."

"Let me tell you a little secret, señora. You're in a new country, and it's nothing like what you left. If you don't let that old world get in your way, I think you'll like it here."

She looked at him, remembering her fear upon entering the fort with the Indians milling around. And she remembered how beautiful the teepees looked at night with the fires burning inside. She had suspended judgments at the fort, and throughout their long journey, and nothing terrible had happened.

She smiled. "That's good advice. Thank you."

He winked. "Good girl."

"So," she said, taking up her fork. "Tell me what you found out about my husband."

"Just like I said, nothing. It's not just that no one knows the name, but no one knows anyone like the man you described. Could he have changed somehow?"

"Changed? No," she said with a frown. "He's large and red haired. Not so much to change. Here he'd be like a penny in the snow—you would see him."

Roger nodded, obviously concerned. Tess didn't know how to help him, so she ate. Happily. There was one thing she'd have no trouble enjoying—food in any guise. She wondered, as the rich sauce burst with flavor in her mouth, then settled warmly in her belly, if she'd ever overcome the fear of hunger.

"Now, I don't want you to take this the wrong way," Roger said, "but do you think he might have been leading you on a wild-goose chase for some reason?"

Tess put down her fork and dabbed her face with the heavy napkin. "Anything is possible, I suppose. If he is not here, there is something amiss isn't there?"

He leaned over. "Tell me the truth, honey. Do you have a husband, or did you make all of this up?"

Fear made her spine rigid. "I did not," she said indignantly. "I assure you I am a married woman, with a husband named Seamus McKenzie." At least that much was not a lie.

"Sorry. I had to ask." He sighed. "I don't know what the hell you're going to do out here alone, that's all. With winter coming on, you're stuck here at least until spring."

"I have money," she said. "And I'm no stranger to hard work. Is there no one who will hire me to clean or cook or sew?"

"I had you figured for a lady who mightn't have the skills to do those things."

Tess laughed. "By now I would have thought you noticed at least that I am no grand lady, only a poor woman who made a good marriage."

"I see." He grinned, and Tess realized he really was a rather charming man with those blue eyes and devilish smile. "And it isn't too hard to see what you might have offered a rich man."

"He didn't marry me for my fortune," she said, lightly. It occurred to her that she'd learned to flirt—and that it was a pleasant activity. "And I did not marry him for his looks."

"Do you love him, this husband of yours?"

"Love him? What does love have to do with marriage?"

"Sometimes it has a lot to do with it."

In a rare burst of honesty, Tess said, "I do not love him." She took a breath. "He saved my brother and me from starving to death, and for that I will remain true to him as long as I live."

His grin bloomed again. "Well, that's a pity."

The conversation echoed one she'd had with Joaquin, and Tess sobered. "Tell me how Señor Morales fares."

Roger looked grim. "He's in trouble. I'm not sure how we'll get him out of it."

"What will happen to him?"

"If we can't find out who killed his father, he'll be hanged."

A fist of something dark and hard and unnamable hit her. She felt winded. "That cannot happen," she whispered. "He saved our lives."

"It won't happen, Tess. Trust me. Raul and I won't let him be put to death."

With a small thread of sorrow, she looked at him. "Did he kill his father?"

"No." The word needed no embroidery.

"Will they let him have a visitor? I mean, would he care . . . might I . . ." She stopped, aware of heat in her cheeks. Quietly, she said, "Would I be able to go see him?"

"You sure can, luv." He pushed back his chair. "I think you might cheer him up considerably."

Tess stood, but hesitated uncertainly, suddenly aware of her unbound hair and wrinkled blouse. She touched her chest, clutched a handful of hair. "Perhaps I should not go out like this."

"Don't be ridiculous. You look fine." He took her hand and led her outside.

All through the meal, the music from the square had drifted into the dining room, a faint, exotic undertone to their conversation. Now, as they emerged into the square properly, Tess was enveloped by the sweet guitars and clapping, by the shouts and singing. It dazzled her. In the dust, she stopped, entranced by the swirling skirts of the women, by the swing of their hair and *rebozos*, by the men in their silver buttons and bright vests. Bright torchlight flickered over all, yellow and cheerful against the looming shadow of the mountains.

The lively scene made her feel unexpectedly lonely. Without knowing why, she thought of Joaquin, and all at once, she could not wait to see him, to make sure he was all right.

Slowly, she moved forward, along the edge of the crowd, following Roger, who kept her hand caught tight, as if he were afraid she'd be swept into the whirling gaiety.

Joaquin was not inside the jail, as she had expected, but sitting on a bench outside. He sat still as a stone, a bottle of some gold liquid dangling near his knee.

A pang shot through her. Just that quickly, she'd forgotten how the sight of him affected her. She'd forgotten the rush of anticipation that swept through her blood, forgotten the low thrumming in her limbs.

Added to all of that now was a penetrating need to comfort him. Her laughing Joaquin, the gentle, courageous comanchero who'd teased her out of a dozen fears, who made everyone around him chuckle and smile, was gone. The laughing man was no longer laughing. His face showed no light, no lurking smile, no joy. Nothing.

As she neared, she saw that signs of the journey had

not been washed from his face, and his hair had come free of the red cloth he used to tie it back. To his shoulders was a rigidness, as if it were all he could do to remain upright.

Roger let her go, and Tess barely noticed. She moved without thinking to sit down beside Joaquin on the bench.

He did not acknowledge her, only lifted the bottle to his lips and drank the liquor within. A harsh sound came from him, as if he had to choke it down. Tess folded her hands and watched the dancing. Joaquin watched, too, his gaze unmoving and flat.

For a long time, they simply sat there, side by side, watching the dancers. Tess did not feel uncomfortable or strange. She did not push meaningless words of comfort upon him, she only sat with him so he'd know she cared what happened to him. And somehow, sitting with him in silence was a better way to spend her time than a hundred things she could imagine to do. She sat with him, her hands folded in her lap, and watched torchlight play on his black, black hair. He drank at intervals and watched the dancing.

After a long time, he said, "I loved my father."

A tendon stood out on his jaw and Tess knew he wanted to weep. She hesitated, then lifted her hand and touched his long back. His hair grazed her fingers, and below his clothes, she sensed the strength in the muscles there. After a moment, she moved her hand away.

He reached out and grabbed it back to him, folding her fingers within his own in an almost crushing grip. He hid the clasp below the fabric of the serape he wore. Against her knuckles pressed the length of his thigh, tense and warm. Without speaking, they watched the dancers for a long time, holding hands.

Much later, a soldier came to take Joaquin back to jail. It was the same man who had arrested him, and Tess saw his slightly regretful expression. "I must take you back inside, Señor Morales," he said.

Joaquin nodded. He squeezed her hand once and stood

up with a bowed head. "Thank you," he said without looking at her.

As she watched him go, Tess felt a wildly sorrowful ache. Never had a man moved her as Joaquin Morales did. Never. And there was nothing at all she could do about it.

17

"Let me help you," Tess said to Sonia, who struggled to reach the ties of her shoes. Kneeling, Tess unlaced the simple boots, worn through in spots, and tugged them off. "You need new shoes."

Sonia nodded wearily. "I reckon you could use some yourself."

"Mine were new when we began. Turn around."

Sonia stood up slowly, a hand to her lower back, and allowed Tess to unbutton her dress.

"Come," Tess said gently. "A good warm bath will make you feel better, I promise."

With the singular exhaustion she'd displayed for two days, Sonia shed her chemise and stepped into the wooden tub that had been brought to their room. Her pear-shaped belly strained the skin, and Tess frowned. The babe had grown too big too fast—she didn't like to think it was not the babe, but too much water within. It might mean any number of things were not going well. Frustration rose in her—if she only had her herbs, or some way of communicating what she needed to one of the women here, as she had with Owl Woman. Sonia needed an infusion.

Since she'd been unable to find the herbs she needed,

Tess gave Sonia a cup of plain camomile tea. Scouring through the bottles and tinctures on the shelves of the hotel kitchen, with an indignant young woman glowering at her, Tess had found the herb with a little cry of glee. The woman in the kitchen told her they called it *manzanilla*, a word Tess repeated over and over to herself.

"Drink this, and soak there a while in that hot water," Tess said now, drying her hands on her apron.

Sonia only nodded, as if speaking were too much effort. The wound on her leg, until now healing well, looked angry, and Tess had not missed the limp Sonia tried to hide. Tess put a hand to her forehead. "Don't be stoic, please," she said briskly. "I'll not be able to help you if you don't tell me what ails you."

"I just don't feel right," Sonia said.

"The baby?" Tess perched on the bed. From where she sat, the gray light from beyond caught on the ridged scars that ribboned Sonia's dark back. Absently, Tess lifted a hand and touched the snakelike scar that marked her own arm and breast.

"The baby is fine," Sonia replied. "Movin' all the time."

"Good." Perhaps Sonia was only very tired, now that the journey had ended at last. In that case, rest and good food would do their work quickly enough. All the same, Tess was not feeling satisfied. "Perhaps I will go down and ask Señora Mascarenas for the name of a good midwife."

That decided, Tess helped Sonia wash her hair and put on fresh clothes that Raul had brought to her—Spanish clothes, loosley cut for her tummy. Tess grinned. "You look quite exotic."

Sonia smiled, touching the beautiful, turquoise-colored skirt with its ribbons of red. "It's real pretty."

"Let me do your hair." Tess combed it with lavender-scented oil and pulled it straight back from Sonia's high forehead. She wove the thick, springy mass into a single, long braid, tied with a strip of deerskin like the one the Indians used. She smiled when she was finished. "You look like a native."

"Not quite," Sonia said with a hint of her usual wry humor. But she leaned back on the pillows almost immediately and closed her eyes. "I ain't never been so tired with any of my other babies," she said.

"I know." Tess put the comb on the small table. "You sleep and I'll see what I can find to help you feel better."

She slipped downstairs. Señora Mascarenas spoke little English, and could make neither heads nor tails of Tess's plea. Frustrated, Tess wandered out to the square, tucking her shawl up over her head to protect her hair from the drizzling moisture in the air. Surely someone here knew where to find the herbs she needed, or how to make a reasonable substitute.

Across the square sat the jail, its walls darkening with trickles of rain. Tess sucked on her bottom lip, fighting the impulse to go inside and ask Joaquin. He knew everyone in town.

But would he respond to her questions? Twice since the night when he'd sat somberly drinking on the bench in the square, she had gone to see him, taking as her excuse plates of food specially prepared by Señora Mascarenas. Both times, Joaquin dully accepted her offering, his eyes lowered, his shoulders unusually rigid. It made her ache to see the life sucked from him this way, but nothing she did or said seemed to make a difference.

Still, after all he'd done for her, she had to keep trying. She headed across the square, knowing she did it not to find answers, but only so she could see him. Perhaps she might find a way to make him smile again, if only for a moment.

The soldier who guarded the jail stood just inside the thick doorway, watching the rain. "*Buenos dias*, señora," he said politely, his thick mustache making it impossible to tell if his lips moved. He stepped back to let Tess pass.

Within, the squat adobe rooms with their small barred windows were dim. She stopped and blinked, letting her eyes adjust.

And there was Joaquin, tall and straight, his back to

her. They had finally let him have clean clothes and a bath, for the long, black hair held a glossy sheen, and the red cloth was gone, replaced with a deerskin thong.

He wore no shirt or shoes, only a pair of close-fitting breeches the color of the desert. Tess had never seen him without the billowing shrouds of his loose-cut shirts, and even then she'd thought him beautifully made.

But oh, 'twas nothing to this! She stared at the lean length of his back, the pale reddish-brown of pinecones. The flesh held a muted, satiny shine. Her gaze dropped lower, to his lean waist and the high, round shape of his buttocks.

As if he heard her quick intake of breath, Joaquin turned, and Tess went weak with longing. His chest was bare and sleek as a seal, and she wanted to put her mouth against the line of his ribs, against the square chin and sober mouth.

He said nothing. Tess swallowed against the sinful visions in her mind and remembered her purpose in coming here. "Sonia is not well," she said without preamble, so she would not lose her nerve. "I must have herbs to help her, and I cannot make myself understood. I do not know the plants here. I don't know what to use. And I can't make anyone understand me."

"My sister would have been able to help," he said. Even his dark mood could not dim the beauty of his voice. "But she is gone."

"I know. Roger told me."

He picked up a clean shirt from the bed and pulled it over his head. The full sleeves fell around his dark hands and he buttoned the placket at the neck. As if exhausted by his actions, he sank down to the thin pallet on the floor.

Tess found herself at his side. "Joaquin, please don't lose faith." She put her hand over his. "Roger and Raul will not let them hang you. Even now, they are gathering the stories of everyone in the village, to help you."

He looked at her hand, and turned his own to clasp her

fingers. His dark lashes, an oasis of softness in so harshly carved a face, hid his eyes. Slowly, he lifted her hand and pressed a kiss to her knuckles. Tess felt shaky as he raised his gaze to hers. "Say my name again," he whispered.

She lifted her other hand to his face, moving on pure instinct, and brushed a stray lock of hair away. "Joaquin."

He squeezed her fingers, his dark eyes aflame with a thousand things Tess couldn't name. There was grief in the mix, and hopelessness, and, yes, yearning. "Come tonight to the square and I will dance with you, Tessita. Carlos will let me out. Will you do that?"

"Yes." The word was little more than a whisper. Emotions thickened her throat. "Though I hope your toes will not hurt too much in the morning."

The smallest tug of a smile lifted his lips, and Tess felt dizzy with victory. She touched the edge of his mouth lightly. "I had hoped to see you smile just a little, for all the times you made me smile."

His eyes darkened, and his grip on her fingers was nearly painful. "Tessita, why did we meet now? So late?"

She shook her head, and smiled sadly. "Perhaps we each simply needed a friend."

"No," he said. "Friends I had."

Gently she pulled away. Afraid of her rising emotions, she stood up and briskly walked to the other side of the tiny space, looking through the bars to the door beyond. A fine trembling coursed through her limbs, and she had to take in a long breath to still it. "I must find someone who can help me with my herbs. Do you know the midwife?"

Joaquin stood and came to stand behind her, his hands braced on the bars to either side of her head, his chest against her back. He bent close, and Tess wasn't sure, but she thought his mouth brushed her ear. "Go see Octavio Valdez, in the house with the blue dog. His wife can help you, and he speaks a lot of English."

Tess struggled to remain still and calm, but each word caused his breath to sough over her neck, her jaw, her ear. "Thank you," she said.

This time, there was no mistaking the brush of his seductive mouth against the side of her neck. His nose touched her jaw. "Till tonight, then," he said.

"Yes."

He released her. Tess turned, her heart pounding, and let herself drink in the uncommon beauty of his face for one more moment. He simply looked back at her, sober and lost and despairing.

And in that moment, Tess knew she'd fallen deeply in love. "Tonight," she repeated, and left him.

A soggy drizzle, dripping from an overhanging pine tree, awakened Seamus McKenzie. He rubbed his face and shook his hair out of his eyes. From this high place, he could see the whole Taos valley, stretching for unimaginable miles to a distant stand of mountains on the western horizon. In the cold, gray light, it was spare and vast, and filled him with an odd fear.

The weather hushed the birds. There were no cocks crying out a greeting to the morning, no soft green haze over the vastness, as in Ireland. He disliked this place with its bristly plants and the terrifying sky that burned an unholy blue on clear days. It made him uneasy. The light broke in unexpected and unsettling ways, in colors he'd never seen. The fields were clotted with spiky plants no man could eat, and he heard the howl of coyotes in the night winds.

Dread grew in him as he stared over the harsh landscape. He told himself the fear was only the legacy of his superstitious mother, the plague of every Irishman born, but he couldn't shake it. The earth spoke, wherever a man walked. In Ireland it wept. In Arkansas, on the banks of that wide Mississippi, so rich with silt, it purred.

Here, it whispered in a language he could not grasp. He heard the menacing voices in the trees, the moan in the wind, the rustling of unseen spirits all around him.

But Tess was down there, with the slave she'd stolen. And to possess his wife again, he would brave the evil voice of the earth in this place.

His blood quickened. Yes. Tonight, he would have her. Tonight, he would begin the long process of taming her. With a heavy hand, he nudged the trapper awake. "C'mon. It's dawn."

The papers from Armijo came to the jail at half past two. Joaquin had been dozing on the pallet. His nights had been restless, filled with twisted visions of his father and Doña Dorotea.

And Tess.

Voices, low and angry, jolted Joaquin from his doze. He sat upright, blinking, and peered through bars. Carlos Pineda argued with two soldiers, their forms blurred by the hazy, gold light falling through the door. It had stopped raining, then. He might be able to dance with Tessita tonight after all.

He ached to hold her close, just once. Perhaps make love to her before her husband came to claim her. Just once he wanted to touch her, taste her, bury his sorrow, shame, and exhaustion in the nourishment her body could provide.

These past days she had been the only light in his dark world. Her face never failed to ease him, if only for the moment he could gaze upon it. Her lilting, musical voice unbound the knots in his soul. She was a clear, cold stream in a hidden valley, his own secret source of strength.

The soldiers rode off, the hooves of their horses making authoritative clopping sounds on the stones of the square. The guard turned toward Joaquin, a letter in his hand. "Señor, I'm sorry to tell you the governor has granted Doña Dorotea's request. You will be shot at dawn tomorrow."

Joaquin closed his eyes. "I did not kill my father," he

said quietly. "But who will believe the son of a slave against the wife of a powerful ranchero?"

"*Sí*." The man put his hands on the bar. "Unless you can find the murderer, you are dead in the morning."

Tess. Her name floated through his mind, giving him a poignant ache. He stood. "The woman who comes here, I want to dance with her tonight. Will you let me bring her back to my cell?"

The guard nodded, his smile buried in the thick mustache. "*Sí*."

"I do not wish to tell her that I am to be executed," Joaquin said.

"The news will be all over town before then. I don't see how you can keep it from her." He shrugged. "Do what you will." He turned away, then paused. "I'm sorry, señor."

Joaquin nodded.

Death at dawn. No more riding the plains in the brisk light of early morning, or rounding up cattle for branding, or laughing at jokes, or playing cards, or eating. No more.

He didn't fear dying, but he liked living. He wanted to hug his mother and his sister again. Wanted to have children of his own and see them grow. Wanted to get back his simple, ordinary life.

As if the execution order were a bucket of cold water splashed in his face, he felt his mind clear, suddenly and completely. The fog of despair and grief that had dulled his senses these past days lifted. Left behind was a fierce resolve—he would not die. Somehow, Roger and Raul could free him. It would be so easy to walk away from the fandango tonight. He would wait until everyone was very drunk, until the guard was deep into a game of—

No, even better. He would have Raul find a woman to seduce the guard. Besides his thick, lustrous mustache, the man was homely—he had a beaked nose and skinny limbs and a bad complexion.

But before Joaquin left Taos forever, he would kiss Tess Fallon. Perhaps she could be coaxed into making love with him, just once, so they would have known each other inside out before fate parted them.

"Hombre!" he called to the guard. "Send for my friends, if you would be so kind."

18

Tess had spent the afternoon with Octavio and his wife. The old man translated her questions so the midwife could answer. The woman was kind and warm, eager to share her remedies with another healer.

Her step was light as she returned to the hotel. She had found a teacher, not only for her herbs, but to give her the language. By spring, surely she would have made great progress on both. And the old woman had hinted that she might be able to help Tess and Sonia find work, too.

The door to her room stood open, and Tess immediately sensed the heavy mood within. Raul sat next to Sonia, holding her hand, and Roger leaned on the window, his face grim.

Tess dropped her package on the table. "What is it?" She hurried to the bed and put her hand on Sonia's head. "Are you bleeding?"

"I'm fine," she said. "As fine as I was when you left, anyhow."

"I brought some herbs from the *curandera*," she said. "I'll have the cook boil some water, and soon you'll be feeling yourself again, though I think you should rest very well the next few days."

"Señora," Roger said.

Tess paused. For a moment, she resisted it, resisted hearing the bad news he was going to give her. Had they killed Joaquin? She felt suddenly cold. She swallowed and sank to a chair, her gaze fixed on Roger's sober face. He pressed his mouth together as if he wished he did not have to speak.

Perhaps it wasn't Joaquin at all. Perhaps it was Seamus, instead, and he'd found her.

Fear made her voice sharp. "What is it?"

"It's Joaquin," Raul said. "The governor sent the execution orders this morning."

"Execution? But you know he is innocent."

"He's the bastard son of a slave," Raul said harshly. "Don't make a lick of difference if he did it or not."

"But they can't kill him!" she cried. "Can't you stop it? Can't you do something?"

"What do you want us to do, señora?" Raul asked. His dark eyes flashed. "You think he means more to you than he does to us? I been riding with him for five years. He gave me a chance when weren't nobody else willing."

Tess stood up, her fists tight at her sides. Raul had treated her badly from the beginning and she was weary of it. "Do not take that tone with me, Señor Libre. I don't know what there is to do, but deciding who loves him best will accomplish nothing."

Raul sneered. "Right. Lady Bountiful comin' to the rescue."

"Raul—" Roger said in protest.

But Raul stood, his face twisted. "Y'all think you can do anything. Just get used to snapping your fingers and having everybody running to do your bidding."

Cleansing anger burned away all the hesitations, fears, and worries that Tess had harbored. She stood up angrily. "You listen," she said. "He will not die by some order from a governor who steals Indian children, who cannot be bothered to find justice but sends orders for an innocent man to die." Unaccountably, tears of anger and resolve rose in her throat. "If need be, I'll ride the square naked. I'll burn the town. I'll kill the soldiers." She set her mouth. "He will not die like that."

Raul gaped at her for a moment. Then a slow smile spread over his mouth, and a wide, dazzling smile it was. "Well, I'll be damned. You're really in love with him."

"He saved my life." Tess dashed away the tears on her cheeks with an impatient hand. "I'd only like to do the same."

Raul glanced at Roger. "Well, as it happens, we do have a plan."

"Tell me."

His eyes narrowed. "If you don't do right, I'll kill you myself."

Tess met his gaze evenly. "Tell me."

"Sit down," he said. "And listen up."

She sat, and listened carefully as Raul outlined their plan to save Joaquin's life. It meant he had to run, had to leave Taos until his name was cleared, which might mean forever. Her heart grew heavy. Never to see him again!

But better he should live, and thrive, far away, than die at a despot's order. She would do what she could.

Raul brought a set of clothing for Tess to wear. She put on the simple blouse and skirt with a sense of excitement tinged with fear. What if things did not work out the way they had planned? What if Joaquin were shot while trying to escape? What if—

No. It would work. It had to.

She spread her arms. "What do you think?" she asked Sonia, who was propped on fat pillows. Her color was considerably warmer than it had been earlier. The tea had helped.

Sonia smiled. "You look like a flower."

With a spin, Tess sent the full skirt whirling out around her. Air swept her bare ankles, giving her a devilish thrill. "I feel so daring," she said. "Even dangerous." The blouse was cut in a low square, and showed far more bosom than even her everyday chemise allowed. Self-consciously, she put a hand over the bare skin. "My father would turn over in his grave."

"Well, he ain't here, is he?" Sonia chuckled. "Maybe you oughta be thinking about what that man out there is gonna be thinking when he sees you like that."

Tess turned to the tin-framed mirror. Candles burned in carved, tin sconces on either side, providing a blaze of light. Her hair was loose on her shoulders and the yellow light gave a sheen to her slim arms and cast shadows over the valley between her breasts.

It was her eyes that caught her attention. She didn't know if it was the clothing or the anticipation—to dance with him!—but her eyes shimmered.

She looked like a woman hungry for sex, and unafraid to show it. "I don't even recognize myself," she said quietly, smoothing the crisp cotton over her stomach. A striped sash of woven red fabric belted her waist.

"Joaquin will recognize you."

Her anticipation leapt another notch. What would he think when he saw her this way? She lifted her hair, preparing to pin it in a loose style with combs. Lifting her curls left her chest bare, and the mirror reflected the thick scar that Seamus had left on her body. Even in the low, kind light, it was an obscenely ugly thing, starting just below her collarbone, snaking over her breast. It disappeared under her blouse, then reappeared on her arm in a twist, where the edge of the whip had snapped around her elbow.

There were other scars, but they had healed better, and left only small white marks. This one had healed poorly, as had many of the marks on Sonia's back, and had marked her for life. With the tip of a finger, she traced it.

"Remember what Owl Woman told you," Sonia said. "A woman's scars are her warrior marks."

Tess dropped her hand, ashamed. "So small a scar, in comparison to those you carry," she said. "'Tis only vanity that makes me wish it away. Were it not for this whipping, we'd still both be in Arkansas with Seamus McKenzie."

"No," Sonia said, her husky voice sober. "I reckon he'd have done killed me by now. And probably you with me."

Tess turned, dropping her hair. "And here we are, alive, in this beautiful place." She grinned and pulled her hair up in an exaggeration. "I should show it proudly, then."

"Yes, you should."

There came a knock at the door, and Tess felt a leap of tangled emotions roil in her stomach. "Come in," she called out, knowing it would be Raul. "I'm nearly ready."

He entered, carrying one of the long shawls the women here wore at all times. It was black, with long fringes. He gave it to her. "You'll need this. It's cold out there."

"Thank you."

He looked Tess over from head to toe—and she felt his gaze catch on the scar. His face turned grim as he stared at it. Then he met her eyes. "So you ain't no fancy lady at all, are you?"

Tess took a breath and shook her head.

"I tried to tell you things weren't what you thought, sugar," Sonia said.

Raul didn't look away. "What'd you do? Steal Sonia and run away?"

Tess looked away, biting the inside of her cheek, wondering if it weren't better to leave things as they were. The less anyone knew, the better. "We ran away, that's all."

He put his hands on his hips. "Nah, that's not good enough. I reckon I'd like to know this story right now. If something happens to you, I need to be looking out for Sonia."

Tess looked over her shoulder at Sonia, who had the old mischievous expression back. With the Mexican clothes and her single, neat braid, she looked like a painting from some man's wild imagination. Tess smiled. "Raul, if Sonia wants to tell you, that's fine. Right now, I just want to go to the fandango."

"All right, then." Raul looked at Sonia. "I'll be back shortly. Don't go anywhere."

Sonia chuckled, the sound low and seductive. "I'll be right here waitin', honey."

When she was almost at the door, Tess felt a sudden urge to turn around and go back. She hugged Sonia and said quietly, "'Twould be better," she whispered, "if you do not . . . if you do not have. . . ." She looked over her shoulder to where Raul stood, big as a bear, by the door. "Intimacies," she finished.

Sonia laughed silently. "More than one way to skin a cat, Tess. You go on now."

Blushing, Tess flung the rebozo around her head, and followed Raul into the night.

Joaquin had dressed carefully. He combed back his hair and tied it neatly. Roger had brought him a vest of red velvet with carved silver buttons, and tight black trousers that buttoned down the legs. His full-sleeved shirt was starched and pressed by Roger's current mistress—the illustrious Elena, who hadn't minded at all that Joaquin's heart had landed elsewhere. Roger, it seemed, had a few hidden talents.

The guard nodded in approval as Joaquin turned around, clicking his boot heels smartly against the floor. "Well done, señor," he said with a cackle. "She'll think you a *rico*."

Joaquin winked, unable to quell his anticipation. "My point exactly, amigo. If I am to die in the morning, I wish to die satisfied."

The guard sobered. "I wish I could—"

"*De nada*," Joaquin said with a wave of his hand. "They would kill you, too. And then two instead of one would die."

"I must care for my sister. She has no one."

Joaquin put his hand on the guard's shoulder. "Say no more." He tugged his vest into place. "*Vamanos*."

Together they stepped into the square. In the east, the moon rose above the shoulders of the mountains. It was nearly full, a bright gold, and cast thick puddles of light over the vast plain. Trees in the plaza rose in silhouette against it, branches making feathery patterns against the sky. Torches in tall sconces burned brightly. Joaquin paused, scanning the crowd for Tess.

It was a moment before her saw her, standing with Raul near a table set up for the occasion. His breath caught somewhere in the path of his throat.

Next to Raul, she appeared very tiny, her waist banded with a red sash, her skirts full, her blouse, the traditional chemise of the local women. Her hair was caught in a loose knot at her nape, wisps of it floating free to trail over her long neck. Light washed over the satiny rise of her breasts, half bared by the low neckline of her blouse.

Beautiful. A thready ache beat in his veins. He wanted to kiss her from head to toe, release the tumble of curls and take the clothes from her body one piece at a time, and make love to every inch of her. Standing there under the wild Taos moon, he clenched his fists against his need of her, and forced himself to remain composed.

Tonight he would flee his home—perhaps forever— and Tess would be left behind. He watched her, laughing in quick delight at the swirl of the fandango, her eyes shining in joy at the beauty before her. She belonged here. Taos made her shimmer, like the light of a candle reflected in a silver sconce.

He looked up at the sky for a moment, and took the beloved air deep into his lungs, smelling mutton fat and sage and fire and pine. He let the music fill his heart, one more time, and at last he stepped forward to claim Tess. It might only be dancing, when he would like far more, but he'd claim what he could.

She didn't see him at first, but Raul caught sight of him and pointed. Tess turned her head eagerly, and scanned the crowd, and found him. Her face blazed with joy, and he saw her take one small, quick step toward him before she caught herself. As if to hold herself still, she clutched her fingers into her skirts, and waited.

Deliberately and purposefully, he moved toward her. Their gazes locked, and Joaquin thought they might have been the only people in the world. His need for her doubled, trebled, and he found himself rushing the last few steps. He stopped before her, just looking at her, unable to speak. Tess seemed similarly stricken. They stood there a long moment, caught in the yellow light from the torches and white from the moon, staring at each other.

"You are so beautiful," Joaquin said, at last, his heart pounding. "I have to kiss you."

Tess did not move, but her face tipped upward and her eyes gleamed. He bent and claimed her ripe, full lips. The taste was so sweet, so alluring and unsatisfying all at once that he groaned, and caught her face in both his hands, and kissed her again. She tilted her head more, and he drank deeply, straining for the hint of moist tongue below her giving lips. A soft, hungry sound escaped her throat, and she kissed him back, opening her lips, tentatively brushing his tongue with hers.

Breathless, he lifted his head. She opened her eyes, and he saw the narcotic haze in them. He took a long breath, brushing her lips with his thumb. "Tessita, I—" He swallowed and stepped away a little. "Will you dance?"

"Oh, yes," she whispered, and let herself be tugged into his arms.

He paused when his body touched hers. His member went instantly, fiercely hard, and he laughed ruefully, pausing to give his body a chance to calm. He felt uncontrolled, undisciplined. "You bewitched me."

"No, señor," she said in a husky voice, "I think it is you who have bewitched me. I'm very dizzy."

"So am I." He heard an old man make a bawdy comment, and Tess evidently understood enough of it to catch the gist, for she blushed. "Somehow, we must dance anyway," he said, smiling to encourage her.

And somehow, they did. She quickly caught on to the simple steps, and their bodies meshed as if made from one length of cloth. Joaquin held her as close as he could, reveling in the gentle bounce of her breasts against his chest, in the nudge of her knees against his legs. It was private and public all at once.

"I love this place," Tess said. "Your Taos."

"I think it loves you, too," he said, admiring her bosom frankly. He meant it as a teasing flirtation, but the alluring shadow between her breasts caught his attention and he found himself aching again—aching to touch, to taste, to possess. He shook his head. "This is madness."

"Is it?" She slid her hand over the velvet of his vest. "It did does not feel mad to me. It feels magical."

He bowed his head, touching his cheek to her hair. Into her ear, he said, "I have tried not to want you, Tessita, but from the first time I saw you, I have thought of nothing else." He brushed his lips against her ear, smelling the deep, mysterious fragrance of her skin. "Only thoughts of you kept me from losing my mind these past days."

A faint shudder passed over her spine. He felt it in his fingertips. Shyly, she lifted her head. "I never knew there were men like you in the world. Tonight, you look so handsome I can barely breathe."

"Do you dream of me, too, *mi* Tessita?" he whispered, moving his hand on her back, pulling her tighter yet. A small sound of hunger or pain, or maybe both, escaped her throat. Already they were so close a hair could not have passed between their bodies.

She softened against him, melting closer. "Yes."

He bent his head close, putting his brow against hers. "We met too late, or I would have made you my woman."

"Don't say it," she whispered. "Just let me hold you like this, dance with you." Her hands tightened. "I want to remember how you smell, how you feel. I wish that night at the fort—"

So did he. He wished he had loved her then, had not listened to his conscience, which urged him to leave her be. Now there was no husband and he had not given her the pleasure she ought to know. And he would always regret it.

"So do I," was all he said aloud.

Tess lifted her head. "It is almost time for the woman to come for the guard. We mustn't forget to keep watch for her."

"I won't forget." But he might. It might be worth dying to have Tess Fallon naked in his arms for one night. Unable to resist the nearness of her mouth, he kissed her again, hungrily, fiercely. Somehow they were swirling slowly, bodies shifting one to the other and back again. Her lips parted and he slipped his tongue inside, inviting hers to come play. Their dance stilled altogether.

Mindful of the eyes of the others, Joaquin backed her into the shadows next to a wall. He leaned against the cold adobe to brace himself, and tugged her tightly against him, aching male and female parts pressed close. He put his hand in her hair, and pulled her head forward, and kissed her properly, deeply, feeling himself slip away. Tess kissed him back with a hunger as deep as his own, her hands catching his face, her body straining against his.

So long he had waited to be lost in her this way! So long he had ached to hold her, to feel her softness against the hard length of his body, her breasts plumply against his chest, her hair tangled in his fingers, her mouth and his locked together in an ancient, inflaming dance.

His member strained at his trousers and she seemed to sense his need, for she rocked ever so slightly against him. He touched her shoulder beneath the *rebozo*, skimming his open palm over the exquisitely soft flesh. She held him so tightly her fingers were almost painful on his sides. With a gasp, he lifted his head.

"I would give all I have to be with you for one night."

"And I," she said, pressing her fingers to his lips, "will refuse so that you live to see another day."

"Ah, you are my woman," he sighed, putting his head against her hair, his heart near to bursting. "You are mine. I claim you, do you hear?"

She pressed her face into his shirt, and he put his hand on the crown of her head. At first, Joaquin didn't hear the commotion in the square, but the flurry of activity finally caught his attention and he looked over Tess's shoulder to see what was causing it.

His body went rigid. On a great black horse was a red-headed man. An enormous man with small, piggy eyes in an unhealthily flushed face. A rotund belly strained at the front of his shirt. He looked filthy and wild and mean.

"Tess," Joaquin said, fiercely clutching her shoulders. "Look at this man on the horse."

He felt her fear in her suddenly stony arms. She turned.

A sharp sound whistled through her lips, and she bolted, tearing from Joaquin's arms so quickly he had no chance to stop her.

"Tess McKenzie!" bellowed the man on the horse.

Without a second thought, Joaquin raced behind her, knowing she would die if she fled on her own.

19

In the dark, winding streets, Tess ran with the jerky terror of a frightened animal. She ran so hard she could not breathe, her side burned, and she lost her slippers. Still she ran, hearing footsteps and horses and shouting. She was glad for the short skirts that did not tangle.

Seamus.

Her heart clenched with the terror of imagining what he would do to her if he actually caught her. He would not be content with a horsewhip this time. No. Nothing so ordinary as that. Shards of terror pierced her, and she ran harder. He'd had a thousand miles to conceive of a punishment for his runaway wife.

She ducked into a dark alley and stumbled on a dog, who raced the other way. Knocked off-balance, Tess went down with a strangled yelp. She took the impact on one knee, and skinned her elbow hard against an adobe wall. Her skirt caught on a nail and she yanked it fiercely, stumbling again as she got to her feet.

Hands grabbed her from behind, one arm cinching her waist, the other clamping over her mouth before she had a chance to scream. Wild with terror, Tess fought with nails and feet, but the grip on her was unbreakable and she ran out of air. Frantically, she inhaled.

And smelled Joaquin.

She went lax, her limbs trembling with the run. He put her down, put a finger to his lips, and took her hand. Stealthily, he led the way to the end of the alley, and poked his head into the street. Only his silver buttons, down his waistcoat and the side of his trousers, caught the soft moonlight. He paused for a moment, then tugged her hand. "Run," he whispered, "to the side door of the church there."

They dashed across the narrow street and into the church. The heavy, carved door slammed shut behind them, surprising a priest kneeling in prayer before the Virgin. Tess crossed herself.

"*Padre*," Joaquin said, and rattled off a spate of Spanish Tess could not dream of following.

The priest, a round, owl-eyed man, looked from Joaquin to Tess, gaping. Time dragged endlessly. The sudden sound of shouts in the street seemed to decide for him, and he rushed forward, waving them to follow. He said something in Spanish to Joaquin, and yanked open a small door at the back of the church.

Joaquin whispered, "*Gracias*," then dragged Tess in behind him.

It was a long, narrow closet. The priest left the door open until they made their way to the back, where a clutter of discarded items were shoved against the wall. Tess ducked down among them and Joaquin squeezed in behind her. He tossed a cloth of some kind over their heads, and the priest shut the door. Utter darkness descended.

Joaquin settled against the wall, his knees on either side of her, and pulled her back against his chest. He pressed a fervent kiss to her temple.

Thick adobe walls surrounded them, cold and impenetrable. The silence and darkness were absolute, and Tess shivered with cold, wrapping her rebozo around her closely. Joaquin rubbed her arms. His scent enveloped her, and in spite of her terror, Tess felt comforted.

She eased against him. Against her ear, his heart thudded loudly, still racing from the run through the streets. A button pressed into her cheek. His body cradled her gently, and she could feel his breath on the top of her head.

But in spite of all that warmth and the protection of the church, Tess began to shake violently. Seamus had found her.

Mother of God, what would he do to her if he caught her?

A wall crumbled in her mind, and memories of his careless, daily cruelties poured through the breach. She leaned her head in her hands, trying to halt them, trying to stem her fear, but like demons, they would not be stilled once they were set free.

Seamus: his face, red and sweating, as he held her still and had his way with her; his eyes, flat and dead, when he wielded the whip over some minor infraction; his smell, sour and dank, when he came in from the fields. The visions spun wildly, pieces of him she'd pushed into a dark corner of her mind: the brutal, beefy hands, the ugly feet, the unclean teeth. She shuddered and pressed the heels of her palms into her eyes.

Faintly from beyond the walls came the sounds of horses and shouts. Tess started lifting her head to listen.

And there was Joaquin, cradling her, his gentle, elegant hands moving in comfort over her arms, her back, soothing her. With an ache, she turned as well as she was able and buried her face against his velvet-clad chest.

Joaquin. Who smelled of spicy cologne. Who spoke in a voice as rich as a song. Who laughed and teased, who gently comforted a terrified woman.

Joaquin, whose eyes were filled with light and laughter, and a burning promise. She nestled closer yet, wishing she had found him sooner, that somehow her life had brought her to this place before she'd given holy vows to another man.

As if he understood, he wrapped his arms around her back and held her close. He stroked her hair and her back, wordless expressions of comfort.

She didn't know how long they stayed there, close in the dark. A long time. Long enough that her knees cramped and her bottom felt frozen from sitting on the cold floor. How much worse could it be for Joaquin?

The door opened, flooding the small space with light from beyond, and Tess went rigid. Joaquin held her still until the priest hissed at them. He spoke again in Spanish, too quickly for Tess to follow, but the words must have been good, for Joaquin stood up, swaying as he found his feet, and pulled her up with him.

"They're gone to the mountains, he says," Joaquin explained. "We have to leave now and get away as fast as we can."

"No. You have only one horse, and I am not dressed for such a journey." Tess shook her head. If Seamus found her, it would be horrible, but if the guards found Joaquin, he would die. "Go!" she said, giving him a little push.

"I will not go without you."

"Look at me!" she cried softly, gesturing at the simple skirt and blouse, alluring but none too warm.

Joaquin sighed, his arms crossed on his chest, and gave the priest a look of long suffering. Tess felt her heart plummet—now he would be gone from her, and she would never see him again. Wrapping the rebozo around her head to hide her hair, she decided she would go to the midwife. They would hide her.

Firmly, she stepped up to Joaquin, bracing herself with her hands against his folded arms, and kissed his cheek. "*Vaya con Dios,*" she said softly.

He grabbed her. "You misunderstand, Tessita," he said. With a swift gesture, he flung her over his shoulder. The air whooshed from her lungs. "I will not go without you, and I'm not staying."

Behind her, the priest chuckled.

"*Muchas gracias, Padre,*" Joaquin said as he carried her out the door.

"Put me down. You don't have to kidnap me. I'll go with you."

He bent and put her feet on the ground. The town around them was eerily silent, the moon flooding cold light over the landscape. Far away, a coyote howled.

"No tricks," Joaquin said. "I mean what I say—you are my woman, and I will not leave you to him." He jerked his chin in the direction of the town.

She nodded soberly.

"You must listen to me carefully, or we'll be dead before dawn." He touched her cheek with one finger. "It would be tragic if I did not get to make love to you after all this."

A tumult of desire and fear heated her cheeks. "Yes," she whispered. "Tragic."

"Perhaps God has smiled on us after all, hmm?" Without giving her a chance to answer, he said, "We're going to move very fast. Follow me, and do not be surprised at anything I do."

She nodded. He put his hand around hers and tugged. "Come."

He led them through the dark streets, over a moonlit pasture, past a stand of cottonwood trees along a small stream. They passed isolated houses, squat as pumpkins against the vast night sky. Chickens, startled by the strange noises, clucked and chattered, and twice dogs barked at them.

Joaquin kept moving.

At one place, he stopped. "Ah, look! I knew she would not disappoint me. Señora Esquivel is a singularly lazy wife." With a grin, he lifted his chin to a line full of flapping clothes. Joaquin crept close and stole a blanket and trousers and men's shirts, then moved quickly back to Tess's side. "Raul and Roger will have put blankets and a serape in my bag. For now, you must put these on."

"Where?" Tess looked around at the open fields.

"This is not the time to be shy, Tessita. Put the shirt over your blouse, and the trousers under your skirt. Then you will be warm. The mountains will be cold tonight."

She did as she was told, feeling slightly ridiculous as

she tied the drawstring waist of the woolen pants. But she'd never donned trousers, and they were surprisingly warm. The shirt was only a full-sleeved cotton, but the warmth was welcome on her bare arms. He gave her the folded blanket, and she tossed it around her shoulders, like the Indians she'd seen.

He gave her a quick nod and a grin. "Good."

They ran most of the way to the grove. Joaquin ducked under the low-hanging arms of an elm tree, tugging her behind him. She heard him laugh, and hurried forward to see what amused him.

He gestured with a flourish. "You see," he said. "Raul knows me better than I know myself."

Not one horse, but two were tethered under the trees. Tess, infected by the moonlight and the excitement of having eluded their enemies, laughed too.

It was only once they were mounted that Tess thought to ask, "Where are we going?"

"To my mother and her people. I have to find my sister. She is the only one who will be able to tell me what happened."

His mother. "To the Indians?"

His smile was wry in the moonlight. "I am half Indian, Tessita," he said, a glitter in his eye. "Have I harmed you?"

She shook her head.

"Trust me." He reeled the horse around. "Now we must ride. It will be a long night, but I have faith in you." He touched her cheek, winked, and spurred his horse.

Tess raced behind him into the night.

The mountains were cold and dark. They rode for hours and hours before they stopped, and Tess sometimes wondered if Joaquin had eyes like a cat. It seemed impossible to have a sense of direction in the vast wilderness. The moon, bright and high, helped, and so did the sure-footed horses, but she was still afraid almost all the way. She thought she saw creatures in the trees, and knew she heard them—scrabbling, squeaking, hooting.

They stopped in a high grove. Tess felt dizzy with exhaustion as Joaquin helped her dismount. She stumbled when he put her on her feet, her legs nearly numb with the cold, long ride.

She looked around her. The grove was small, deep inside a narrow canyon. Above, the moon had moved across the sky, and now hung in the west above the rocky face of the canyon wall. They had ridden nearly all night. "We will sleep here?"

"Yes. Wait here. I must check for snakes before we go in."

Tess looked around. Snakes? Joaquin ducked into a dark opening in the wall, half-hidden by a boulder and a collection of scrub oaks. When he did not immediately return, she sank to the ground, cushioned by pine-needles. The grove was not still—in the trees she heard scratching of small animals, and the sharp, beautiful song of black-birds singing in advance of the dawn.

Every bone, every muscle, every joint of her body ached with fatigue. She felt as if she could curl up in the blanket and go to sleep right there, with no care for what might happen to her. She tipped to one side and lay on the ground, pulling the blanket over her face.

So tired.

She dozed lightly, weaving the night sounds and the shining moon into a confused dream. And then she smelled the faint trace of cologne left on Joaquin's jaw, and his arms were gently surrounding her, his voice urging her awake. "Tess, come with me. I have made you a bed where it is warm. You can sleep comfortably there."

"Yes," she said, and sat up. He knelt beside her, still dressed in his Spanish clothes with their silver buttons and rich fabrics. Overcome, she put a hand on his face. "Joaquin," she whispered.

He kissed her, lightly, quickly, and tugged her to her feet. "Come inside."

They had to duck into the opening of the cave, and Tess immediately felt the warmth as he led her into a room chiseled from solid rock, tall enough for Joaquin to stand easily. It smelled faintly of sulfur.

Tess straightened, and looked around in wonder. The cave was as large as an Irish cottage, the walls smooth and ancient. A buffalo skin and blankets had been laid out neatly, and Tess recognized the blanket that Joaquin said his grandfather had woven. Oil lamps sat on ledges, thick, yellow flames smoking in their glasses, but she saw no other fire to account for the warmth.

Instead, butting up against the far wall was a wide pool of greenish water, its edges sandy. It made a quiet gurgling sound. A brook sprung from one side and traveled a carved path in the rocks to the outside. Her arms and legs tingled at the warmth in the room after the cold ride. "Why is it so warm in here?"

"It is a hot spring. The walls trap the heat."

Tess knelt and put her fingers in the brook. It was, indeed, warm. Warmer than bathwater. Now she could see the faint steam rising from the large pool. She looked at Joaquin. "It is!"

He smiled. "If you wish, you may bathe in it. I will give you privacy while I tend the horses."

All at once she was aware of the unfinished business between them. Now at last they were alone, and uninterrupted, and . . . A wave of longing, mixed with embarrassment over her wantonness, filled her. She lowered her head, nodding.

"Tessita, there is no rush." He knelt beside her and tucked a lock of hair behind her ear. "I will not hurry you. Do you understand?"

She closed her eyes and pressed a kiss to his palm. "Yes. Thank you."

He left her alone. Tess removed the overshirt and put it on a rock, then the trousers. Now she hesitated, feeling shy. But from outside, she heard Joaquin talking to the animals in his usual way, and decided she was being foolish. Quickly she shed the chemise and skirt and her drawers.

And for one shameless moment, she stood there, nude,

enjoying the strange sensations of outdoor air on her bare skin. Air currents washed over her breasts, and kissed her belly and swept her thighs in soft gusts. Tucking her hair up more firmly, she walked to the edge of the pool.

The first touch of the water on her cold toes nearly burned, and she gasped a minute, waiting for her flesh to adjust. After a moment, she waded in a little at a time. The pool was much deeper than it appeared, carved from eons of bubbling water that must have dripped into the natural basin. At its deepest point, she could stand and feel the water lap her ribs. It smelled earthy and rich, and flowed elegantly over her skin. Her dulled senses awakened and stretched, and she felt a bolt of pure joy.

Feeling like a wood nymph, she submerged her breasts and shoulders and moved in a circle, closing her eyes to feel the caress of the warm water on her body. Her stiff, sore joints eased, and she felt sensation return to her cold feet. Inadvertently, her toes discovered the source of the spring, bubbling up from some hidden place, where the water was very, very hot. She made a quick, pained noise that echoed on the walls.

"Tessita?" Joaquin called from outside. "Are you all right?"

She laughed. "Yes!" she called.

Then she turned toward the cave opening, thinking of him standing out there, still cold and tired. She thought of his mouth and his hands, and how much she wanted him. And Tess Fallon, who had never been forward in her life, backed against the back wall of the pool for strength, and called his name. "Joaquin!"

"Yes?"

She swallowed. "Come in, please."

The water covered her to her neck, and she knew all he could see was the reflection of the oil lamps wavering atop the water. Still, her face was flushed with embarrassment as he ducked into the cave.

He stopped just within. "What is it?" he asked quietly. His eyes glittered.

Her heart pounded, just looking at him, so tall and lean and comfortable, the dark hair coming loose from the queue, his skin dark against the snowy shirt. Her voice deserted her for a moment.

His mouth quirked into the crooked smile she found so endearing, and he stepped closer. "Do you need something, Tessita?" he asked. "Someone to wash your back, maybe?"

Tess stared at him. Then she nodded. "Yes. I'd like you to come wash my back."

His teeth flashed. "I think I can do that."

"Shall I turn around?"

"Only if you want to." He began to unbutton his waistcoat, then sat down on a rock to pull off his boots. "Are you too shy to watch me undress?"

"I don't know."

He inclined his head. "You look very pretty in there." Lazily, he shucked the fine waistcoat, folded it, and put it atop her chemise.

He looked very pretty, too. Tess bobbed against the wall, her hands flat behind her, staying safely hidden, and watched him undress with a sense of painful anticipation. She did not feel shy, only hungry to feast her eyes on him, and she wondered if she were a wanton, after all.

Next came his shirt. He unfastened the buttons down the front and let it gape over his lean, brown belly and chest. A quickening bloomed in Tess's nether regions. He skimmed the shirt away, leaving his torso bare, and paused. "Are you sure, Tessita?"

"Oh, yes," she said. Even to her own ears, the words were thick and husky.

He unbuttoned his pants, and skimmed them from his body, then stood there a moment as if to allow her a moment to admire him.

Tess willingly complied. He was splendidly made, his long legs and arms in perfect harmony with his flat belly and wide shoulders.

All brown and smooth and hard, all of him. She looked at his face and saw him smiling.

"Do you like what you see?" he asked.

"Oh, yes," she whispered. "You are more beautiful than any man I've ever seen or imagined."

He held out a hand. "It would be only fair to let me admire you, in return."

Tess hesitated, afraid he would not be as pleased with her as she was with him. She was not perfectly made, but too large in the hips and not full enough in the breast. Her skin was pale as sand, too.

His smile disappeared. "Please," he said softly. "Let me see you."

So Tess moved, first straightening her knees so her shoulders came out of the water, then her breasts. She walked toward him, fiercely aroused by the expression on his face as he looked at her. She walked up the slope, feeling water sluice away from her body, exposing her tummy, her thighs, her knees. There she stopped, and they faced each other, naked across the small slip of water.

He swore a mildly profane curse under his breath, and reached a hand across the small space to put the tips of his fingers on the pearled point of one breast. "Not even in my best imaginings," he said, and swallowed, his fingers moving slowly, "were you so beautiful as this."

Tess trembled at his touch, and more as he stepped closer, and put his other hand on her other breast, so he cupped her in both hands, his thumbs moving in a wildly arousing caress. She stood still and let him explore, with his hands and his eyes. He kissed her.

The kiss was unlike any he'd given her before. He captured her lower lip in his mouth and suckled, his thumbs still moving in that slow, erotic way over her nipples. Every brush of his thumbs sent stabs of sensation through her body, and his hot mouth on her lip somehow intensified the feeling.

When he lifted his head, his eyes were black with desire. "Touch me," he whispered.

"Where?"

"Wherever you like."

Tess nearly swooned. He backed her into the warm water, and pushed close to her, taking up his slow caress once more. Tess lifted her hands and put them on his upper arms, where the satiny flesh swelled over ropes of long, hard muscle. She touched his smooth chest, let her hands fall down his sides. As if to encourage her, he made a low, growling sound of approval, and she let herself go farther, to his hard thighs below the water, and around back to the firm round of his buttocks.

He slid his hands over her body the same way, and Tess wanted to cry out at the absence of the heavy, thrilling weight of his palms on her breasts. As if he knew she ached for that touch, he murmured, "Slowly, my love," and claimed her mouth once again, and teased her, the tip of his tongue flickering at the corners of her mouth, over the sensitive center dip, lightly, so lightly.

A restlessness rose in her body, and Tess let her hands roam over him. The water made his manhood nudge her belly, and instinctively, she reached for it, wrapping her hand around it. He groaned, and his kiss took a fierce turn. She stroked it lightly, and touched the swinging weight of the sacs below, and he stilled utterly for a moment, his fingers tight on her shoulders.

They had waited too long for the teasing to last. With a fierce noise, Joaquin lifted her out of the water, and carried her, dripping, to the pallet of buffalo robes on the cave floor. For one moment, he paused, touching her face, his eyes sober and luminous and hungry. "Tessita, I can barely breathe for wanting you."

Tess put her hands in his hair, pulling free the thong that held it back, and it tumbled free around them. Her heart hurt with the beauty of him. She put her fingers on his lush mouth, spreading them wide. "Everything about you makes me think of making love."

He smiled. "Then make love we will."

He kissed her, long and deep and hard, pressing his

naked body close to hers, his arms and legs engulfing her, tangling her close. Every brush of his tongue raised her desire, every sweep of his hand, every tiny, hungry noise he made. Restlessly, she explored his long, hot back, and his legs. She kissed his cheekbones and his jaw, slowly, reverently.

He stroked her breasts, and kissed her throat, and then there was a new urgency in his movements. His hand skimmed her belly, then fell lower still. And to her great frustration, Tess felt herself tensing in fear.

He suckled her breasts, and his fingers dipped into the folds between her legs. She stiffened.

Joaquin halted instantly, and he lifted his head. "Your husband, he was rough?"

She nodded, appalled to find tears streaming down her face. She wanted him—why couldn't she simply take pleasure in the way he moved, the way he touched her?

He dropped his dark head to her breast, pressing his forehead against her flesh. His hands tightened on her upper arms. "I would like to kill him for what he's done to you. For this," he kissed the long scar, "for this," he gently touched the place between her thighs. "For making you afraid and not treating you the way he should."

Tess shook her head. "I'm sorry," she whispered. "It isn't that I don't want . . . well, you know."

He lifted his head, and the quick grin flashed. "No, I don't know. Tell me. What is it that you don't not want?"

She hesitated. "You."

"I know, Tessita." He kissed her, lightly, sweetly, and smoothed her hair. "There is no hurry." With a quick movement, he pulled the pile of blankets and furs over them, then pulled Tess into the cradle of his nude, damp body. "This is sweet, too, our bodies hot and warm together like this. Let me just hold you."

Tess felt the press of his skin against hers. "I want to please you," she whispered.

His hands moved on her arms. "You please me now. Except this."

"What?" She lifted her head, and he plucked the pins from her hair, then threaded his hands through it to make it fall around her.

"There," he said, and pulled her down into the hollow of his shoulder, tucking her next to him like a treasured child. "Now go to sleep, Tessita."

"Joaquin—"

"Sleep," he whispered, and kissed her hair.

His body was hot against hers, his arms a delicious weight, but Tess felt relief that she did not yet have to face the lurking terrors of sex. The tension in her body flowed away, and in moments, the long day and night caught up with her, and she was indeed asleep.

20

Joaquin lay in exquisite agony for hours, watching sunlight bloom in the canyon beyond the cave and streak in through the door to lay in bands over the floor. He listened to birds tweeter and squirrels scold and the water chuckle in the pool. And all the while, a naked Tess slumbered peacefully in his arms.

Against his ribs rested the bare round weight of a breast, soft and giving against his flesh. Her silken hair spilled over his chest and arm. Her thigh, warm and surprisingly sturdy for her small size, rested on his own naked leg.

He could barely breathe for his need, and did not know how he could be gentle when she awoke, did not know how much longer he could bear to be still this way—temptation so close and yet so far.

When the light had reached an almost noontime yellow, he shifted ever so slightly to move his arm from below her. She stirred, her hand skimming his stomach, brushing the rigid length of his erection.

He could not bear it. Turning on his side, he pulled away. Tess shifted and he watched her tuck a hand beneath her cheek.

The scar on her breast and arm gleamed a dull purple

in the bright light, and he tugged the buffalo robe back a little to look at it. This was the mark of her brutal husband—the one who made her bolt in terror, the one she had supposedly gone to Taos to meet. There was no doubt in his mind now that she had run away from him.

Drawn by some force beyond himself, he traced the line with one finger, watching her cinnamon-colored nipple tighten in anticipation as he neared it. He smiled, thinking he'd very much like to give it what it desired. Her breasts were very sensitive—it was a mistake to think all women felt thus, but she did.

He leaned over her. Without touching her in any other way, he put his mouth around that aroused point and began to flick his tongue over it, around it, giving a tiny tug every so often. Tess made a quiet sound of satisfaction, and encouraged, he continued.

She shifted a little, restlessly, as if she missed the sensation. He moved to the other side and repeated the swirling, teasing movements. She stirred, and opened her eyes.

"Joaquin," she whispered, and the sound was raw. He caught her hands gently before she could touch him—he did not think he could bear it, and wanted to save the long-held seed for the right moment.

"Let me taste you," he whispered. "Do not move, only let me love you."

"Not move?"

He bent his head and kissed her breasts. "No moving."

He pushed away the robes until she was exposed to the bright light, and skimmed a hand down her body. White breasts, a rounded little belly, chestnut curls at the top of her sturdy thighs. A pear-shaped body, and beautiful to him. He kissed her tummy, and belly button, then her hipbones and thighs—every inch of her, until she was restlessly moving, waiting for something she didn't even recognize. He knew, and moved there.

She reached for him. "Joaquin," she protested.

He smiled at her. "Trust me, Tessita," he said, nudging

her legs apart. He touched his tongue to her, and she went completely rigid. With skill, he teased and moistened and caressed, making a slick path for his fingers to continue when he moved away to suckle again at her breasts.

She arched against him, and he moved his hands ever so slowly until he knew she was very, very close to exploding.

And he stopped, moving his hand away, moving up to kiss her, slowly and thoroughly, tracing a path over her body with light flickers and play.

She moaned. "Joaquin, please."

"Please?"

"Please let me touch you!"

"Oh yes, you may touch me as you like."

Her pale green eyes, reflecting the light of the pool, opened, and he saw the dusky sensuality there. She rose on her knees and bent over him, and he nearly lost control at the sight of her, wild hair tangled over her shoulders, breasts pointing, her mouth wet. She kissed him, her hands roving down his body, until her small fingers closed around his organ. With a strangled sound, he seized her wrist. "Wait," he gasped. "I cannot—"

Her fingers moved gingerly, and urgently he sat up, taking her in his arms, kissing her fiercely. Her own arousal now matched his own, and she shivered in his embrace, a low sound coming from her throat. With as much restraint as he could manage, he shifted her until she lay on her back and he was over her.

And there, he paused for a moment, his hands on her thighs. His breath was harsh, and his hands were not steady. The sight of her, bare and trembling with passion for him nearly undid him right there.

But he needed to hold on one more moment. He brushed her cheek with his fingers. "Look at me, Tessita," he whispered, "let me see your eyes."

Soberly, she did. "Are you ready for me, Tess?"

She reached for him. "Yes. Oh, please."

He eased, slowly, slowly, into her, fighting for control

until at last he thrust himself all the way home. Tess made a low, gasping cry of pleasure, and he knew all was well. At last.

At last. He grasped her hips and moved. They cried out together this time. And then they were lost, lost together in the perfect melding of their bodies, the long-awaited joining of heat and love and passion. She fit him perfectly, and met his thrusts as if they had made love a thousand times. He heard the increasing pant of her breath, felt the gathering ripples of her body, and at last he let go, lifting her against him fiercely, feeling her come apart, even as he at last spilled his seed into her precious body.

At last.

Spent, Joaquin slumped close against her, and Tess clasped him close, reveling in the feel of his face against her neck, his body tucked within her own, his long back against her palms. His hair, cool and heavy, fell against her cheek.

Her body still pulsed faintly around him, giving her little shocks of pleasure unlike anything she'd ever known existed. A smile tugged her mouth and she pressed a kiss to his ear. "Oh, Joaquin!" she breathed, and laughed.

When he lifted his head, he was smiling, his beloved face alight with the same almost delirious pleasure she felt herself. With one big hand, he smoothed her hair from her face. "Did you like that?"

Laughter rose in her chest. "Yes, yes, yes." With each yes, she kissed him. "Yes."

"I thought I would die before you awakened." He kissed her, softly, slowly. Bracing himself on his elbows, he cupped her face in his hands, and his eyes were still and clear. "I love you, Tessita. I did not think it would happen this way, and there are no promises I can give you." He swallowed. "But I love you."

Cradled in his arms, so unimaginably far from the place she had once called home, Tess gazed up at him. She took

in the high forehead and the sloping planes of his cheekbones and his rich, full mouth. She saw the gentleness and
strength that lived easily in him, side by side, and it
seemed all her life had led her to this moment. "I am not
free to love you," she whispered. "But I do."

He kissed her again.

Tess lifted a hand to his thick hair, wondering what it
would be like to bear a child with hair such as this, or a
daughter with his easy laughter, his dark and shining eyes.
She moved her mouth on his slowly, savoring the particular taste of his mouth, the swell of his lower lip, the bow
of his upper. Joaquin's mouth.

And then she was lost in him, lost in the wonder and
the joy and the freedom that he had given her.

Lost in Joaquin.

Across the vast, high plain west of Taos, late-afternoon
sunlight collected in pockets of shimmering gold, catching on bare-fingered trees and casting queer shadows that
seemed to have no source. Seamus McKenzie, mounted
on his horse, stared at the patterns grimly, disliking the
superstitious unease they gave him.

He disliked everything about this place—the language
and the customs that were so alien, the food that all
looked like slop for pigs, and the dark skins of the
Mexicans and Indians who lived here. Most of all, he
hated the land itself. Low-lying dread had not left him
since they rode over the mountains yesterday morning. He
felt it on the back of his neck, prickling, making him as
jumpy as a rabbit.

Irritably, he looked at the ragged trapper who'd been
his guide through the mountains. "What the hell is taking
so long?"

Horace shrugged. "Doña Dorotea wants everything
just so," he said. "She ain't about to pay for a posse that
don't turn up the body she wants."

Seamus eyed the small woman who commanded the

attention of the gathered Mexicans. No taller than a gnome, her head was covered in a black-lace scarf fastened with some kind of comb underneath. Seamus recognized quality when he saw it. It was written in the imperious tilt of Doña Dorotea's head, in the winking diamond buttons on her dress, in the heavy cuffs of silver at her wrists, and the pendulous earrings swinging in her pierced ears. But it was written mainly in the way the men gathered around her and listened when she spoke.

Horace leaned over and said quietly, "Word is she's probably the one who killed her husband. Don't look the type, does she?"

Seamus lifted one brow. "She killed her husband? Maybe to keep her husband's bastard from taking the ranch. Can't say that I blame her."

"Yep. She'll double the reward if anyone brings her the head of Joaquin Morales."

"Well, now, that's pleasure I'd like to grant."

"We'll find him. No doubt about that."

A roiling burn of fury rose in Seamus as he thought of their quarry. Joaquin Morales. Everywhere he'd gone, he'd heard the name. Joaquin Morales. In memory, Seamus saw his Tess in the shadows of the square, dressed like a native, showing all her bosom for the world, rubbing up against the bastard savage.

If Doña Dorotea wanted his head, Seamus wanted to be the one who severed it.

At last there was a shout of finality among the men, and they mounted, led by a soldier with a thick, black mustache. He yelled loudly in Spanish, and waved them to follow.

Seamus spurred his horse.

In the cave, darkness began to fall. Joaquin left the nest of furs and blankets to light the oil lamps. Tess watched him moving with a glow of love and barely sated hunger.

Her body tingled and burned all over, and she still wanted him back next to her, touching her, kissing her. Loving her.

He fed the horses and came back in with jerked meat and apples and a roll of tortillas wrapped in cloth. He dropped them next to her, already tearing into the meat as he sat down and pulled off his boots. "You've given me an appetite like a bear, *mi amada*."

Tess smiled sleepily, admiring the lean stretch of his stomach. She shifted to one elbow, carelessly tucking the blanket around her breasts, and picked up one of the apples. She felt marvelously wanton, her hair spilling free over her back, her body nude below the robes. "Me, too," she said, biting into the fruit. It tasted marvelously sweet and crisp.

They grazed on the food in comfortable silence, hands and legs touching. Joaquin finished and wiped his fingers. "Somewhere in here," he said, scanning the room, "is a bottle of pulque Raul stashed last time we were here."

"Do you come here often?"

Joaquin looked behind a rock, then moved and lifted another. "Sometimes. We found it by accident. We got lost in a storm and wandered up here by mistake, thinking it was a pass into Taos." He checked behind a small boulder against the wall. "Ah!" Victoriously, he pulled out a nearly full green bottle of the liquor, waving it in the air with a grin. "We'll have to drink it from the bottle."

"We?" Tess echoed. "I tasted a bit of it in Taos, and I'll not be sharing it with you."

He unstopped the bottle, stuck with a small corncob, and took a swallow. His hair, loose and long, tumbled over his bare shoulders and down his chest. It somehow stirred her desire once more, and she sighed. "Come here, señor," she said huskily. "Let me try it again."

Devilment glinted in his eyes. "What do you want to try again, señora? This?" He held up the bottle, coming closer to her. "Or this?" He gestured toward himself.

"Both," she said distinctly.

The dark eyes grew heavy-lidded as he squatted next to her and deliberately lifted the bottle to his mouth, then bent to kiss her, the liquor still on his lips and tongue.

Tess grabbed his arm to steady herself, and the robes fell away from her breasts. The kiss was fiery with liquor and heat, and she pulled away, licking the taste from her lips. "Mmmm." She grinned. "Let me try again."

He gave her the bottle and she gingerly took a taste, feeling the burn all the way down her throat. She coughed a little, and he laughed. "Go slowly."

Tess tried again, an even tinier sip, and the golden flavor was apparent now. She held the tiny taste in her mouth and lifted her mouth to his, swallowing it just before she kissed him. His tongue swirled in, as if to capture a drop, and the invasion sent a ripple of shock through her body.

With a small, mocking sigh, she said, "I'm afraid you've turned me into a wanton, señor."

"*Bueno*," he said with a chuckle, then took her hand. "Let's go in the water."

"I'd rather have you join me here," she said.

"And I would please you, but we will not be able to walk tomorrow, much less ride, if we don't rest our bodies."

Tess blushed. "Oh."

He chuckled again, lifting a finger to the burning color on her face. "Do not be shy, Tessita. I know a little about this water, eh?" He winked. "It heals fast."

Understanding dawned. "Oh," she said with a wicked smile. Even as she grinned that way, she was amazed at the transformation he'd wrought in her in a single afternoon. She felt like a goddess, like a queen, whole and perfect and beautiful. Without shame, she tossed the blankets aside and stood up, ready to wade into the water.

Joaquin grabbed her with a groan, his hands capturing her legs, his mouth falling on her belly. "*Madre de Dios*, you are a woman like no other."

She laughed, pushing him away playfully. "The water,

remember?" She waded in. It was deliciously hot, as before, but as it reached the nether portions of her body, she felt the slight stinging evidence of their ardent love-making, and sucked in her breath.

"Here," he said, wading in behind her. "Drink a little of this. It will help."

Carefully, Tess found a submerged shelf to sit on, and accepted the bottle. Again she took the tiniest sip, and another, liking the warmth of it in her throat. "I don't know how you can take those big gulps," she said, giving it back.

Joaquin settled opposite her, on another shelf. Across the pond, his feet found hers, and settled comfortably over her ankles. "Long practice."

They soaked amiably. "I will have to describe this place to my brother," Tess said. "He will not believe me."

"I brought Miguel here once. He was afraid to take off his clothes." He swigged the pulque. "But I got him drunk and we had a good time after that. It did not take much to make my brother drunk," he said with a grin. Then he sobered a little, gazing at the bottle. He stood up abruptly and poured a dollop on the rocks outside the pool. "For Miguel." Then he poured a larger one. "And my father."

Tess felt the shift in his mood like a drop in tempera-ture. He stood there, in water to his waist, the ends of his hair damp and sticking to his back in points, his head held at a stiff angle. He stared at the small pool of pulque on the rocks with a stricken expression.

She moved in the water silently, and pressed her face to his back. "I'll not think you unmanly if you weep for your father," she said quietly.

His back was very straight and stiff. "I have passed weeping," he said roughly. "I cannot believe he is dead. That we will never sit together again, and drink. I will never tell him of what I've seen on my travels, or listen to him scold me about taking a wife." He turned, and gath-ered Tess close. "He will never know you."

Tess smiled up at him. "Perhaps he does know me.

Perhaps it was your father who brought you to me after that raid."

At this possibility, his face softened. "You are so good for me, Tessita. Perhaps it is true."

He put a hand in her hair. "And my mother will know you."

"Will she like me?"

The crooked grin reappeared. *"Sí."*

He settled back on the shelf where he'd been sitting, and tugged Tess down into his lap. "We leave here with first light," he said soberly. "Doña Dorotea will have men behind me, and I doubt your husband will let you go so easily."

Tess sighed, resting her head on his shoulder. "No, he won't. He'll come after me, of that I'm sure."

"So we must go, tomorrow early."

"To your mother?"

"Sí. But first to El Pueblo. I think my sister may have gone there, and if not, they will know where the Cheyenne are camped."

Tess took a breath. "If I allow myself to think of it, I am afraid of going to the Indian camp."

"You will be with me," he said. "You will be safe."

She nodded, thinking lazily of the teepees lit from within, glowing in welcome. "I trust you," she said quietly.

He bent his head and tipped up her chin and kissed her. "I know."

21

At some point in the darkest part of the night, Tess awakened abruptly. A single oil lamp still burned low, and she blinked, wondering what had pulled her from sleep.

Next to her, Joaquin cried out again. The wordless cry held notes of anguish and hopelessness, and she knew he dreamed of his father's murder. She turned and put a hand on his chest, making a circular gesture meant to ease him. But still he dreamed, a deep and painful dream.

Tess shook him lightly. "Joaquin," she said.

He awakened suddenly and half sat up, blinking. She saw his cheeks were wet with tears. It pierced her. "It was only a dream, my love." She kissed his wet face. "Only a dream."

He buried his face in her neck, pressing his mouth to her throat. His hands swirled over her and cupped her breasts. All at once, he was all around her, over her, his mouth on her lips, devouring, then on her throat, suckling with enough force that she knew there would be marks in the morning.

Her body, in spite of the long afternoon, made itself ready for him instantly. When his urgent mouth fell to her breasts, she could not stop the small cry of need it culled from her, and she opened easily when he moved between her legs.

This was no soft and gentle joining. He thrust hard into her, and the deep pressure made her nerves ripple all over her body, tightening her nipples against his tongue. She lifted her legs around him, pulling him closer, and he grasped her shoulders firmly. In an age-old gesture of welcome, Tess put her hands on his buttocks, thrilling to the shift of muscles as he rocked against her. Her breath came in little gasps.

And all at once, she was not Tess, and he was not Joaquin, but they were one being, as if his act of need and her act of giving formed some new creature melded out of pieces of his heart, her soul, his voice, her dreams.

She arched and met his thrusts, and reveled in the fierce clutch of his fingers against her shoulders, the pounding need of him inside of her, with a joy unlike anything she had ever known.

He reached release with a throaty, long groan of relief and satisfaction, shifting her body upward to take all of him, and there, against his pulsing, Tess let herself go, accepting all of him, giving him all he wished, knowing they were, from this moment forward, irretrievably bound.

In all her life, Tess had never been so happy as she was over those next magical days. The weather, though cold, was bright and clear. They followed a high pass through the mountains, bordered by a rushing stream, through forests of thick pine that smelled of spice and earth. Towering above the landscape as they rode were two great mountains, dazzling with their white crests. Joaquin told her they were called *La Tetas de Madre*. The Breasts of the Mother.

Tess smiled when he told her, and looked up at them. Yes—like great blue breasts, rising voluptuously to points high above the earth. They seemed benevolent mountains, too, as if they exuded a special protectiveness.

The land was truly beautiful, but Tess knew she also viewed it with the eyes of a lover. She would never think of this ride without remembering Joaquin riding beside her, laughing and teasing. He gave her little presents as they traveled, pretty stones he found along the creek, or a gathered bunch of dried flowers that still smelled of summer, or a perfect pinecone.

He told her the names of the trees, the mountains, and the streams, and patiently tutored her in Spanish, chuckling when she made silly errors. Once he doubled over, putting his head against the neck of his horse when she accidentally said a brother-in-law hopped through the fields instead of a rabbit hopped through the fields. Bewildered, she'd only watched quizzically until he gained control of himself, and when he explained, wiping tears of mirth from his cheeks, she laughed with him.

He seemed to know everything about everything— about the land, about their trail, about the animals and the sky and the weather. He spoke his native Spanish, and English, his mother's Cheyenne, and bits of other languages. He could read, which amazed her, and sing, which thrilled her.

And yet, for all that, he remained a simple man, who confided his simple dreams: a house with a patio in the middle where he could sit on summer nights, a comfortable bed, animals, and a garden.

And children. He had, he confessed without looking at her, begun to wish for children of his own. Tess did not reply. The thought of carrying their beautiful children in her womb was so powerful it stole the words from her— and brought forward the memory that she was still married, that if she had his babies, they would be bastards, as Joaquin was. It seemed a very cruel thing to do to him.

By necessity, he still wore the black trousers with their silver buttons down the side, and the full-sleeved shirt that gave him so exotic a look. The silver shone in the sunshine, emphasizing his long, long legs and the hard-heeled boots he'd worn for the dance. Tess sometimes watched him when he was focused on the road and a clutch of wonder would seize her heart, so fierce and powerful an emotion that she could barely fathom it.

So this was love. This wild, almost painful joy that she felt when she was with him. How could she bear to ever be apart from him again?

The days were sweet, filled as they were with new horizons and adventures, but the nights were like stolen water, a phrase Tess remembered from the days her father had read her the Bible—sweeter than honey, sweeter than mead, sweeter than anything she had ever known or even dreamed existed. They spent long hours exploring each other, touching and kissing and playing, making love with still soberness, and wild abandon, and sometimes even with laughter edging their voices all the way through. Tess had not known it was possible to actually be laughing and make love all at once, but it was a heady, delicious pleasure.

And sometimes, when he was sleeping, Tess would watch his face for long moments, feeling overcome. When had that slope of cheekbone become so unbearably precious? When had that mobile mouth become the most beautiful in all the world?

Yes, it was love. She loved him with such power it frightened her. If she spent a hundred years of days and nights with him, it would not be enough.

The thought brought tears to her eyes. She pressed her forehead against his chest fiercely, willing herself to love him now, to take in the scent of his skin and the feel of his hair, and the feathery wings of his eyebrows.

Never enough, she thought, her brow on his skin.

He stirred, and seemed to sense her dismay. He put a hand in her hair. "Tessita, what is it?"

Tess raised her head and pressed a kiss to his mouth. "I did not know I could love anyone this way," she said, and suddenly, tears fell over her face.

He drew her close and wiped away the tears with his thumb. "Nor did I," he said. His fathomless eyes held a sober light. "I never dreamed there was a woman like you in all the world—I had not thought to dream so big a love, even when I saw one between my parents."

His words did not ease her. "How will I bear to ever be without you?"

"You have me now, *mi amada*," he said, and kissed her. "And for as long as there is breath in my body." He pulled away, cupping her chin in his long-fingered hand. "Know that, Tessita—even if we are not together, I am with you."

Tears flowed afresh and she kissed him, knowing there were things beyond their control. He was marked for death unless he could clear his name, and even then, there was Seamus to contend with. "I will not go back to my husband," she said, her hands tight on Joaquin's arms.

"I won't let him take you." He kissed her as if to seal the vow, and Tess greedily drank of the flavor of his mouth, tucking the moment away for all eternity.

And at last she understood what Sonia had said to her all along—there was no hope of controlling the future, so a person had to live fully every minute, and pray for the strength to face whatever came.

Tess had this moment in Joaquin's arms, with his kiss upon her mouth. She had these days they had spent together. She could not bear to think of the world without him, and she could not control the future, so she would take now. Live now. "Make love to me, Joaquin," she whispered.

He did.

All too soon, they rode into view of El Pueblo fort. The structure was similar to Bent's Fort, with its adobe walls and battlements, but this one was much smaller, and around it were small adobe houses, and fields from which a crop had recently been gathered. Tess could see a bright orange gleam of pumpkins peaking through a withering vine.

The fort sat at the confluence between two rivers, where trees grew thick. It was a very pretty spot, but Tess viewed it with regret—now their idyll would end.

It was midafternoon, and there were men and Indians milling around outside. Tess eyed the Indians curiously— they were not like the Arapahos and Cheyennes, nor the Pueblos she had seen in Taos, but yet another nation. These men were tall, with handsome faces and wide mouths, and long hair they wore loose. She looked at Joaquin with a rueful expression. "How many different kinds of Indians live in this place?"

He grinned. "Many. You have not even seen half of them."

"And they all have different ways and languages?"

"*Sí.* Some much alike, some not so much." He lifted his chin. "These are Utes. They live all over the mountains."

Tess admired them discreetly. Before she had come to America, before she had come West, her mind had held a single picture of Indians—red skinned and painted men on horses, savage and wild. It was dizzying to realize how much difference there was among the tribes, in the ways they did things and what they wore and the language they spoke. "'Tis a vast land."

He smiled at her. "You do not need to master it all at once, Tessita. One little bit at a time is enough."

"Are these men friendly?"

"Friendly enough."

Their arrival sparked curiosity and shouts. Mexicans and Indians seemed the only inhabitants, in spite of the fact that they had crossed the Arkansas River into America again. Men came out and greeted Joaquin. They were a rough lot, and eyed Tess with a curiosity that did not have the same edge of lustful imagining that had made her so uncomfortable at the other fort. Tess soon saw the reason as a small knot of women and children emerged.

As she dismounted, a gaggle of children rushed up to her, touching her arms and her hair with the unself-conscious curiosity that adults outgrew. Tess smiled, letting a little girl finger her hair. She glanced at Joaquin, but saw that he was already deeply engaged in conversation with a rough-looking black man with astonishing eyes. Already the conversation seemed a grave one. With a shrug, she looked back to the children. *"Buenos tardes,"* she said.

A little girl giggled. Probably, Tess thought, without rancor, at her accent. The women, three of them, watched Tess with no lack of friendliness in their bright gazes.

"Mama!" one of the little ones said, *"muy bonita mujere!"*

Tess laughed and touched the child's head. One of the women came forward and said something too fast for Tess to catch, but she understood "water." For washing or drinking? Tess didn't care. She nodded and allowed herself to be led inside.

Joaquin watched Tess being gathered by the women of the fort, smiling at the way she managed to keep from tripping over the little children who gaped at her. They'd never seen a woman like her, he was sure, and were as astonished by her appearance as Tess was by yet another new tribe of Indians.

Beckwourth, an infamous trapper who had lived among the Crow, listened grimly to Joaquin's story. "I ain't seen your sister," he said. "I reckon she's gone to your mother."

"Where are they camped, do you know?"

Beckwourth spoke to one of the Indians sitting comfortably in the warm sun against the wall. The Indian, a squat, dark-skinned man of advanced years, shrugged without much interest. He heard, he said, that they were going to the waters, to heal some of the band of their ills.

Joaquin grinned. The waters were a name for a mineral spring not far north. He and Tess could sleep in his mother's camp tonight. And Juanita! He'd not seen her in months, and longed to see for himself that she was well. He clapped Beckwourth's shoulder and thanked him.

"Not so fast, now," Beckwourth said with a mischievous drawl. "Can't get away without a little gossip in payment." He took the straw from his mouth and gestured toward the fort. "Who's the woman?"

"My woman, you dog."

"Is that right? They were talking about her at Bent's last time I was there. A big old mean Irishman was after her. I saw him myself." He salted his telling with a meaningful pause. "He claimed he was her husband."

"Seamus McKenzie," Joaquin said, sobering. "You met this man?"

"Met is a generous term. He wouldn't have nothing to do with niggers and Injuns, you know." A glint of amusement sparked in the man's eye. "But once he heard his wife had been there with another man, he was fixed for bear, I can tell you that."

"I saw him in Taos."

"Watch your back, *mi amigo*."

Tess came out of the fort, carrying a small child. The child, a boy of about two, flirted with her, touching her cheeks and burying his face in her breasts. Tess laughed at him, touching her nose to the crown of his head. Joaquin, watching, felt a stab of longing for that to be his child on her hip, his child at whom she smiled with such gentle happiness.

"She's a pretty little thing," Beckwourth commented. "Where'd you find her?"

"The spirits led me to her," he said lightly. "And I intend to keep her."

"Well, you let her know your good friend at El Pueblo is willing to take care of her, anything should happen to you."

Joaquin made a derisive noise. He made for his horse, and gestured for Tess to follow. She put the boy down and expressed thanks in her halting Spanish, then moved toward him. "We will not stay?"

"My mother's camp is nearby. We will be safer with her." He glanced up as Beckwourth sauntered over, his wild hair glinting in copper streaks in the sun. Joaquin raised his chin toward him and told Tess in a voice loud enough to carry, "That man is Jim Beckwourth, one of the most notorious womanizers in the land. Whatever you do, never turn to him for help."

Beckwourth laughed. "Don't listen to him, ma'am. I've a heart as big as those mountains."

Tess smiled at both of them. "Men," she said, mounting with the athletic ease she'd gained these past months on the trail. "All of you lie."

They both laughed. Joaquin raised a hand in farewell, and they rode north. To his mother's camp. To his sister. To find safety, and perhaps some answers that would give him back his freedom.

For now, he was a hunted man, exiled from his home. Until he could prove Doña Dorotea lied, he would remain so.

He glanced at Tess, riding gracefully astride. Her face was tanned from so many days in the sun, and her hair, caught loosely in a ponytail at her nape, had become laced with threads of bright yellow. Whatever happened, he could not regret these past days. Not ever.

As he admired her, his body stirred, and with a wicked grin, he rode close to her. "Come ride with me, *mi amada.*"

She glanced sideways at him, the blue eyes glinting. "But why, señor? I am perfectly comfortable where I am."

He reached out and grabbed her around the waist, laughing when she squealed. He put her down in front of him, and she wriggled into place against him. "Comfort is not what I had in mind," he said, low against her neck. In the warmth of the day, she had shed the serape, and wore the Mexican blouse with its drawstring neck. He put his mouth against a slice of shoulder and kissed it.

"No?" she inquired softly.

"No." He slid his hand upward from her tummy, to

cover her breast with his free hand. The warm soft flesh fitted neatly into his palm and he sighed against her neck. "I like your breasts," he said quietly.

She leaned backward against him. "I love your hands."

"Yes?" Her eyes were closed. Joaquin looped one finger through the bow that held her blouse closed, tugging the tie slowly. "What else do you like?"

"I love your voice, the way you talk."

The bow came undone without her noticing. Joaquin grinned and gave the fabric a quick tug. It tumbled from her shoulders, revealing her breasts and shoulders to the wind. Reaching around her, he lifted the soft white flesh in his callused hands, watching the tips pearl against the brush of the air.

With a scandalized little cry, she tried to catch the fabric. "Joaquin! What are you doing? What if someone sees us?"

He nuzzled her ear, tasting the lobe and the tender flesh hidden below. "Who will see us? That hawk?" He chuckled, moving his fingers in the teasing way he knew she liked. "Let me see you, Tessita, all in the sunshine, in the light." He kissed her shoulder, the back of her neck. "Let me touch you."

"'Tis wicked!"

"Yes," he murmured, kissing her jaw, feeling her soften against him. "A delicious wickedness. Have you ever felt the sunlight on your breasts?" Her arms relaxed and she leaned against him languorously.

"You've turned me into a wanton woman, Joaquin," she whispered, arching a little into his caress. Her hands fell to his thighs and moved restlessly.

"Not wanton, *mi* Tessita," he murmured. "I have only freed you to your passion." He skimmed the fabric lower, so her whole torso was naked. "Does it not feel sweet to have the wind caress you, to have the sun kissing your breasts?"

"Yes," she said.

"You are so beautiful," he said, feeling that wild

strange wholeness rise in him, making sacred even the most secular of his touches. Her skin was a prayer, her soft sounds of pleasure, a psalm, and his need of her grew so ardent that he knew he could not simply tease her this time.

Clasping her tightly, he took the reins and led the horses into a copse of trees nearby a small river. There, on a soft rise of grass, with the sound of the water chuckling by, Joaquin worshipped her, as he was born to do, and vowed he would find some way to end the lies. So he would be free to love her thus always.

22

Clouds knotted up over the mountains, swirling from the south to darken the day, abruptly and ominously. Seamus heard the others in the posse grumbling about the threat of Indians.

They made camp in a sheltered clearing, high in the mountains. Out of fear of raids from the Utes, who were known to be fierce about intruders, they had no fire, and made do with hard bread and dried meat for supper. As he drank cold water from a tin cup, Seamus longed for the comfort of hot coffee.

Rolled in a blanket on the hard, cold ground, he thought of the feather bed he'd shared with Tess at the plantation, with its fluffy white coverlet, kept in perfect repair by the army of slaves—like the floors that never grew dusty, and the windows that shone like diamonds all times of year. He'd thought Tess would take to a life of such ease. He'd thought it would please her.

How could a woman who'd suffered so much toss such ease away? It bewildered him. She hadn't taken to the notion of slaves, that was sure, but 'twas not an uncommon reaction among soft-hearted women. They grew accustomed to it soon enough.

But Tess had not. She babied them, especially Sonia,

and the longer she spent among them at the plantation, the stiffer she grew in Seamus's bed, ever more resistant to his needs and orders.

Sharp wind howled through the narrow canyon, and Seamus huddled deeper in his blankets. A rock bit into his back and he shifted to his side, pulling his hat low. Snow dropped on his face, wet and cold. Wind pushed into his ear, and as if in protest, he felt a sharp, deep twinge, way down deep.

A bolt of fear penetrated his vague, growling discomfort. As a child, he suffered vicious earaches, from which there had been no relief. His mother would mix onion juice with warm oil, and drip it in, and hold him, and sing, but she had died of a fever when he was eight, and after that, he simply lay in agony when they came on. As he grew, they got better, and he'd not known an earache in twenty years.

This was likely just the cold from the long ride, and the shifting pressure of riding up and down the passes as he had these last few weeks.

He covered the ear carefully with a blanket, leaving his feet bare, and the low twinge eased. He let go of a breath. Just the cold. Nothing to worry about.

Thick snow had begun to fall by the time Tess and Joaquin reached the Indian camp. The storm came suddenly from the south, blotting out the bright sky with low, dark clouds, heavily laden.

Joaquin said, "I'm glad we'll have shelter tonight."

"Yes." Tess thought of that shelter, and her stomach gave a little jump. She'd been carefully avoiding the thought of the Indian camp. In one way, it seemed an adventure, another chance to learn something new—for had she not liked most everything she'd learned of this vast, strange, wild place?

But as long as she lived, she would not forget those painted warriors who had swooped from the mesas and killed the traders, who would have killed her, too. She still heard their cries at night, in her dreams.

Tess and Joaquin had not yet come within sight of the camp, before men very like the ones she feared rode out in a party to meet them. There were four of them, riding horses of a very fine caliber, their manes grown long. The men wore buckskin instead of the bare chests of the warriors of her memory, but their hair flowed loose and free in the wind, and their faces had no welcome.

"Do not be afraid, Tessita," Joaquin said. He lifted a hand in greeting, and called out something in the Cheyenne language.

One of the younger men smiled, and called out something even Tess could tell was teasing and cheerful. His companions laughed.

Joaquin grinned, and translated for Tess. "He says it's good we've come, or they would have had to marry my sister to Summer Killer, a very ugly old man, who has no more teeth."

Tess nodded uncertainly, not really understanding the joke. Joaquin smiled at her. "When you see my sister, you will understand. Men always want to take her to wife, and she turns them all away."

"Why?"

He shrugged. "She says she has not found the man for whom she will make a good wife. The rest will only be miserable with her."

The warriors escorted them toward the camp. Under the gray and blue day, the lodges were pale, and dry snow caught on their sides. Curious children ran to the edge of the meadow to see who rode into their midst, and Tess saw with amusement how they stared at her. Her strange appearance caused a stir wherever she went.

Suddenly, there was a cry, and a woman bolted through the children, holding her skirts up so she could run. "Joaquin!" she cried, her black hair flying behind her.

Joaquin leaped down and rushed out to meet her,

catching the slim, tall woman in his embrace. He whirled her around.

It could only be his sister. She wore a calico blouse and a plain gathered skirt, a knitted shawl with very long fringes around her shoulders. On her feet were beaded moccasins. Tess saw the beads flash as Joaquin spun her.

They were very alike. The slanted bones and clean lines that had made Joaquin's face look so unique and powerfully beautiful to Tess, became more sensual, a little softer in Juanita's face, and her mouth was fuller, brighter than her brother's. The effect was breathtaking.

Joaquin put her down on her feet and kissed her cheek. Taking her hand, he turned to where Tess still sat on the horse. She felt underdressed and strange. Juanita's face showed no expression as Joaquin said only, "This is my sister, Juanita. This is Tess Fallon, who has come a very long way with me to find you."

At a gesture from Joaquin, Tess dismounted. She was all too aware of the warriors, and the children, looking at her clothes and hair, and white skin. She knew from some of the giggles that she was as odd to the children, especially, as a hen among peacocks.

But she took courage from the bright, gentle light in Joaquin's dark eyes, and lifted her chin. Joaquin touched her shoulder and drew her into the circle comprised of himself and his sister.

It was hard to look at the face of Juanita; the dark eyes and cheeks of dusky rose and bold red mouth were too bright, and Juanita was very tall, too. Her breasts were deep over a waist that cinched in, only to swell roundly once more over shapely hips. Tess only looked at her, words stolen from her mouth. For comfort, she raised a hand and touched Joaquin's fingers on her shoulder.

At this unconscious gesture, Juanita slowly smiled. "You are the one, then," she said. She touched Tess's hair. "He has waited for you a long time."

Tess looked at Joaquin, a trill of apprehension sounding in her brain. What would Juanita think of her if she knew Tess fled her husband? That in truth, she was no better than an adulteress? The scriptures did not say, "Do not commit adultery, except if you truly fall in love."

"She is my woman," he said simply, and lifted his hand to touch her cheek. "But I am going to have to fight a little longer to have her."

Juanita laughed, the sound husky and full of zest. "Come, *mi hermano*, your mother needs you."

As they walked, Joaquin said, "How is she?"

"As you would expect," she said grimly. "You'll see for yourself."

A youth of about twelve, and a younger boy, about seven or eight, ran up to meet them. Both had the same distinctive blend of Spanish and Indian features that marked Joaquin and Juanita. Joaquin laughed and touched them in his way, telling Tess they were his brothers. The older one was Red Tree, the other was Little Mouse.

Juanita interrupted, touching her youngest brother's shoulder. "He is Kills a Rabbit now."

Joaquin lifted a brow. "Ah. You're becoming a man."

"It was a big rabbit," Juanita said, without a hint of indulgence. "He caught him with his hands, and broke his neck."

Kills a Rabbit lifted his chin and tried to look nonchalant. Tess kept her own smile firmly hidden when he managed to look pleased and modest at once.

At a lodge set some distance from the others, beneath a trio of sheltering pines, they all ducked into a doorway covered with a hide. Tess hesitated, a lump of nervousness in her throat. This time, it wasn't a fear of the lodge, or the Indians around her. All had been chased away by the realization that she was going to meet Joaquin's mother. His mother.

The youth, Red Tree, paused politely to hold the hide up for her. In his face she saw the shape of the man to come. Armando and Sleeping Bird had made very beautiful children indeed.

She put her hands on her stomach to calm the roiling,

and ducked inside. It was dim in comparison to the light beyond, and Tess had to pause to let her eyes adjust. While she blinked to clear her vision, she smelled a rich combination of scents, pine smoke from the fire, a hint of meat fat, the earth below them. As her vision cleared, she saw the fire burning yellow and low, its smoke venting into the sky through a hole near the top. The interior gave a feeling of much more space than she had imagined. Buffalo hides covered the floor, and a trunk sat against one wall, and there was a pole strung between two others to provide a place to hang blankets and clothes.

Joaquin knelt next to a woman who sat on the floor, the needlework in her lap forgotten. Her black hair was chopped irregularly around a gaunt face with hollow eyes. The grief was so evident in that ravaged face that Tess wanted to cry out at the unfairness. Had she not paid enough of a price for her love of Armando, without him being murdered on top of it?

Joaquin spoke quietly in Cheyenne, and gestured to Tess. The woman raised her eyes, very solemnly taking in Tess who stood quietly for the examination. Then Sleeping Bird inclined her head, and gestured for Tess to come sit next to her. As if by some prearranged plan, the others left. Sleeping Bird took her hand, and said in English that was halting but clear, "Welcome, daughter."

After everything else, it was too much. Tess felt tears of relief well up in her eyes. "Thank you," she whispered, and bowed her head to hide her emotion.

Joaquin, lingering at the doorway, heard what his mother said and smiled. Then he took Juanita's arm, shooed his brothers away, and walked into the trees. They did not speak until they were well away from the village. Juanita sat on a boulder, her hands loosely held in her lap. "I am so glad to see you, brother. It's been a hard wait."

"You should see it from my side." With a sigh, he sank into a sitting position. The ground was only slightly damp here, in spite of the snow swirling around them. "When I rode into Taos after the trip, there were soldiers waiting to arrest me."

"Arrest you! For what?"

"For killing our father."

She closed her eyes. "Joaquin, I am so sorry. I did not dream she would accuse you." Her mouth tightened grimly. "But I should have known it. It was to keep you from having the land, that she killed him."

"Doña Dorotea killed him?"

Juanita nodded soberly. "She shot him with his own gun. I saw it."

He had known she had been behind the murder somehow, but he'd never dreamed she had actually killed her husband herself. *"Dios!"* he exclaimed, covering his face. "She's gone mad at last."

Juanita nodded. "Miguel is all that kept her sane. When he died, she had nothing but the hacienda to remember him by. If you take it, she has nothing."

"I would give it to her if it would bring my father back," he said, and the enormity of the death swept over him again. "I miss him so much."

His sister gathered him close. They clung together, weeping at last for the man they had both adored all of their lives. "He was a good man, Joaquin. He has God's favor. All of this will end well." She lifted her head. "Are you cleared, or did you escape?"

He made a face. "I escaped, but mainly for Tess. She—" He stopped. "It is a complicated story."

"She is in trouble, too?"

"She has a husband, who will chase her to the ends of the earth, I think. He followed her to Taos, and we ran."

"Ah," Juanita said. "It would be too easy for you to find a woman of your own class and race that wasn't married, I suppose? What is the challenge in that?"

Joaquin frowned. "I did not look for her, Juanita. She fell in my path, like an angel."

"You love her, this Anglo?" she asked with some bitterness. "You're going to give her your children so they can be washed out, their blood thinned even more than our own?"

Her bitterness shocked him. "Why are you angry? I did not spurn some woman of my race and class, as you say, to choose this one."

She leapt up, and gathered her shawl around her. "They are coming, Joaquin. So many of them. There is talk of war, coming here. The Ojibwa and Lakota fight to beat them back, but for every white person they kill there are ten thousand more." She looked at him. "It was not enough for you to see our parents suffer as they did all their lives, for love?"

"Did they suffer more than they loved?" he asked quietly. "When our father lay on that ground dying, do you think he thought of Sleeping Bird and wished he'd never seen her face, or did his spirit fly away to her, to make a place for her when she came?" His voice caught in his throat. "Until you love, Juanita, you will not know why it does not matter what the world thinks or how it will end."

Tears fell over her ruddy cheeks. "You think you will pay for your love with your life."

He looked away.

Juanita hit him. "Don't you dare. I've lost my father, and my Miguel, and I will not let you die with them."

He took her arms. "I will live," he said, and it felt like a vow. "But you must come to Taos with me and tell them what you saw."

"They will not listen to me, Joaquin! Armijo only wants to get fatter and richer, and we are only the children of a *genizara!*"

"You must try. They will execute me if I cannot prove my innocence." He shook her slightly. "Where did Papa put the papers for the ranch?"

Juanita bowed her head. From the pocket of her skirt, she took a sealed document. "Here. When I saw her kill him, I went to his desk and took them, and ran."

Jubilantly, he kissed her forehead. "You are a wise

woman, *mi hermana!*" He put the papers back in her pocket. "For now, keep them. I must go tell the war leaders what I think will happen, to warn them."

"What do you think will happen?"

He chuckled. "That is a business for men," he said, knowing it would annoy her. "Go to the women, where you belong."

Juanita made a noise and rolled her eyes, but she moved toward the lodge of his mother amiably enough. When she was near to ducking under the trees, he remembered. "Juanita! Tess is a healer. She seeks one who will teach her the ways of our medicines."

For a moment, Juanita only stared at him.

"What is the matter?"

Juanita closed her eyes. "I dreamed of a healer with strange eyes, who saved your life."

He inclined his head. "And so she has," he said.

23

When Seamus awakened, he was soaked through. The blanket over him was sodden, and his clothes felt damp and cold against his skin. The snow, thick and wet, had melted when it fell upon the warmth of his body.

Sitting up, he moved his head to test the faraway pain he'd felt last night. In his ear was a low, faint hum of noise, but it didn't hurt. That single fact allowed him to face the other miseries with less annoyance than he might have.

The rest of the posse was not so forgiving. Wet and irritable, they quarreled between themselves. An argument broke out just before dawn, and half of the posse rode out—not toward their quarry, but back home. Their departure left seven men, including Seamus.

They eyed one another in the cold, bright morning. Frost hung in the air with their exhalations. "What is it going to be?" one man asked. He was a Mexican soldier, the kind of man Seamus respected—tough and terse. "Are the rest of you going to run like women, or fight like men?"

Only one more left after that, and the rest of them rode northeast, coming out of the mountains to a wide, flat, golden plain about noon. Nothing had ever looked so fine to Seamus. This was land he could understand—flat stretches of unbroken grassland. The mountains still surrounded them, and rode along the horizon as the sea did in Ireland, but if he could help it, Seamus would never set foot upon them again.

Just past midday, the posse met a small band of Utes on the trail. They were returning from a small fort on the Arkansas, and were willing enough—for the trade of a rifle—to tell what they knew.

Seamus sat on the sidelines while the Indians and the Mexican soldier rattled on in rapid-fire Spanish. Listening to them, Seamus scowled. What kind of language was that? It would likely strangle him if he tried it. Annoyed with the wait, he glanced off toward the pair of mountain peaks, dusted this morning with a coat of snow.

And in that single instant, as if a dart had been flung by a brownie intent on mischief, pain blazed in his left ear. Not a dart's worth. An arrow, cut into the deepest part of his skull.

He reeled, as if struck, and clamped a hand protectively over the ear, but it seemed to only close the pain in, trapping it like a nest of wasps. He grunted.

The trapper who'd been traveling with him since Bent's Fort, rode up. "Your ear painin' ye?"

"Goddamn right."

"Mountains do that to some folks." He reached into a saddle bag and pulled out a flask. "Put a little white lightning in the cap and let it drip inside your ear. Works better hot, but it might help anyhow."

Seamus glared at him. Whiskey for an earache? What kind of idiocy was that? But the buzzing pain loudened, and he grabbed the flask. He'd cut the bloody ear from his head if it would help.

He dripped a little in his ear and held his head sideways, feeling the heat of the liquor slide inside. To his astonishment, it dulled the pain somewhat. To be safe, he took a hearty swallow by mouth, as well. "Thanks," he said gruffly, handing the flask over.

The trapper waved it away. "Keep it. I'll stock up at El Pueblo."

The Indians rode off, and the soldier turned to the rest of the party. "Joaquin Morales is with the Cheyenne, camped at the spring up north that the Indians call the 'healing waters.' We'll ride on into El Pueblo and spend the night, then head out in the morning."

"Thought nobody wanted to ride into an Indian camp," Seamus said.

"We will not. It is too dangerous." His horse moved restlessly, and the soldier flipped the reins. "No, we'll settle some distance away, and wait for Morales to leave camp."

"And how you gonna get him to do that?"

The soldier winked. "Trust me, señor. He has a beautiful woman with him. Would you not find a way to sneak away with such a one?"

Seamus smiled slowly. Perfect. They could drag Morales back for his hanging, and Seamus could drag Tess to her punishment. They were so close he could almost smell her now.

Tess felt suspended in some kind of magical world, as enchanted as if she'd stolen away to a fairy camp in the forest. The world of the Cheyenne was immensely different, and fascinating, and somehow pleasant in a way she had not anticipated.

Juanita gave her a soft, deerskin dress and moccasins to wear—the freedom of such clothes, without the constriction of undergarments pinching and pushing, was heady. She liked the joy of the children, who ran and played and chased under the watchful eye of all the adults in the tribe. They were expected to perform their chores, like all children, but she liked the freedom they also had to just be themselves.

As she went about the tasks Sleeping Bird and Juanita gave her to do—shucking corn in preparation for drying, scraping buffalo hides for tanning, even learning a little of the magnificent beadwork so many of the clothes boasted—she mentally composed a letter to her brother, which she then wrote at night.

Liam, she would write, you would love this place.

> *The people live close to the land, just as the Irish have always done. But there is more wisdom in their way than in ours, or perhaps the land is not so weary as it is at home, so tired from trying to feed too many hungry people for too long. Wild food is abundant here—nuts and berries and wild onions, growing everywhere. Game birds fill the trees, and the prairie boasts rabbits of a size you would not believe.*

> *But most amazing of all is the buffalo. I had eaten it and slept upon their robes, but had not seen the animals until yesterday. Joaquin and I walked out to a low bluff nearby here, and there in the valley below was a herd of them so vast one could almost not see the end of it. Big, heavy animals they are, so many they would feed all of Ireland and still be swarming all over the plains. Joaquin ran back to tell the others, and a hunting party went out. We feasted, I can tell you, and today the women are tending to the hides, which will be used for clothes and the walls of the lodges they live in, and blankets that are so soft and warm I can't even tell you how they feel.*

Oh, yes. Liam would like it very much. He'd often cursed the way of their miserly farming life, and mourned the days when their ancestors had taken wild boars and rabbits and deer aplenty from the forests of Ireland. Here, he would see that life could yet be lived the way he dreamed.

She wanted him to come to America, come to live with them. How happy he would be among these people!

At night, she slept close to Joaquin, but in his mother's lodge they did not make love, though he insisted his mother would not object. Tess could not bear the lack of privacy, however, and he respected her wishes.

Tess felt most comfortable with Sleeping Bird. Their conversations were awkward, for Sleeping Bird spoke little English, and Tess little Spanish, but they got by with Juanita's help. The woman was plainly grieving the loss of Armando, and deeply, but it was also plain that Joaquin had inherited much of his good-humored ways from her. She teased her sons, Joaquin, Red Tree, and Kills a Rabbit. Her only daughter was Juanita, she explained, and that was why she was so happy to welcome Tess into her brood.

At this revelation, Tess blushed. Miserably, she looked at Juanita. "Does she know we are not married?" she asked in English.

Juanita laughed, and evidently repeated the question to her mother. Sleeping Bird inclined her head.

"She wants to know why, if you are so in love with her son, you do not tell the other husband you will no longer be his wife."

Tess shook her head. "If only it were that easy. Is that how you do it, just say you aren't my husband, and he goes away?"

"Not always quite so easy as that," Juanita said. "But not like with priests."

Sleeping Bird leaned forward earnestly, putting her hand on Tess's arm. She spoke slowly and clearly. "My son loves you like you are the sun."

Tess swallowed a lump in her throat. "And I love him the same."

That was all that was said on the subject, but later, she walked up a stream, thinking on it for the first time since they'd arrived in Taos.

She had always been a good Catholic girl. She believed her prayers were heard, that God listened, and there was only misery because humans did not listen well enough in return.

But there seemed to be a whole other side of God in this wild land. A much kinder, more understanding God who would not punish a woman for spurning a man who was cruel.

From the dirt beside her, she plucked a handful of pebbles. All of them were shades of clear-pink quartz with veins of dark gold, darker pink granite, deep-red sandstone that could be carved. In the sunlight, something shiny shone in the granite, and Tess held it in her palm, admiring the sparkle.

Would God punish her? One by one, she tossed the pebbles into the stream running beside her moccasined feet. Would Joaquin even want her if they could not be properly wed?

She had enough sense to realize she was suspended for the moment in a magical place. The rest of the world was not like the Indian camp. Taos, as beautiful and rich as it was, was a Catholic village, and her infidelity would be a shameful thing. Could she bear that shame for love of Joaquin?

The shame would be worse for Joaquin, for it was in his village they would live, where he was known. Would he resent her once the first flush of passion had worn away?

She sighed, leaning back against a pink boulder speckled with black. The stream, made plump by the recent weather, rushed over the rocks in its path with a somewhat comforting noise. She touched the dress over her knees, feeling the soft leather with her palms, and looked at the sky, visible between the points of pine trees. The color stunned her, a blue so dark and rich and it seemed unreal, especially in contrast with the furry, dark green of the trees.

The beauty chased away her gloomy thoughts. She smiled a little, thinking how approving Sonia would be—Tess was learning, slowly, to be happy in the moment. As if in reward, she saw Joaquin duck under a tree and come toward her.

He, too, had shed his town clothes for Indian garb, a simple shirt made of deerskin with fringes, worn with long leggings. He wore his hair loose, and it fell over his shoulders in a thick wash, shiny and somehow alive in the bright light.

He no longer looked dangerous and rough, like the comanchero who had rescued her. Nor like the grand Spanish gentleman he had seemed in the velvet vest and silver buttons. Today, he looked like his brothers, like a Cheyenne. And as he came toward her with his easy, loose-limbed lope, she realized he was all those things, and none of them.

He was Joaquin. Her Joaquin. And she could never be ashamed of her love for him. As if he knew what she was thinking, he smiled and knelt to kiss her, thoroughly, sweetly, passionately. She touched his hair, and smiled. "You look very handsome this way," she said.

"I'll wear it for you every day, then," he said, his eyes glittering as he settled next to her. "As long as you promise"—he added wickedly, sliding his hand under the soft deerskin dress, all the way up to her thigh—"to leave your drawers off under your skirts for me."

His slow caress was delicious and arousing. Tess grew aware of her lack of undergarments in a whole new way, and slapped his hand. "Be good!" she whispered, looking back toward the camp.

"I will be," he promised, and grabbed the hem of her skirt, pushing it up to show her knees. "I promise." His laughter fell on her ears, as richly musical as the stream.

They had not made love since coming to the camp, and Tess suddenly ached to feel him. The camp was more than a half-mile downstream, and no one would find them. She put a hand on his thigh and slid it upward, to the place where his sleek, brown hip was uncovered. "I like this."

His dark eyes shone. "Do you?" He stroked her legs, shoving the dress higher.

Now she realized he, too, would be without undergarments, and the knowledge sent a rippling stir through her body. "I remember when I first saw you," she said. "I thought you were an Indian, and you would kill me."

He lifted a hand and touched her breast over the soft leather, bringing the tip to a visible point. "And instead, you are alive."

"Yes. As I never have been." She watched hunger make his eyes liquid as his gaze traced the path of his fingers. Thick need washed through her body, and she slipped her hand below the breechcloth he wore. As if it had life of its own, his aroused organ nearly leapt into her hand. She laughed in delight, and Joaquin kissed her smile, pulling her backward on top of him as he laid back in the sweet-smelling leaves.

"I think Anglos should take up Indian clothes," he said, pushing up her skirt again, this time clear to her waist.

With a little thrill, Tess felt the air on her buttocks, and boldly straddled him. "Why do you say that?" she asked with mock innocence, moving her body against his arousal.

His eyes glittered. "Maybe they wouldn't be so grim all the time."

Tess swayed forward and kissed him, taking his precious face in her hands. "It isn't the clothes that will improve their natures," she said.

His hands skimmed her buttocks, lightly, teasingly. Feeling the power of her position, Tess smiled and moved her hips against him, laughing low in her throat when a soft groan escaped his lips. "No?" he managed.

"I don't think so," she said calmly. She pushed his shirt up to put her hands on his lean, brown chest, and on his hard belly.

"What, then?"

"This," she whispered, leaning forward to press her breasts against him. He let go of a heartfelt sigh, and clasped her close. Urgently, he lifted her enough to free himself, and then with a single thrust, joined them together.

The sensation was so acute after the days of wanting

him that Tess was momentarily stunned. He didn't move immediately, holding her close and deep for a moment, the sun cascading around them, the birds chirping in the trees, the stream singing over her path. Tess could not quite catch her breath, for the joining was too acute, too rich, too precious.

Joaquin looked at her. "This?"

"Ah—yes," she whispered, and urged him to move. "Yes." And once again, she was lost in the joyful swell that was Joaquin—loving him, touching him, feeling him. Once again their spirits dissolved into one mass that swirled between them, through them.

Making them one.

24

From his vantage point, fifty feet up the mountains, Seamus McKenzie peered through a glass, staring down at the pair of them through a haze of red fury. The anger made his earache intensify, swelling a degree with each beat of his heart. He was nearly mad with the relentless ache. Not even onions and warm oil had soothed it. He'd been drunk almost three days, and even that failed to help it anymore.

Now Tess Fallon McKenzie, his legal wife, humped a redskin in the open air, and the agony in his ear rioted like a thousand soldiers without pay, stomping through his head.

When had she learned to be so wanton? He didn't think he'd ever taken her by the light of a candle, much less the blazing light of a full noontime sun. Outside, no less.

He let the glass skim over her hips and the silky thighs. In his groin, he felt a faint nudging stir, but it disappeared in a haze of pain from his earache.

Which made him even more furious. After all this time, the very least he deserved was a good fuck. He narrowed his eyes. When both of them were lost to the act, Seamus made his move. Stealthily and quickly he went down the mountain. His feet slid two or three times, but he doubted the pair of them would notice.

Thirty feet, twenty, ten. He stopped, narrowing his eyes. The camp was about a half-mile downstream, and he heard no sounds save the panting cry of his whore of a wife. Below her, Morales wore the expression of a man in heaven—which Seamus reckoned he was.

He stared virulently at them, disgust churning in his belly. How could she rut with a savage? What he wanted was to grab her by the hair and make her ride him the way she rode the Spaniard.

How to take her? The breathy cries increased in tempo, and he knew his narrow window was closing. Impulsively, he knelt and picked up a rock, a little bigger than an average man's hand, flat and heavy. He hefted it once to gauge the weight, then crept forward, waiting.

He didn't look at Tess—he couldn't bear the temptation. Instead, he focused on the savage, listening. Tess's voice rose on a swell of such sweet pleasure that Seamus wanted to tear her limbs from her body.

Seamus struck with precision, hurling the rock at the savage's head. When it struck him, hard in the temple, he let go of a loud, grunting cry. Tess didn't immediately notice. The cry sounded much like the others. Her head was flung back, her throat exposed, and every muscle in her body was taut. Seamus leapt forward, growling in his rage, and grabbed her by the hair, dragging her from the savage like a dog in heat.

She screamed. Seamus took pleasure in the terror in that single note. She stumbled as he dragged her, and cried for her lover. "Joaquin!"

Blood poured from a deep gash on Morales's head. He lay unmoving on the ground, his mouth slack. For one instant, Seamus wondered if he'd been lucky enough to kill the son of a bitch. He was good at killing, after all.

But the moment's gloating cost him. Tess made a low, animal noise and came at him with her hands and feet and teeth. He didn't let go of her hair, but she didn't seem to notice. She roared forward, her face a feral mask, teeth bared. Her nails gouged his face before he could catch her wrists.

"Goddamn it, Tess, you're my wife!" he bellowed, and caught her wrists in one hand, slapping her hard with the other. She made a noise, and kicked him, the flat of her foot landing just short of her target—his groin. He sidestepped and she fell, crying out as she landed too hard on one arm.

He seized the moment. Bending, he caught her from behind, and wrapped her wrists around her body so she could not move. Roughly, he hauled her to her feet and took out his gun. They'd already made a lot of noise, and he didn't want an anthill of Indians swarming after them. His arm firmly around her waist, he said in her ear, "You come quiet, and I won't shoot him. You make another sound, and he's dead."

A small, tight sob came from her mouth, and he felt her body go limp. Morales had not moved, but fresh blood continued to spill from the wide gash on his head. A scarlet stream poured over his cheekbone. Not dead yet, but maybe he'd never wake up.

"C'mon," he said roughly, and shoved Tess in front of him, the gun in hand. He'd kill her before he let her leave him again.

In a state of stunned horror, Tess trudged through the forest. Behind her, Seamus panted heavily, cursing. He shoved her when she slowed even a little, trying to give Joaquin a chance to awaken and find them before—

Her stomach roiled. Before Seamus could wreak his revenge. She couldn't even bear to think what he would do. Her nerves recoiled.

But as they walked, her mind began to clear. She was no longer the weak, starving Irish villager Seamus had bribed from her home. The months of her journey and the good food had made her strong. She could feel the power in her arms and legs, could feel the heightened endurance she possessed. The rising, falling landscape barely winded her, but Seamus could not speak for shortness of breath.

If she stayed alert, perhaps she might have an opportunity to run away. He could not catch her, not given the difference in their endurance.

At a turn in the stream, he made her sit down. "You try and run, and I'll kill you," he said, gesturing with the gun.

Tess eyed the firearm, wishing she'd paid some attention to the guns of the trappers and comancheros. But she had not. This one was long, with beautiful metalwork along the barrel, but she did not even know how to fire it. She sat on a rock.

He squatted to drink from the stream and Tess fiercely imagined kicking him into the water and sitting on his head to drown him.

She stared at him, at the filth caked on his clothes, and the matted red hair. How she hated him! It was not a new emotion, but never had it been tempered with so little fear. He was an insect of a man, a bully who used his tremendous size and lack of conscience to make his way in the world.

He straightened and caught her virulent expression. For the first time, Tess saw his face clearly. His flesh was almost deathly pale, his eyes hollowed. The healer in her recognized his illness, and she felt a flare of hope. He touched his ear, and a ripple of pain twisted his features for a second. "Goddamn you, Tess."

She simply gazed at him without speaking.

He pursed his lips. "You look like an Indian in that dress. Take it off."

Distinctly, quietly, Tess said, "No."

"If I end up taking it off you, you won't like it near as well." A brightness touched his eyes. "But then, again, you've changed, haven't you?"

She met his gaze without flinching. He could take her life, but he would not take her pride. Not again. She would never let Seamus McKenzie humiliate her again.

He shook his head wearily. "I ain't gonna bother with it now. Let's get moving."

Calmly, Tess stood, straight and strong, feeling power gather in her, as if she took nourishment from the very air. He was ill, and weary. Her chance would come.

She would not let herself think of Joaquin, lying so still and bloody. Not yet. It would weaken her.

In the sunny clearing, Joaquin stirred slowly. He felt the sun on his face, and smelled the pine-laden breeze that brushed him. His body felt oddly heavy, and for a moment, it seemed too much effort to open his eyes.

Slowly, slowly, he surfaced. The light behind his eyelids was red, and there was air on his body—on his stomach and his groin and upper legs. He shifted and groaned as a blaze of pain shot through his head and neck.

He opened his eyes, lifting a hand to the source of the pain. He lay in a grove, and his head hurt. Thick stickiness met his questing fingers. A fall?

Tess.

Abruptly, he sat up, remembering. They had been making love, wildly. And something happened. What?

His mind felt thick as sludge. Carefully, he stood up and walked unsteadily to the stream, blinking to clear his vision. On the bank, he swayed unsteadily for a moment, then slowly bent over. He splashed water on his face, and dipped to rinse the cut. The stream flowing away from his head darkened with blood. The cut stung. But soon the icy cold numbed the feeling, and brought a little life back into his brain.

Where was Tess? How had he gotten cut?

He looked over his shoulder to the place where he had lain. Nothing. He frowned and stood, then walked around the place carefully, examining the ground.

There, just beside the black-speckled boulder, were footprints. The signs of a struggle, and movement. His blood went cold.

Seamus McKenzie.

He stood up and shouted, "Tess!"

The cry was swallowed by cushioning trees, but he tried again, listening intently for any whisper of an answer. Nothing.

Blood trickled into his eye. Desperately trying to concentrate, he brushed it away. The tracks led away from the clearing, over the stream and into the wooded foothills. Joaquin followed them.

Seamus's ear made noise, a deep, burring buzz of pain that came in steady waves. The air seemed too thin to breathe, and he took gulping mouthfuls, trying to get enough into him. At the edges of his vision, black speckles appeared and disappeared, in time to the waves of pain in his ear.

Doggedly he put one foot down, then the other, over and over again. Ahead of him, Tess walked without strain, her back straight, her head high. Her long curly hair, touched with shimmery copper in the bright sunlight, was caught in a braid that tumbled down to the hips that swayed below the deerskin dress. That hair had bewitched him for years, even when she was a little girl, and he kept his eyes on it like a sailor watching a beacon in the night. Now it was all that kept him going.

They came out of the trees suddenly and Tess stopped. He heard a soft exclamation come from her mouth. A jolt of fear touched him, and he hurried toward her, to see what caused her to make that sound. The way his luck was going, there'd be a whole new nation of Indians waiting for them.

Instead, there were rocks. Seamus stopped in his tracks, as awed as Tess, who stared without speaking. Dark red rocks, bare and ragged, rose hundreds and hundreds of feet into the air. Centuries of wind and rain had carved them into blunted shapes and towering pinnacles. They rose like mute gods, the color a vivid contrast against the sharp blue of the sky and the sage green and gray at their feet.

Seamus knew the land. Even with his ear blazing, he could hear the land in this place. It was a hushed and holy voice, for it was a holy place.

Tess spoke quietly. "I've wronged you, Seamus," she said quietly. "But perhaps it was meant to be, so both of us could come to this land. Perhaps there is some great fate awaiting you here."

Her lilting voice, soft and warm, sounded of Ireland. How he longed for it, for the cool mists and the rolling green hills. "There's no land for me but Ireland," he said gruffly. An ache rose in his throat. "The thought of it burns in me, the farther I come among all these heathens, to this screaming land that never has the right voice."

"The right voice?" she asked softly. "Tell me how the voice of Ireland sounds, Seamus."

As they had been standing there, the buzzing in his ear had stilled a little. His breath, too, had slowed. He looked at her, to see if she made sport of him, but she only gazed up at him with that curious glint in her gray-green eyes, eyes the color of moss in the forest, or the sea as it rushed the rocks at Galway.

So he said, "She sings, and weeps, she does. Crying for the bloody English to leave her to heal her wounds, and feed her children. She sings at night to lull us to sleep on her soft breast."

He felt a curious calm steal over him at the words, and to his surprise, he glimpsed tears shining in Tess's eyes. "Don't you miss her?" he asked.

"What voices have you heard here? In Taos?"

The dark dread of that place growled through him, kindling the flame in his ear anew. "There's a demon there," he said.

"A demon?" she echoed. "That wasn't the voice I heard."

"What then?"

She turned her face toward the towering red rocks, and

Seamus was slain by her profile, so sweet and pure, the most beautiful face he'd ever seen.

He watched her lips move when she spoke. "I heard welcome and peace. Until I rode into the valley, I had been missing Ireland, dreaming of it at night." She shook her head, and looked at the sky, as if there was something written there. "When we came into the town, I felt I had come home."

He could not breathe for love of her. It had been thus, forever. And she'd wed him. "It did not welcome me."

Tess looked at him. "There will be such a place for you, Seamus. I know it." She touched his arm. "Let me go back to Taos, to the life I may build there, and you go on, and find yours. We are not suited, you and I."

"We're married," he said, narrowing his eyes. "You've given a vow and must keep it."

Her fingers tightened minutely. "I never pleased you, Seamus." Her lips turned up in the barest smile. "You'll not hurt my feelings if you admit it. You're a big man, with big appetites, and there are women you can take to wife who will pleasure you as I never could."

The black speckles pulsed at the edges of his vision, in and out, dancing with the sword thrust in his ear. It made it hard to think, to remember why he'd come so far. She made it sound so simple.

He was so tired.

As if she sensed his mood, she pressed his arm. "Sit down, Seamus," she said kindly.

He did. She knelt next to him and pressed her hand to his ear, covering the searing pain with a cool, gentle touch. "You had these earaches as a child, I remember. We heard you weeping. My da said it was a terrible thing for a child to have such pain so young."

He closed his eyes. Somehow, her hands brought comfort. "A trapper said the mountains do this to some folks. Even them without a history of it."

She frowned, touching his brow. "You need to be in bed, resting. You're burning with fever."

Waves of dizziness and exhaustion ripped through him, and he felt himself drifting into a half-aware state. It seemed, vaguely, that he should not do that, that he should remember something important, but the black edging his vision pushed outward in, obscuring his vision.

"Seamus," she said. "Seamus, can you hear me?"

With effort, he opened his eyes. Her face wavered, caught against the blaze of the sky, and he blinked hard. "Aye," he said gruffly.

"You're very ill. There are onions by the water. I want to get a few of them, and some mud."

He grabbed her arm fiercely. "No. Stay here."

"You'll lose your hearing, Seamus. I don't want to stay with you, but you must know a healer can't leave a man to go deaf. I promise I'll return."

The pain swelled suddenly, doubled, then tripled, then raged like a whirling knife inside his head. He grabbed his ear and cried out. "Go, then. If you leave me, I'll only find you again."

She touched his face. "It will only be a moment."

The whirling knife in his head blotted out all other thought. He did not care. He wanted it to end.

Tess raced down the small incline to the stream, where she could get mud. Although she'd told Seamus there were onions there, she was less sure than she had pretended.

At the edge of the water, she paused. Her instincts told her Seamus would fall into insensibility if she left him alone. Eventually, he would probably die of thirst and exposure, for the ear was virulently infected. She had smelled it when she got close to him.

He would not know for hours that she had not returned. Even when he would notice, his agony was likely to be so deep he would not be able to find her.

She could run now, make her way back to the Cheyenne camp, tend to Joaquin's wound, and be free of

Seamus forever. He thought he would chase her, but she knew he would die.

A battle kindled in her breast. In her mind's eye she saw Joaquin, lying so still and bloody in the field. Head wounds bled profusely, and he might have been momentarily stunned, but she did not think the blow would kill him.

It would hinder him, however. Even if he wished to follow and mete out justice to Seamus, Tess was on her own. She could tend his wound and let him live, or leave him lying senseless on the mountain to die.

If he lived, could he be talked around? She thought he might be persuaded to let her go. There had been such weariness in his face when he spoke of Ireland, the weariness of a man dying.

If she left him to die, he would haunt her forever. It would not then be her vows that weighed down her soul, but the guilt of a healer born and trained, who let a man suffer and die when she knew she could help him. Seamus McKenzie was a brutal, violent man—but how much in him had been twisted by pain and privation?

No, she could not run, not while he lay in such agony. She could treat him, then go, if another possibility presented itself.

She walked up and down the bank, looking for wild onions, but she found none, nor anything else she recognized as a useful herb. At last she gathered handfuls of cool mud and carried it back up the small incline. Even before she reached the top she heard the low, agonized moans. Seamus lay on his back, writhing, both of his hands clutched to his left ear. His eyes were wild with pain.

"Seamus!" she cried, and rushed to him. "Lie still," she said, "let me—"

He roared, like a wounded bear, and struck out at her. Tess ducked quickly, and his dizziness knocked him off-kilter. He got to his knees, rocking, then doubled forward, falling with all his weight on his elbows, his head clutched between his hands. Out of him came a noise like a woman in the late throes of labor, long after her strength was gone, and the babe still would not come. Tess had only heard it when a woman was going to die.

Seamus rose up and suddenly gagged, as if he was going to vomit. Fear shook her—she was afraid to go closer, afraid to leave him, and in this wild land where the plants were unfamiliar, she could not help him. "Seamus!" she cried. "Let me put this mud on your ear. Please. Lie down. Let me help you!"

"Tessita!"

The voice, so beloved, came from behind them. Tess leaped to her feet, looking for Joaquin, wanting to warn him to stay back for the moment. He came from the woods, running. Blood darkened his brow, and stuck his hair to his head, but he looked strong enough. She held up her hands. "Joaquin! No! Go back!"

Seamus gave a horrible scream, and Tess turned to look at him. From between the fingers clutched over his ear came a rush of fluid, tinted dark with blood. He roared, his face tilted toward the sky, and Tess saw the rabid look in his eye. He lunged for the gun and used it to stand up.

Tess ducked the arm he swung toward her. His balance was off and she thought he might still be dizzy. He stumbled, but righted himself, and with horror, she saw the pain leave his face, as if it had suddenly eased.

Joaquin ran toward them, his face a blank, intent mask of hatred. Seamus raised the gun to his shoulder, and she screamed, "Joaquin, no!"

He had to be mad, rushing a rifle like that.

Then she saw the horsemen behind him, coming fast from the forest in pursuit of him, and she knew he was going to die, from one or the other.

She whirled and flung herself at Seamus, throwing all her weight into the shoulder that barreled into his ribs. The gun fired at the same instant, and there was a cry. She couldn't tell who had made it.

Seamus tumbled backward, and Tees went with him, tumbling over and over, down the hill. They landed in a tangle at the edge of the stream, Tess on top. Seamus shoved her and she went into the water, but she cried out, grabbing at his shirt, his pants, whatever she could grab.

"No, Seamus!" Her voice sounded strained and she realized she was nearly hysterical with her need to make this all turn out right.

"We can all live!" she cried, grabbing a hank of his hair. "Stop this now."

He shoved her away. "He stole my wife," he said with extraordinary calm, and stepped around her, his clothes dripping. "For that, he dies."

Tess saw the rifle on the ground, gleaming in the sunlight. She stood unmoving until he bent to pick it up, then launched herself at him. She landed on his back. "No!"

He flung her off like a fly, and Tess landed hard on the ground. The air whooshed out of her. On the ridge above, she saw Joaquin, between two Mexican soldiers, his hands up. She saw the rifle Seamus raised.

She rolled, gasping for her lost wind, and flung her body into his legs. A shot rang out, exploding into the day, sending birds screeching into the blazing sky. Dust or needles or gunpowder flew in her eyes. She couldn't see. She could only cry out, "No!" and cling with all her might to Seamus McKenzie.

25

The bullet went wild, disappearing into the sky. From his vantage point on the bluff above them, Joaquin said, "Do not let him harm her, and I give my word that I will go with you peacefully." He did not look away from the struggle. "Please."

McKenzie staggered from the recoil of the rifle, and seemed unable to see. Tess, covered with red dust from her struggle, rolled to her side and got to her feet.

"Kill him," Joaquin said raggedly. He could barely speak for the tension in his throat.

Everything in him, every thought, every prayer, every shred of concentration he owned was focused on Tess. He dared not move, for fear the soldiers would shoot him—and then Tess might be distracted, and she might forever be in the clutches of her enemy.

Dressed in the soft deerskin dress, her hair dulled by dust, her face fierce and dirty, she hardly seemed the same woman he had found on the prairie. But even then, he'd sensed her strength, the scrappy, tenacious strength of a street cat who'd lived by its wits.

She was strong. And as she scrambled to her feet, gauging her next move, he saw that she needed to fight this fight, that she would never be whole without resolving it.

Afraid and proud and aching with love, he willed her to succeed.

Seamus was turned away from her, struggling with the rifle. Tess bent and stealthily picked up a stout stick. Hefting it in her hand, she crept toward Seamus. With a great cry—he thought it sounded like, "God forgive me!" she lifted it and brought it down on his head. At the same instant, a gun roared.

Until he saw the stain spreading over the Irishman's chest, Joaquin did not know where the sound had come from. Seamus fell heavily to his knees in bewilderment, then looked at Tess. She covered her mouth with her hands.

The soldier next to Joaquin made a move, as if to go down the hill. Joaquin forestalled him with a raised hand. "Wait."

Seamus put a hand to his wound, and surprise came over his face. He looked up at Tess, and spoke. She collapsed in front of him, putting her small hands on his bearish shoulders.

The Irishman listed and fell sideways, and Joaquin saw him reach for her hand. Tess was weeping, he could see it from the slope of her shoulders, and he wondered what she found to mourn in a man so cruel, so warped as this one was. A man who would have killed her over setting her free, a man who could put the mark of a whip upon the flesh of another. How could she mourn him?

Seamus clutched her hand tight, and spoke once more. Tess reached over and brushed her fingers over his eyes. She made a movement like a cross over his chest, and bowed her head.

The soldiers next to Joaquin crossed themselves.

And oddly, even Joaquin was moved by her gesture, by her attempt to send even a loathed enemy from the world in a state of grace.

Slowly she got to her feet, and walked heavily toward them. On her face was dread and defeat as she eyed the soldiers, and he could see the smears her weeping had left on her face.

Joaquin turned to the soldier on his left. "Give me one moment with her before we go."

They stepped back several paces, and Joaquin turned to wait for Tess to come to him. At last she came over the rise, and walked up to him and put her head against his chest. He held her while she wept, smoothing her hair, stroking her back.

At last she raised her head. "Fate is unkind," she whispered. "I am free, and now you are going to be dragged away."

He touched her lips with his own. "I love you, Tessita."

"Señor!" cried one of the soldiers.

Tess gripped his arms. "No!"

"Go to my sister, Tessita, and tell her what has happened. She will know what to do."

"Joaquin!" She touched his face. "What if I never see you again?"

He closed his eyes to clear them of everything he had ever seen, and looked at her. "Then you must remember how I loved you."

Before he could see her tears, he turned and let the men lead him away.

"Joaquin," she cried, "I love you!"

He turned, so she would know he had heard, and raised his hand.

Tess struck out stubbornly as soon as the riders disappeared over the ridge. For a moment, she felt disoriented and terrified—how could she find her way back? She looked up, and found the great peak that dominated the landscape, then thought of the stream. If she followed the stream, it would take her back to the Cheyenne.

It turned out she did not have to walk all the way. Dark had begun to fall, and the shadows frightened her. She started violently when she heard horses coming toward her. Quick as a fox, she hid in a tumble of shrubs, praying the twilight and her brown dress would hide her from the intruders.

When she saw Joaquin's brother and two other warriors from the camp, she emerged from her hiding place, and stood there mutely, unable to tell them what had happened. "Joaquin—" she began helplessly.

One of the warriors held out a hand to her. Tess allowed him to help her up, and she rode back to camp on his horse. Juanita was fetched, and Tess poured out the story to her.

"He said to tell you," she finished, "that you would know what to do."

Juanita looked away, then stood up without a word and went to speak with one of the elders, who called Sleeping Bird.

At some point, a woman pressed a bowl into Tess's hands and she ate, but there was a curious dullness in her, as if life left her with Joaquin.

It was decided they would leave at daybreak. Tess, Juanita and her brothers would go, along with Sleeping Bird and a small band of warriors for protection.

And so it was that Tess Fallon, poor Irish villager, came to be riding across the vast plains of a new land in the company of a band of Indians. Fierce warriors who never seemed to be watching or caring what went on about them, but could kill a snake with an arrow before Tess had even seen it. Warriors who could shoot a bird right out of the sky, warriors who laughed and teased each other in a musical language that lulled Tess to sleep at night.

In the early mornings, Juanita walked with Tess through the trees or along the streams, teaching her the names of plants used for healing and spells and charms. As they rode, Tess smelled the samples she'd taken, and tasted them, and kept watch for them in the fields along their path. She chanted their names to herself, loving the roll of them on her tongue, the taste of them in her mouth—*plumajillo* and *yerba del pasmo* and *altamisa*.

The plants were her only focus, the anchor to which

she clung. She felt as if she had become separated from
the center of herself, as if some cruel knife had set her
adrift from her moorings. She feared she might shrink and
shrink and shrink, until she was only dust, if Joaquin did
not live, if they killed him before the party arrived in Taos.
It was too terrible to contemplate.

She said the names of the Spanish herbs as if they were
an incantation that might save him, as if there was magic
in the roll of syllables that might be at home in his mouth.
She thought of his crooked grin when she mutilated a pronunciation, and the way he'd laughed helplessly over her
bigger mistakes.

Every moment of their time together, she remembered
and relived. Every detail of him, she reviewed to keep new
in her mind. The fall of thick, black hair, the way he
moved with such easy, confident grace, the mischief eternally lurking in his eyes, the rich sound of his laughter, his
gentle, elegant hands.

She loved him with an almost unbearable force. And to
that, too, she clung. For if anything could hold off the
spirit of evil, surely it was love as wild and deep as this.

In the pass above Taos, only one more day's ride into the
town, they had to sleep. Knowing Joaquin was down there,
only hours away, made Tess anxious and restless. She did
not sleep well, and even when she managed to drift off, her
dreams were tangled flashes of bright and dark.

Toward dawn, she awakened with a start. Her stomach
roiled dangerously. She rushed from the camp, into the
sheltering trees, and vomited. As suddenly as it had come,
the illness disappeared.

Tess burst into tears. She was exhausted and lost and
very frightened. The trips—from Arkansas to Taos, then
to the Cheyennes and now back yet again—had taken
their toll. She wanted only to sleep for a month, and
recover her lost strength.

Sleeping Bird, evidently awakened by Tess's abrupt
movements, appeared at her side. She knelt next to her,
putting a hand on Tess's shoulder.

Ashamed of her weakness, Tess tried to wipe away her tears, but more followed behind. Sleeping Bird made a soft, comforting noise, and gathered Tess close. Overcome, Tess wept long and hard, wailing out her rage and terror, and the dull, never-ending ache for the arms of her love.

Sleeping Bird rocked her, and sang. The sun came creeping on yellow feet into the spice-scented wood, and birds whistled in merry greeting. Tess, finally spent, quieted, but she did not move from the comfort of Sleeping Bird's shoulder.

"*Mi hijo te ha sembrado un niño,*" Sleeping Bird said with a chuckle. "This is good."

Tess frowned. It was only when Sleeping Bird put a gentle hand on her tummy and said, "A baby, no?" did she realize.

She lifted her head, gaping, and saw in the dark eyes that were so like Joaquin's, a glimmer of new joy that chased away some of the sorrow there. With a sense of wonder, she covered her belly.

Was it possible? She tried to remember how long it had been since she'd had her courses. So much had happened, so fast—

But she did remember how difficult it had been to maintain privacy for such matters while they were on the road. On the pass into Taos, Sonia had helped her, and together they'd found means of keeping the whole business as private as it should be.

How long had that been?

A sharp, bright thread of hope unfurled within her, casting light through the dull darkness she had carried these last days.

A child. Joaquin's child.

"Joaquin must live," she said fiercely, gripping Sleeping Bird's hands. Until she'd said the words, she didn't know she could say it in Spanish.

Sleeping Bird smiled radiantly, returning Tess's grip. "*Sí,*" she said. "He must live."

26

In the company of warriors and women, Tess rode into Taos. Her heart pounded as she looked for a gallows or some other sign that Joaquin might already have been killed.

Instead, there was a strange air of festivity permeating the town, which told her the execution was yet to come. Her stomach rolled dangerously.

Riding in with Indians was different than coming to a place with others, she discovered. Clearly the Indians in their exotic clothes and bright adornments, riding on their beautiful horses, were a source of awe and fear and wary respect. Tess found she rather liked the power.

She spied Roger, off to one side of the square. He caught her eye and grinned. The familiar rapscallion expression gave her reassurance. She dismounted and hurried over to him. "What word?"

"They've got him in jail, but he's still alive."

Tess closed her eyes, briefly. "Thank God."

A uniformed officer, high ranking by the look of his fine boots and the braids and buttons of his uniform, came out of the jail. Tess had never seen him before, and her heart sank. The governor must have sent him to see that nothing else went wrong.

He planted his feet in the square, eyeing the Indians with far less awe than the curious townsfolk. Putting his hands on his hips, he boomed out a question in Spanish.

Tess looked at Roger. "You must tell me what they are saying."

Roger said, "He asked who is in charge."

The warriors, resplendent in the bright afternoon sun, sat unmoving on their horses. Sleeping Bird and Juanita dismounted. They approached the officer, backs straight.

"We have no leader," Juanita said.

His lip curled contemptuously. "Slaves and *genizaras?* What can you say that I would care about?"

Sleeping Bird said, "My son, who sits now in your jail, is going to be put to death for the murder of his father. I wish to speak to Doña Dorotea before it is done."

The officer laughed. "Why would she talk to her husband's whore?"

Tess widened her eyes as Roger translated this last bit.

The unmistakable crack of a rifle being readied echoed into the sunlit square. The officer eyed the Indian who had done it, his smile fading.

Sleeping Bird said, "Tell her I wish to speak of Miguel."

"Miguel?" Tess echoed. "What does he have to do with it?"

Roger shrugged.

From behind the officer came the jailer Tess recognized, the plain man with his thick mustache. He bent and whispered into the officer's ear. The officer listened, then looked at Sleeping Bird for a long moment, then to the warriors sitting so still and alert on their horses.

"Very well," the officer said aloud. "I will speak with Doña Dorotea." He called for his mount.

"What's happening?" Tess asked Roger. "I don't understand."

"Nor do I, good lady. But it looks as if Gonzales is going to ride out and speak to her personally."

"What do we do?"

"We wait."

But Tess had waited long enough. She pushed through the knots of curious onlookers, past Juanita and Sleeping Bird, and stopped before the jailer. "Take me to him," she said.

His face went stony. "You tricked me."

Tess shook her head. "Not on purpose."

For a long moment, he stared at her, his black eyes glittering with unreadable emotion.

"Please," Tess said quietly. "If he is to die, I want to see him one more time."

The man hesitated, then stepped aside and let her pass.

Inside it was dim, and Tess could see nothing. She stood just beyond the door, waiting for her eyes to clear, and suddenly, they did.

Joaquin stood at the bars of his cell. His hands were wrapped around the bars, and Tess thought again how beautiful they were. Now that she looked upon him, she felt all the air leave her lungs, and she could not think; she moved in a kind of stillness and put her hand over his. He sighed, as if in relief, and leaned his head forward. Tess put her forehead close, and though the bars prevented their actual touch, she felt the comfort of his flesh close to her own.

"My mother is with you?" he said at last.

"Yes. She sent for Doña Dorotea."

"It will not help. They are going to execute me at dawn. My sister has the will my father wrote, the second one, but—" He took a breath and let it go. "I do not think it will make any difference."

She put her hands to his mouth, halting his words. "Shhh. You will not die, my love. I have come too far to find you."

His eyes were bleak, and he reached through the bars to touch her face. "*Mi* Tessita. You are more beautiful everytime I see you."

"You will not die," she repeated, more fiercely this time. Firmly, she took his hand and drew it through the bars, and put it on her belly. "Here I grow your babe, and I don't intend to be raising it by myself."

His big hand spread wide, nearly covering her from hip bone to hip bone. A stillness came on his face, then he reached for her, putting his other hand around her neck and drawing her close to kiss her. "Then no matter how it goes, all is not lost."

"If you die, *I* will be lost, Joaquin," she said, putting her hands on his precious face. "Without you, my life will mean nothing. You *must* live."

He did not answer, only kissed her again. "Stay with me," he said softly.

Tess nodded. "Yes."

Just past dusk, the jailer came to Tess. "The *genizara* wants you," he said. "Doña Dorotea has come, and you must be there when they talk."

"Me? Why?"

"I do not know, señora."

Tess looked at Joaquin. He smiled, and she realized it was his old smile, the mischievous one that always seemed so free and alive to her.

"*Vaya con Dios*," he said, and winked.

"She can't be so terrible as all that!" Tess protested.

His grin broadened.

In exasperation, Tess shook her head. Only a man could be so thick as to joke about a dragon woman when his head was on the block. Only a man would think it enough that he should plant a babe in his love's belly before they carted him off to a fool's death.

She scowled. He was no doubt relishing the ballads they would compose about him, which would make all the ladies weep for the brave and falsely accused Joaquin Morales, who died with a kiss from his lady upon his lips.

Over her dead body. "I'll be back," she said, and hurried out.

With some trepidation, she met Juanita on the bricked patio outside the hotel. "Be strong," Juanita whispered, and squeezed her hand. Juanita's was very cold.

Within, candles burned in silver sconces, and a fire leapt in the corner hearth. When Tess and Juanita entered the salon, Señora Mascarenas stoppered a crystal decanter of ruby red wine, and put it on the table near a small, imperious-looking woman. "If you require nothing else, Doña Dorotea," Señora Mascarenas said, shooting a pinched look toward Sleeping Bird, "I will be close by."

She left, shutting the heavy, carved door behind her.

That left four of them. Sleeping Bird sat in the straight-backed chair, and she had changed into a white dress made of softest leather, beaded elaborately in bright colors. Her moccasins, fringed and tall, matched. Over her shoulders, she had draped a silk shawl with very long fringes that whispered around her hips on currents of unseen air. In the gentle glow of the candles, her skin gleamed as dark and smooth as the oiled pine of the furniture in the room.

Opposite her, across the polished table, sat the small, imperious woman. She could only be the infamous Doña Dorotea. She, too, was dressed with exquisite care. Tess had seen other Mexican widows, and they seemed to don black upon the deaths of their husbands, never to emerge from it again, but Doña Dorotea wore a gown of deepest wine-colored silk, trimmed with black lace. Her thick black hair, her only beautiful feature, was swept into a sleek arrangement, fastened in place with jeweled combs. Her rebozo was black lace.

Tess stared at her curiously. She was not an attractive woman. Her nose was beakish, her mouth thin and severe, her eyes small and black. The unfortunate arrangement made Tess think of a crow, a metaphor only exaggerated by the black wings of hair.

To her surprise, Tess felt pity rise in her. She had not expected to feel anything but loathing for this mean-spirited woman, and she did not like the softening effect that pity had on her hate. Only with hate could she face down her enemies.

But like it or not, the strange empathy was there as Tess sat down in the chair Sleeping Bird indicated. It would have been painful to be the plain Dorotea, prim and well-bred and nearly barren but for the one son she'd born, when her husband's mistress was vivid and free and fecund.

Juanita sat next to Tess, and when the two older women began to speak, she translated into English for Tess.

Sleeping Bird said, "This is a meeting of women only, and our secrets need not go beyond these walls. But it is women who will settle this problem."

Doña Dorotea sipped her wine. "It is already solved."

"We both know it is not." Sleeping Bird inclined her head. "You did not love Armando, Dorotea. You never did. But you were his wife, and in the end you won. You took him from me forever."

Doña Dorotea did not smile. Her black eyes grew hooded. "I did not kill him," she said.

"That is not the matter at hand," Sleeping Bird said. "I am here to free my son to take the place his father made for him." She leaned forward. "He is Armando's son. His only Mexican son."

"He had a son!" Doña Dorotea burst out. And flushed.

Sleeping Bird smiled. "So you do remember."

Tess shot a glance toward Juanita, who shrugged, as bewildered as she.

The air in the room grew very still and charged. Doña Dorotea put her glass carefully on the table, as if it would shatter otherwise. She did not speak.

Sleeping Bird went on very quietly. "I have brought my daughters to witness that promise made between us so long ago."

"That promise died with Miguel!" Doña Dorotea protested. "You cursed him!"

"No. He was a fine son, a beautiful son. He was a gift like no other—no one who knew him could help but love him. He was the most loved man I have ever known."

Doña Dorotea's face began to crumble. Tess saw her grip the arms of her chair. "None loved him as I did."

"That is true, and is as it should be. No love ever matches that of a mother for her children."

"He was mine!" Doña Dorotea burst out. "He might have been born to another, but he was my son. I suckled him from my own breasts."

"I know your barrenness made you suffer," Sleeping Bird said. "I know, too, you suffered for the love Armando—"

"Do not speak his name!" Doña Dorotea stood up suddenly, drawing herself to her full height. "Because of him, my son died. He never loved Miguel as his own. He never loved him as he loved Joaquin. You told him our secret and he never loved him!"

Juanita translated this last in a bewildered tone of voice.

Sleeping Bird said softly, "Armando never knew. He died believing Miguel was his own." She stood. "I kept your secret, Dorotea, and I gave you your son. I ask you, in front of these witnesses, to give me mine in return."

"Mama, what—"

With a wave of her hand, Sleeping Bird silenced Juanita. "This woman," Sleeping Bird said, gesturing toward Tess, "holds in her belly my son's child. That child will be the only one who will carry on Armando's name and bloodline."

Dorotea trembled violently. Still, her chin was high. "I did love him, when I was a girl. I wanted to be a good wife, and he would not let me."

Sleeping Bird looked as if she would reach over the table, but stilled herself. "We all suffered for laws that have no meaning in the face of human emotion."

"Yes."

Deep silence fell. Dorotea opened her mouth and closed it, like a fish. She sank down in her chair, her face in her hands.

Sleeping Bird said, "He was as kind as he was able to

be, Dorotea. He did not flaunt me. He sent me away so
you did not have to see us together. I kept our other children with me. I brought the baby the warriors found so
you would not be shamed by—"

"Stop!" Doña Dorotea cried. Tears flowed over her face.
"Do not speak it aloud, I beg you. Not here and now."

Sleeping Bird said, "These daughters of mine will know
our secret, so you do not rise up to threaten our line again.
But I will spare you the recounting if you give me my son
now."

Doña Dorotea nodded. "I will do it, in honor of our
promise." With a sly cock of her head, she said, "I do not
know who killed my husband."

Juanita gasped a protest, but bit her lip.

"I will tell them I was hysterical and grieving my son
and my husband, and blamed Joaquin because I wished to
see someone punished."

"And the ranch?"

Doña Dorotea lowered her eyes. "I will go to my sister
in Mexico City. The ranch will be Joaquin's, as Armando
wished." She lifted her head. "But if there is ever a whisper of what was said here today"— she looked at each of
them in turn— "I vow you will never rest for fear of me."

"Then it is done," Sleeping Bird said, and rose. "Go to
them, and free my son."

27

Joaquin heard the cock crow, just before dawn. He had not slept, not in two days, and the sound shot a bolt of dizzy awareness through him. Almost dawn.

Today, he would die.

On weary legs, he walked to the small, barred window in his cell and looked out to the square. It faced east, and he saw the mountains, huge and blue, their details indistinct in the predawn twilight. Beautiful mountains that had framed his life.

He watched the sun pale the night sky, washing away all the darkness as it pushed against the ceiling of the world. Birds twittered in some unseen tree, and through the square, a yellow dog ambled.

Which wall would they choose?

He had not seen an execution since he was a very small boy, and he couldn't remember where it had been. Only that there was noise, and a great, red stain when the man fell.

His insides recoiled. He frowned, not liking the idea that he was a coward, that he could not look death in the eye like a man, his chin upraised, his eyes open.

But he did not particularly want to die. Not now. Not when he'd at last fallen in love, when at last he would have the child he'd dreamed of, when things might finally have come full circle for him.

At the front door of the jail came a sharp rap. A sticky blot of fear stuck in Joaquin's throat, and he looked over his shoulder.

At dawn, they'd said. It was nearly dawn now. Would they let him look at the mountains? The mountains and Tess? And maybe he would not disgrace himself with weeping.

Carlos, dozing with his hat over his face, jumped to his feet and rushed to answer the summons at the door. An unfamiliar soldier stood there. He muttered something to Carlos that Joaquin could not hear. Carlos bobbed and closed the door.

He turned. His face was grim. "I am to take you to the general now, Señor Morales."

Joaquin took a breath. He nodded. Why had Tess not returned from the mysterious meeting? He'd thought she would want to stay with him this last night.

Carlos bound his wrists and led him out into the morning. It smelled damp and sweet. A breeze touched his face. Squaring his shoulders, Joaquin walked with his chin upraised. What would be on the other side? Would his father and Miguel be there, waiting, laughing? Or was that all a myth?

Who knew?

"Where are we going?" he asked after a moment. "Where are the people?"

They rounded a corner, leaving the square proper, and Joaquin saw them—a big crowd. Everyone who lived in Taos, even some of the Pueblo Indians in their handsome blankets. And there were other Indians, too; warriors from his mother's band waited toward the back, arms crossed, legs akimbo, their horses grazing in the open prairie beyond.

All eyes were fixed upon Joaquin.

He stumbled, and shamed at this display of weakness before such proud warriors, lifted his chin arrogantly. Let them take him. He would not be the first man to die unjustly.

The general waited near a plain, whitewashed wall. Of course. They would not want that blood on the town square, where it would serve as gruesome reminder of his death. The general wore full dress uniform, and his hands were clasped behind his back.

Near him stood Doña Dorotea, her face wearing not the gleeful mask he would have expected, but a bitter, pinched expression. Not a shred of color broke the deep mourning she wore. He saw Raul, grim-faced, standing with Sonia, who had been crying, and Roger, whose blue eyes were bloodshot.

And there—there with his mother and his sister, was Tess. His heart leapt to see her. In the deep, gold light, her hair glinted with bright color at each turn of each curl. Her eyes, those water-colored eyes, met his steadily, with the strength he'd seen in her from the very first moment.

She smiled. Her whole face glowed.

In his exhaustion, he could not see a reason for so wide a smile.

"Joaquin Morales," the general pronounced. His voice seemed very loud in the silent gathering.

With effort, he looked away from Tess. "Yes."

"You are the eldest surviving son of Don Armando Morales, lately deceased?"

Joaquin frowned. "I am he."

The general nodded to the guard. "Unbind him."

Carlos cut the ropes binding his wrists. Joaquin looked at him, and Carlos shrugged. Rubbing his wrists, Joaquin waited.

"A document has come to my attention," the general said, raising a sheaf of papers. "It names you heir to the Morales Hacienda, and all the land, crops, and livestock therein. Do you understand?"

Joaquin's heart sped. He looked at his sister, his mother, and Doña Dorotea, who did not protest, but only stared at him with the same virulent hatred she had always harbored toward him. "I am my father's heir?"

"New evidence has come to light about the murder of your father, and I am convinced you did not kill him. Therefore, I pronounce this will in effect immediately, and release you from the holds of the government of Mexico."

A great cheer rang out from the crowd. Joaquin, stunned, stood where he was, rubbing his chaffed wrists, staring dumbly at the general. He couldn't even summon the wits to ask a question.

All at once, Joaquin was surrounded by people, all talking simultaneously, clapping his shoulders. An old woman embraced him, weeping. Raul gave a great whoop. The general gave the sheaf of papers to Sleeping Bird and mounted a horse.

Over the heads of the townspeople, Joaquin looked at Tess, who smiled broadly at him. She lifted her skirts and moved toward him, and he realized that she was laughing, and then she was running.

And it sank in. He was not to die this morning. He would live. He would love her. He would marry her. He would have a baby and it would have his legal name, and live in the grand house his father had built.

He was, in a word, rich.

The thought struck him as absurd, and he started to laugh. It rolled out of him in great, booming waves, enormous and easing.

Later, Juanita would tell him the story as it had unfolded. She would tell the truth about Miguel, who had been stolen from a family in northern Mexico by Apaches. Slowly the baby went from hand to hand until it reached Sleeping Bird's band. Doña Dorotea had been deep in the throes of an hysterical pregnancy—her belly swollen with nothing but her desperate need for a child. Sleeping Bird, wanting through kindness—or at least no cruelty—for Joaquin and Juanita, who stayed with their father delivered the infant to Doña Dorotea herself.

But now, Joaquin was jolted into action. He pushed

through the throng surrounding him, and met Tess, who flung herself in his arms with a loud, chortling cry, raising her fist in the air. He pulled her close and swung her around, and she put her hands on his face and kissed him, victoriously.

He put her down on her feet. The shine of her eyes blazed through him, a light so vivid and brilliant it would light his days and nights forever more. Suddenly it seemed impossible for him to find words to tell her how he felt.

"I am alive," he said simply.

"Aye, that you are, Señor Morales." She grinned. "And a good thing, too, since I find myself in dire need of a husband."

"I don't know," he said with a mock sigh. "I am rich now, you see, and there will be many mamas who will want to marry me to their daughters."

Her face fell. He caught her close. "Oh, Tessita, how can you think I'd ever take another? I was only teasing you."

"Do not tease me just now, señor." Her fingers curled hard into his arms, and she rested against his chest. "I am feeling faint with all that has happened."

He kissed the crown of her head. "You are my only love, Tess Fallon. As long as I live, I swear I will never sleep apart from you. Do you hear?"

"I hear."

"You will never want for anything, Tessita," he said, and again the amazement of such a vast fortune in his hands—horses, cattle, sheep, and land, so much land!—rushed through him. He chuckled. "I really am very rich now."

"Well, it's no sorrow to me, either, I can tell you." She lifted her head and cocked an eyebrow. "Very rich?"

"Very."

Her face grew still, and she lifted a hand to touch his face. "It would not matter, Joaquin, if you were the poorest man in the world. I love you, rich or poor. Always."

Soberly, he kissed her palm. "I am only glad because you need never be hungry, and I can take care of you." He closed his eyes and held her tight, aware of the sun filling the whole Taos valley around him. "You are my woman, Tessita. Always."

EPILOGUE

Taos
August, 1845

Of all the rooms in the hacienda, Tess loved the salon best. It was long and cool, with doors at both ends, leading to other rooms. Vigas carved from pine boughs made runners across the ceiling, and the floor was polished and covered with a rich rug imported all the way from Spain. Hammered, silver mirrors and sconces hung on the thick adobe walls.

But it was the windows she loved—three of them, all facing the courtyard beyond, filled now with crimson hollyhocks and lilies and the slow beginnings of her herb garden. It was in here that she came to read and write, to nurse her daughter Fiona, now three months old and the very image of her *Tía* Juanita. She smiled fondly at the child, who slept on a thick sheepskin in a shady place near the wall.

The late afternoon sunlight held a deep burnished hue as it fell across the table, where Tess laid out the supper dishes. "It's so beautiful," she said for the third time.

Sonia, nursing her eight-month-old son, chuckled. "How many times you gonna say that?"

Tess smiled. "As many times as I like."

"See what happens, honey-chile," she said to her son. Nathaniel, already Nate to all of them, gazed up at her with big dark eyes, as if he was seriously listening. "Give a woman a big, ol' house, some servants runnin' around all over to do her every little chore, and some fancy china— and she goes and gets all uppity."

Nate smiled, and lifted his head, pushing away to look at Tess. He cast her a sidelong look, as if she would rescue him from his mama, who was trying to put him to sleep. "No, you don't, boy," Sonia said. "Time for your nap."

Tess smiled and adjusted the precise setting of a plate.

The china—white with pink flowers and gold trim— had come all the way from Bent's Fort, just this afternoon. Joaquin had surprised her for her birthday, and she'd wept with pleasure, insisting they had to have Raul and Sonia over to eat on it for the first time. Roger had taken the business of trading as his own, and was gone for the moment.

"China!" Sonia exclaimed in wonder. "You got what you imagined, didn't you?"

Tess looked at her. "Everything. As have you."

Sonia lifted her hand to admire the gold band on her wedding finger. "I never expected to be married, to tell you the truth."

"That man would walk through fire for you."

"Yes, ma'am, and the feeling goes both ways. He's a good man." Something in the courtyard caught her attention. "Who's this comin', I wonder."

Tess glanced out curiously. Joaquin, fresh from the horses, walked with a tall Anglo that Tess had never seen before. He was a very large man, with a loping, easy stride and bright gold hair that gave off sparks in the sunny day. "I don't know."

The two men ducked into the hacienda, and she heard a mingling of male laughter as they came closer. She smiled and smoothed her skirt. Whoever it was, Joaquin was happy to have him.

They came into the dining room. The man was young, with a raw-boned, handsome face. His shoulders were as broad as a buffalo's, and his head nearly scraped the ceiling. It was rare that Tess saw a man taller than Joaquin, but this one dwarfed her husband.

He inclined his head, looking at Tess, then propped a big hand on his hip. The gesture tugged her memory—

"Well, now, that's a fine how-do-you," the man said with a thick Irish brogue. "I come thousands of miles, across oceans and a whole continent and my own sister doesn't even know my face."

For one long second, Tess gaped. "Liam?"

"You look a sight better yourself, girl. A little food'll do wonders for a person's looks, you know."

She shrieked and flung herself across the room into his robust embrace. "It is you!" she cried, and pulled back to look at him again in amazement. Now that she knew, of course it was obvious. Her brother's blue eyes twinkled, and she knew she was aghast, but—"What a handsome man you've become!"

"So I was ugly before, is that it?"

"That's what she told me," Joaquin put in with a teasing grin.

"She told me the same," Sonia said from her post in the rocking chair. Her son sat up and gurgled.

"I did no such—"

All three of them laughed. Liam caught her. "Ah, Tess, you're still so easy, girl!"

"Oh, tease me if you will," she said. "I don't care." Eagerly she looked at her brother. "So you must have gotten my letters."

"Aye. Who would have thought you'd be the one to have all the adventures?" He gave Joaquin a sidelong glance. "And find yourself a rich husband."

"Not to mention devilishly handsome," Joaquin added.

Tess realized for the first time how much alike they were. She glanced over her shoulder. "I must have been mad."

Sonia smiled.

Joaquin put his arm around her shoulders. "Set another plate for your brother, Tessita, while I go find my sister and bring her to dinner, no? We can use all your fancy china."

She laughed. "Yes, that would be perfect." She kissed him, and then kissed her brother's cheek, and when Fiona cried, she kissed her, too. She'd kiss Raul and Juanita when they came in, just for good measure. "Supper for everyone tonight!" she said, and smiled.

Let HarperMonogram Sweep You Away

BURNING LOVE by Nan Ryan
Winner of the *Romantic Times* Lifetime Achievement Award
While traveling across the Arabian desert, American socialite
Temple Longworth is captured by a handsome sheik.
Imprisoned in *El Siif*'s lush oasis, Temple struggles not to lose
her heart to a man whose touch promises ecstasy.

A LITTLE PEACE AND QUIET by Modean Moon
Bestselling Author
A handsome stranger is drawn to a Victorian house—and the
attractive woman who is restoring it. When an evil presence is
unleashed, David and Anne risk falling under its spell unless
they can join together to create a powerful love.

ALMOST A LADY by Barbara Ankrum
Lawman Luke Turner is caught in the middle of a Colorado
snowstorm, handcuffed to beautiful pickpocket Maddy
Barnes. While stranded in a hostile town, the unlikely couple
discovers more trouble than they ever bargained for—and
heavenly pleasures neither can deny.

DANCING MOON by Barbara Samuel
Fleeing from her cruel husband, Tess Fallon finds herself on the
Santa Fe trail and at the mercy of Joaquin Morales. He brands
her with his kiss, but they must conquer the threats of the past
before embracing the paradise found in each other's arms.

And in case you missed last month's selections...

MIRANDA by Susan Wiggs
Over One Million Copies of Her Books in Print
In Regency London, Miranda Stonecypher is stricken with
amnesia and doesn't believe that handsome Ian MacVane is her
betrothed—especially after another suitor appears. Miranda's
search for the truth leads to passion beyond her wildest dreams.